PROJECT
VI

JAMES BADKE

Project VI, by James Badke
©2012, James Badke, First Revision 2025
ISBN: 978-0-9916846-5-6

Author Blog: jimbadke.com

Other Books by James (Jim) Badke, available on Amazon:
- *The Mummy of Fisher Creek*, 2018
- *As The Eagle Walks*, 2021
- *The Camp Liverwurst Series*, 2022-24
- *The Island and I*, 2024

To my patient wife, Sarah

I

"Why does anyone live here?" On the other side of Allie's laptop, raindrops streamed down the windowpane. Drop merged with drop until they were heavy enough to race one another to the bottom, and one could never tell which collective would break free first. At the start of a new project, any distraction was welcome. She knew that soon, creative juices would flow and she would become immersed in the social patterns of the world's wealthiest-per-capita nation. But not yet. Her reluctance to open a new document persisted.

Finally, Allie typed at the top of an abysmally blank window, "Project 6." She stared at it momentarily, then hit the delete key once and changed the number to "VI." Clever. This was going well already. Except it was already five o'clock and time to pick up Laney from after-school care. Not that Laney went to school, but mother and daughter needed some sanity time from one another. Where did this day go? She sighed, saved, and closed the laptop.

"How was it, Laney?" Serious six-year-old eyes dared her to guess her opinion of Sunshine Lollipops Daycare. "Not so good, huh? You don't have to go back if you don't want to. What happened?"

"All they talk about is pooping and farting. And I was the only one my color."

"The kids, Laney? You couldn't find nice kids to play with? And who cares what color you are?" Allie knew Vancouver was multicultural, but she was still surprised that no other white kids were at the daycare.

"The farting kids didn't care. Why do you think I ended up with them?"

Allie sighed again and steered her Japanese rental down the next

1

exit, hoping it led somewhere familiar.

"Can we do something fun today, Mom?"

"I don't know, Laney. It's almost suppertime."

"Mommy, Mom, Mom, Mom!" Laney gestured excitedly out the window. "Mini-golf! Can we go play?"

"Closed, honey! See? No cars in the parking lot. Besides, it's raining again."

Silence for three blocks.

"How about we pick up a pizza and watch a movie. Okay?"

First smile of the afternoon. "Yes! Can I pick the movie?"

"Laney, I can't watch Dr. Dolittle one more time."

"Okay, but it's gots to have animals, Mom. Gots to."

"'Has to,' not 'gots.'"

"I agree! It has to have animals."

"Do you know what a manipulator is, Laney?" She glanced at her grinning daughter. "Yes, I think you do."

Long after kissing Laney goodnight, Allie pounded the keyboard. She hadn't traveled from New York for a vacation. The parameters of the project came easily, as they were much the same as previous ones. All her research would have to agree unanimously that Pearson, Boyle and Fitch could only gain by propagating itself all over Vancouver Island in the form of Internet cafés, and that they should move immediately. Mind you, "should" was a given; "could" was the sticky question. Not even McDonald's had succeeded. She typed the word, "Why?" and sat highlighting it and changing the font repeatedly.

Google offered very little on Vancouver Island for her efforts. Of 19,739,391 entries for "Vancouver Island," she already knew that 60% invited the residents of the Canadian city of "Vancouver" to flee to one "island" or another in the tropics. Not surprising, if the city socked in like this every day. A more specific search brought up many news articles about the tiny offshore nation that she could vaguely see through the mist from her hotel window. She read few that were helpful. So speculative, so little firsthand info. And she wondered again at her incredible luck.

The letter—the only reply to the many she had written—said in simple terms that the Directorate of the Sovereign Nation of Vancouver Island was pleased to grant a three-month Market Research Visa to Allison Grey Simpson. The visa commenced on April 15, and to her surprise was conditional on bringing with her the infant daughter, Laney Anne Simpson, age six. Allie hadn't mentioned Laney in her application, which meant someone was doing their homework. The Nanaimo School Authority would provide Laney with temporary educational opportunities for the duration of their stay. A home-schooler by conviction, Allie had no intention of sending Laney to school. But she wasn't about to compromise her invitation by telling them so.

Everyone in the New York office came by her desk to look at the letter. It was hard to say what wowed them the most: the parchment, the gold seal that was not a sticker, or the genuine signature at the bottom. Mostly they came because everyone knew the Directorate of Vancouver Island never issued commercial visas, let alone a research visa. It was a scoop of epic proportions, and they drooled at the sight of it.

The visa unleashed a flurry of flight arrangements, piles of outdated data from every department, long meetings with her newly appointed team and even one with the CEO of the Company. The only surviving partner of Pearson, Boyle and Fitch, Donald George Boyle terrified her for 23 minutes to let her know he was still as sharp as a whip, then smiled and assured her she "was doing the Company proud." Before she had time to process the magnanimity of it all, Allie and Laney were coasting to a stop in a jumbo jet at Vancouver International Airport. In the rain.

She shivered and suddenly felt very alone. Their commute to the island tomorrow would be a big day. The heaviness of the raindrops on her hotel window made her shrink in significance deep back into the sofa. Not bothering to brush her teeth, she pulled her old wool blanket tight around her as if wishing someone would tuck her in, and fell into a troubled sleep.

"Mommy," in a hoarse and urgent whisper, "I gotta go pee! Now!"

"Not good timing, Laney. I don't think we can leave this line."

"Gotta, Mom. MOMMM!!"

"Can I help?" Uniformed woman, looking more like a stewardess than a government official. VI insignia on her shirt—Vancouver Island. Warm eyes. Nope, gorgeous eyes. "I'm afraid you cannot leave the line at this point. But I would be glad to escort your little girl to the toilet." The slight British accent was soothing.

Laney let go of Allie's hand and dragged the uniformed woman down the corridor, creating a wave of quiet and reserved amusement along the short but unmoving line of colonists and a few visitors.

Allie felt out of place and overdressed. No one in the line talked, not even the families, but the atmosphere was unlike any she had experienced in airport security in New York. No impatient glances at the clock, no irritated expressions. These people seemed comfortable with one another, like they were glad to be going home but had all the time in the world. The line hadn't budged in 20 minutes.

Laney and her new friend returned with smiles on both faces as if they shared a private joke. As Laney waved goodbye, Allie thanked her savior, choking a bit on the loudness of her voice in that silent room. Laney returned to her hoarse whisper, which echoed on the pale green walls. "The bathroom had couches and a coffee table, Mom! You shoulda seen it! I used a real towel and threw it in a basket after!" Big eyes.

The line shuffled by inches. Or centimeters, rather, since this corridor and all beyond it were VI sovereign territory. Laney sat on the floor and traced with her finger the intricate design of the ceramic tiles. She also seemed to have limitless time. Allie did not. She laid her hand on the arm of a passing official/steward and asked if they were in danger of missing the noon ferry.

"None, ma'am. The ferry won't leave before this line is on board. If your papers are in order, you will have no problem. May I see them?"

Flustered, Allie had not enough hands. The official waited patiently as she juggled purse, passport pouch and day bag. He glanced at the visa, smiled directly into her eyes and said, "See you on board."

Thirty minutes later, she wished it were that simple.

"Yes, I read the information that was sent to me and I knew about the mandatory vaccination. But I would prefer my daughter not to have it. All of her AAP vaccinations are up to date, as you can see in her documentation, and that must be enough!" This official didn't look like a stewardess, and her firmness was increasing at a rate that matched Allie's impatience.

"Allie." The use of her first name surprised her into a moment's submission. "It's simple. Laney doesn't need to receive the vaccination. All you have to do is walk back down the corridor and return home."

"Mom?" Laney's eyes were full of questions and a little fear. Allie wished she had a mother she could have dared to leave her daughter with. Not the last time.

"It's okay, sweetie. Let me think." If these people had all the time in the world, they could spare a moment for her. What was in this vaccination? Though they assured her it had the approval of the World Health Organization, the VI officials weren't permitted to reveal the contents of the vaccine apart from potential allergens. Allie didn't even trust flu shots.

"I don't mind, Mommy. I wanna go on the boat. Will it hurt?" This to the official, who smiled for the first time.

"It's nearly painless. Most little girls don't even flinch."

"I won't filn… flinch, Mom. Honest." Allie sighed and

nodded.

The official was wrong. It did hurt, and Laney wailed. This surprised Allie, who to relieve Laney's apprehension had received her shot first, which she hardly felt at all. Laney wasn't crying wolf either; an ugly bruise formed quickly on her thin arm. Medical staff clustered, fussed and bothered around them for several minutes, then cleared the way for a man who looked like a doctor.

"Our deepest apologies, Allie." Everyone here seemed to operate on a first-name basis. "This rarely happens, and we greatly regret your little girl's discomfort. We would like to give her some children's aspirin, and would ask that you have her checked by a medical professional on the island if the swelling doesn't go down in the next 24 hours." That seemed reasonable. Allie was too exhausted to argue. They left with a cold pack wrapped in a real washcloth. Laney held up to her nose an elaborate candy necklace a nurse had placed over her head.

"You're a brave little girl," she told her.

Laney wasn't easily placated. "I'm not little. I'm six."

Overwhelming beauty. Warm blue skies stretched across chill blue water, ending in dark clouds still hovering over distant Vancouver. More beach than Allie thought possible stretched out beneath her bare toes pointing skyward as she lay back against a log. Parksville—a good name for a town that seemed to have no other reason to exist than the enjoyment of its citizens. Laney shrieked as she found yet another civilization of tiny crabs beneath a rock. She was already soaked from sitting in sparkling shallow pools of saltwater. Allie closed her eyes for the full 20 seconds that she dared and breathed deeply. It was as if she hadn't lived until this moment.

Her phone. Irritating ring, one she couldn't change on her phone, indicating a roaming call. The world rushed in and gathered her up.

"No, you're right," Allie sighed. The droning voice of her supervisor continued as if Allie hadn't spoken. "Listen, I will have a full report to you tonight. But really, I've only arrived. Haven't even had a chance to… No, I have no difficulty with office protocol. I'll send it… Right. Good-b…" The phone slammed at the other end. Allie wondered how far down the beach she could throw her phone with all the angry energy she felt inside. Six months ago, Rebecca Young became the head of Allie's department, and she made it her mission to keep Allie in miserable subjection to policies even Donald George Boyle had forgotten.

Allie let her head fall back against the log. The warm sun beat against her eyelids and told her that Laney was fine. Apart from the vaccination incident, yesterday was a genuinely perfect day. The service on the ferry was practically cruise ship quality: they spent most of the trip feasting on smoked salmon croissants, curly fries and an amazingly crisp salad, seated at a window table from where they could look straight down at deep green water. Someone announced killer whales off the starboard bow. Lacey squealed her delight as three tall fins rose out of the water below them, followed by large, rubbery, black and white bodies, cleaving the waves in perfect rhythm. The orcas kept up with them for several minutes, then dove deep and didn't reappear.

The colonists seemed as excited to see the whales as Laney and Allie were. One elderly citizen told Laney, "That, young lady, was a sight you don't see every day!"

Allie returned to consciousness with cold water dripping on her neck and an escaped giggle from Laney. Something scrabbled across her chest and Allie opened one eye. "That better not be a crab, my young guttersnipe!" Of course it was. Allie jumped up and chased the shrieking Laney down and up the beach, splashing through the pools and falling in a laughing heap with her on the soft sand.

"I love it here, Mommy! Can we stay here all day? Can we stay forever?"

7

"Got work, Laney…" Crestfallen expression. Damn phone! "But we can stay until lunchtime. How about something from that concession stand?"

Their fast-food lunch was far beyond Allie's expectations. Whatever cuisine her company planted here, it would have to be healthy and of high quality. She expected hot dogs at the little stand near the washrooms; instead, they were serving veggie pizzas on flatbread, a perfect combo of taste, crispness and freshness. She never saw Laney eat so much. By the time they drove back to the condo, the little girl was fast asleep. As Allie carried her up the stairs, she wondered again why kids weigh more when sleeping.

She took the opportunity to look again at Laney's arm where she had the injection. Not swollen, but the yellow/gray tone of the skin meant a nasty bruise was forming. Laney told her it was itchy, and she had evidently scratched it already. Allie would put a bandage on it when Laney woke up.

In the meantime, back to that bloody report.

Not only was the Directorate of Vancouver Island willing to grant Allie a research visa; it was also amazingly accommodating in getting her started. The package waiting for her at the condo was every researcher's dream—stats, demographics, maps, history, the latest census, websites—stuff that normally took her days to track down. Determined to have something to include in her report to Rebecca Young, Allie spread out the contents of the package on the dining room table and began absorbing it as she had been trained to do.

Vancouver Island. Positioned at an angle off the west coast of Canada, jutting below the forty-ninth parallel. Area of 31,285 square kilometers, roughly the size of Maryland. Population a mere 725,000, spread mostly along the east coast and thinning toward the north. Plus another 25,000 on numerous smaller islands on the same side. Vast mountains marched along the center of the island, and temperate rainforest ruled the west coast. Hardly worth her firm's attention, except that the GNP per capita of this tiny nation was more than twice that of the USA. We're talking serious wealth, thought Allie. Luxembourg came a distant second, with nearly the same population but only one-twelfth the landmass. How did this happen?

European explorers immediately recognized the raw resources of this island paradise. In the mid-nineteenth century, the United States and Britain engaged in a tug-o-war over it, and largely through the influence of the then-massive Hudson's Bay Company, Vancouver Island became a British Colony in 1849. Conflict of interest aside, the entire island was immediately leased to the HBC, becoming essentially a "company colony" in which virtually every citizen was an employee. No police, no civil law, and only one civil servant—the appointed governor, who soon resigned in disgust and returned to England.

Thus Vancouver Island was at its beginning a commercial enterprise, running rough-shod over government and its original inhabitants, doing whatever it damn well pleased. Britain appointed the Chief Factor of the Company, Sir James Douglas, as the new governor, who made some attempt to balance his civic and corporate power, but reigned supreme from the Fort of Victoria nonetheless. His powers of commerce included convincing the 30,000 remaining aboriginal inhabitants of the islands to relinquish title to all lands except the villages they occupied, in exchange for some goods from the Company. The natives accepted the blankets as a token of further payment to come, as was their own practice, but blankets were all they ever received.

And there was gold. Well chronicled are the gold rushes of the Thompson and Cariboo regions of New Caledonia (later known as British Columbia, locally termed "the Mainland"). Allie grew increasingly impressed with Douglas' politico-capitalism—he made a point of collecting license fees from every boat that passed up the Fraser River to the goldfields, though he had no jurisdiction. What is less accounted for is his careful, thorough and extremely lucrative extraction of gold from the island itself, or what happened to it all. Unlike the gold rushes on the mainland, this was no first-come, first-grab business. As best as could be surmised, every ounce went into one pocket, to resurface years later.

When the gold fever subsided, the new-founded mainland colony of British Columbia and the colony of Vancouver Island, by now both governed by Sir James Douglas, began to suffer financially. The increasing number of colonists who weren't connected to the Hudson's Bay Company instigated a Reformation movement in protest against the governor's power and apparent inability to keep the colonies solvent. The media campaign against the governor seemed to spell his expulsion, or at the very least, his retirement. A loud cry went up to amalgamate the two colonies under a new governor.

It's hard to know exactly what happened next. Perhaps it was a back-room deal—Allie couldn't help thinking that massive sums of money were involved—but suddenly Douglas withdrew his authority from the mainland, and the colonies of British Columbia and Vancouver Island went their separate ways. British Columbia continued to struggle and eventually became Canada's sixth province in exchange for the payment of its massive debt.

But on Vancouver Island, colonists abruptly ceased their protests and ignored the press. Far from bankruptcy, the government seated in Fort Victoria suddenly seemed to have no limits to its spending power. Roads and infrastructure grew at a frenzied rate, new industries received all the start-up help they could wish for, no one was asking for taxes and levies, and no one seemed to mind any longer bowing to the name of Sir James Douglas. By the time of his retirement a few years later, Douglas' (literally) gold-plated reputation was unanimous, and his place inimitable. Rather than desecrate his station with a replacement, his right-hand men became a Directorate, and for all any colonist knows (or cares), that group of 190-year-old men is still in power today.

Allie gradually noticed that except for the computer screen, the condo was dark, suppertime was long past, and Laney was still asleep on the couch with her one-eared teddy bear grasped tightly in her arms. She stretched, groaned and cursed her protracted attention span. Kraft dinner and beanie weenies for dinner, and a grumpy Laney to contend with tomorrow on her first day of school, to which Allie had grudgingly given in. She put the pot of water on to boil.

II

Staying here forever sounded like a good idea. Allie loved this island. Never had she felt so... what was it? Satisfied. Back at home, she and everyone she knew were on a desperate quest for more of everything. Here, she daily met people who were ridiculously content. They seemed to have time to spare. It helped that they were all well off, but it was more than that. She had to find out what, and not only because it was part of her job.

She had an amiable chat with an older gentleman who owned a small coffee shop, and who claimed to have never stepped off the island in his life. "Aren't you curious?" she asked in amazement. "This is an enormous world, with many cultures and places to explore! Haven't you ever wanted to get on a plane and go?" She plunked down several large coins with the image of an elderly Queen Elizabeth II on one side, payment for a lemon-ginger tea.

His smile was kind, but not condescending. "Where have you been?"

That caught Allie off-guard. "Um, well, a few places. I went to Mexico sometimes with my parents. Germany twice—my mother had family there. Thailand, after I graduated from college..." Thailand. She hadn't thought about Thailand in a long time. "New Zealand briefly."

"Tell me about Thailand."

Allie swallowed the sudden knot in her throat. "Fascinating. Overwhelming, really. Beautiful beaches, lush vegetation everywhere. You walk the streets of Bangkok and the smells and sounds are unlike anything you have ever experienced." She knew she sounded like a travel agent, and stopped.

"Try again," he coached.

Allie closed her eyes and considered. "It was the people. I've never seen people so generous, so ready and willing to help. I remember ordering a drink at a sidewalk bar, and the waiter went down on his knees to serve it to me. True, I was the rich American and the source of his income, but it was so genuine and respectful…"

She opened one eye, and the gentleman's eyes were also closed as he listened intently. She continued, telling him about her first few days in the city. "I saw children playing in the water, others fishing. The water was far too dirty, but I wondered what it would be like to be one of them, with nothing else to do that day. I watched them a long time, but I wasn't one of them and I found myself lonely…" Wait, what are you saying? Allie's defenses regrouped themselves. Dangerous territory. "Warm and generous people. That's what I remember about Thailand."

She opened her eyes to find the gentleman looking at her with a penetrating gaze that made her drop her eyes. After a minor crisis of silence, the man chuckled. "Thailand is like here, then." She looked at him questioningly. "Except, our water is clean. For a moment, I thought I had missed something by not going there." He was laughing at her with his eyes. It annoyed her—a lot. "Your tea is cold. Let me get you another."

He gave her no time to protest. She really should be going, though. These visits to the "competition" were typically a few minutes long, enough to size them up and gain a sense of the atmosphere. She had been here nearly an hour, and she had to pick up Laney from school.

Looking up from retrieving her keys out of her bag, she found the gentleman holding out to her a fresh cup of tea—on his knees. "Thank you for telling me about Thailand. I guess we can learn things from another culture after all." The laughter in his eyes was gone, replaced with empathy and compassion. "Please come and tell me more sometime."

His tenderness almost disarmed her, but not quite. She took the tea and drank it as quickly as she could without scalding herself, watching the gentleman's back as he carefully washed dishes—by hand, despite the stainless-steel dishwasher behind the counter. He didn't see her leave.

It was surprising to get a call from the Vancouver Island Information Bureau in Victoria, offering even more help with her research. Her name was Sandra, and she suggested meeting Allie at one of her favorite spots: a small café overlooking the tiny harbor town of Genoa Bay. Allie dropped Laney off at school, watching wistfully as several little girls grabbed both her hands and whisked her away, all talking at once. The road to Genoa Bay was hills and curves and pretty in the morning mist, which cleared to bright sunshine as she wound down into the bay. She instantly knew Sandra could be a friend.

"Now, I'm instructed not to influence your research by being too inquisitive about your company and its objectives. So don't tell me, please! I would rather get to know you and offer whatever support I can." Sandra threw her long, dark hair behind her and dug into a briefcase packed with papers and pamphlets. "I understand this island better than anyone I know—yes, I'm pretty confident!—so, please ask me anything you like!"

"How old are you?" They both laughed.

"Good one, Allie! Okay, I'm at the ripe old age of 29, though I don't feel a day older than 22. You?"

"I'm 35, and I have a wonderful daughter named Laney, who is six going on 22. You would get along well."

"My, this is turning into truth or dare! Please tell me, what's it like to turn 30—is it truly awful?"

"Only if men are an issue. In my case, it didn't bother me at all."

"Oh good! I got engaged last week—" Allie congratulated her. "Thank you—so only one man is an issue, and he loves me for who I am. I take it Laney's father is out of the picture?"

"And good riddance. I didn't even know I was pregnant before he disappeared."

"I'm sorry, Allie! Has it been hard?"

"No, really, not that hard. My daughter is the joy of my life, and I don't mind not having to share her. Most of the time."

Sandra set a pile of paper and leaflets on the table. "How is the research going? How can I help?"

"I'm amazed—all the information left at my condo, that was from you?" Sandra nodded. "It saved me days! I've been using the time to explore and engage in as many conversations with... um, let's say... hospitality providers as I can. I'm having a great time!"

"And what are you finding out about this place?"

Allie thought of a way to say it. "I think this very well might be the best place on earth! Sometimes I've thought that if I could..."

"Find a way to live here?"

"Yes! To put it bluntly! I'm sure it must be nearly impossible, or this island would be wall-to-wall people, which would ruin it. But if I could..."

"People do immigrate here, Allie. It is quite a process, but maybe you should look into it."

"No easy path?"

"Well, only one, but judging by your comment about men a minute ago, you might not find that one appealing!" Allie sighed. "But there is a more conventional route, and worth trying. Okay, back to business. Ask me a question."

Allie searched her notes. "History. And politics. How did this country happen and how is it run? I read a fair bit, but I'm still curious."

"Wonderful! I love history and I'll do my best with the politics." She paused. "It may be helpful to think of this place more as a company—a business—than as a country, both in its origins and the way things happen here. Do you remember anything about the first Europeans who ruled here?"

"Sir James Douglas, and the Hudson's Bay Company. I remember being impressed with his way of running the colony, a man who could get things done."

"Exactly. Not always popular, especially at first, but he was definitely the one who got this country on its feet and set the direction you see today. You should see us on 'Sir James Douglas Day'—July 16th—the biggest event of the year for us. They pull out all the stops: fireworks over the water; free food everywhere; great wine flowing like water. It's an all-night party! If we had nothing else to thank Sir James for, that day would be enough!"

"That's the day after I leave! Maybe I can rebook my flight."

"Maybe! See you there! Anyway, back in the mid-1850s, not long before the gold rush in British Columbia, Douglas sent geologists throughout the island in search of minerals, especially gold. One of them was a hunter, guide and translator for the Hudson's Bay Company, a colorful Iroquois character from Lower Canada named Tomo Antoine. He traveled up Cowichan Lake, about an hour's drive from here, and chanced upon a group of native hunters using unusual shot for their HBC muskets. They couldn't afford the lead pellets sold at company stores, so they made their own—from pure gold! The hunters took Tomo up one of the rivers that flowed into the lake and showed him a cave of quartz, lined with heavy seams of high-grade gold."

Allie shook her head in amazement. "What gave James Douglas the rights to all the gold on the island?"

"Like I said, he was a powerful man—Chief Factor, Governor, practically Emperor. But he was also shrewd, and not greedy. He envisioned a land where people would never have to worry about how to pay their taxes, where avarice wouldn't call the shots. And that's what he created."

"Okay, that clarifies what I read, but what happened next? How did the country become a democracy?"

Sandra sat back and looked pointedly at Allie. "Allie, forgive me for saying it, but that was such an American question! Why would you assume this is a democracy?"

"It's not?"

"Hardly. We have never had elections, not even municipal ones. Remember, think of this as a company, not a country! Could you imagine Wal-Mart holding elections for CEO?"

"But you have, like, a Minister of Transportation, and mayors and school trustees and council members. Who chooses them?"

"The Directorate. People apply for the positions, and they choose them."

"And who chooses the Directorate?"

"Allie, are you sure this has to do with your research anymore, or are you just curious?"

"You got me—I'm so curious."

"Well, I will have to leave you that way, because I have no idea. I assume that when they need a new Director, they choose one."

"So, you have never taken part in an election. Never dropped a ballot in the box."

"No. And frankly, I wouldn't care to. Maybe if they ran this country poorly or unfairly, or if it was in a mess financially, I would want the ability to choose a new government. I think it's more likely I would leave. But as you know, that's not the case, not by any means."

The food arrived. Their conversation became mostly business but always gravitated back to getting to know one another. They talked until Allie had to leave to pick up Laney, finishing with a list of favorite hiking spots. Sandra stood to leave. "I don't know if I've helped you with your research as much as made a friend and sold you on moving here. But it sure has been fun."

That evening, Allie daydreamed about becoming a colonist and making the island a home for her and Laney. Maybe even the "unconventional" way. There had to be at least one man in this paradise she could tolerate, who could be a good daddy to Laney. She envied her new friend, so satisfied with life, a ring on her finger and everything to look forward to. She tucked Laney in, kissed her forehead and dreamed big dreams for her.

Allie took the first opportunity to consult Sandra's hiking list and explore on her own. A brochure from Sandra listed a trail at Cable Bay, south of Nanaimo, with good views of Dodds Narrows. Her GPS was less than helpful, but by chance she found herself on the right road and saw a small wooden sign designating the trailhead. The day was the coldest she had yet experienced on the island; her clothing choices were not enough to stay comfortable. She came through the trees to a "beach" of sandstone and picked her way along the fast-flowing tidal water for some distance.

What would her family say? She didn't care what they thought of her, but she anticipated the uproar if she told them she was moving across the continent to live on an island. They would label her a dirty hippie, throwing her life away. And what would she do here? She would need some job offer if she were to have any hope of making it through the immigration red tape. Vancouver Island probably had little call for market research analysts.

The wind was biting cold along the water, and Allie decided to turn back when she reached the next headland. She came around a small bluff and nearly walked into three men gathered around a fire on the leeward side, protected from the wind. She froze. They were cooking something in a pot over the fire, and several tall, forked spears leaned against the rock wall. The men were First Nations and as surprised as she was. Apprehension flooded her mind, partly based on stories she heard about natives but mostly on stereotypical fears, all telling her she was in serious trouble.

"Whoa, you scared us, lady! Hey, come out of the wind and warm up by the fire." It would be a reasonable suggestion if she weren't alone on an isolated coast with three men who might have grounds to be antagonistic. But there was no casual way to turn around and leave. She was practically in their space already. She moved to the fire and held her numb hands to it.

"Do you like crab?" This from another of the men, the one minding the pot. He reached in with a set of large tongs and pulled out a bright red one. "Needs another minute." She nodded, and the men gave attention to the fire and the pot and the fast-flowing water beside them.

"I'm Mike," said the crab man. The others introduced themselves—Joe and Tom—and Allie did the same.

"Hey, you're from New York, aren't you?" Tom asked.

"How did you know?"

"Got cousins there; you sound like them. Visited a couple of times. Whew! Not my cup of tea. Too many people, too little space. What do you like about it?"

Allie relaxed slightly. "Um, I must say, it's the people I enjoy. Shopping at Christmas and it's like a river of people on the sidewalks. I like it." She realized at the same time that this was true. Would she miss the crowds if she left there to live here?

"I guess. But isn't it weird that none of them talk to each other or even look at one another? Each in their own little world, no matter how big their city is." Tom used two sticks to draw a long, thick package from the coals under the fire. He pulled a corner of the aluminum foil back. "Mmmm… done. Nothing like sockeye salmon roasted in the fire. Will you join us? Or are you in your own little world?" His eyes sparkled with amusement as he said it, and Allie accepted a spot on a log and a plastic plate.

It was surreal to sit at a fire eating the produce of the sea like people had done for centuries—apart from the plastic plates. Allie discovered that Mike, Joe and Tom worked at a local sawmill and had the day off. Their families expected them to bring home a feast, but they had already caught plenty of fish and crab and didn't mind doing a taste test for lunch. They invited her to come home with them and join the feast, even after she explained about Laney and the need to work on her project all evening. But they were content watching her enjoy the taste test, which was fabulously messy and delicious.

"Can I ask something, hoping not to offend you?" Their shoulder shrug said, Whatever. "What's it like, living as a native of this island with all these colonists? I read about how the Hudson's Bay Company took your lands and gave you only blankets in return. This whole island was yours! Do you ever want justice done?"

They sat and looked in the fire for a long while. Tom spoke again. "Allie, thank you for your concern, but it was a long time ago. Since then, my family has never gone hungry, and we live with dignity and pride in our heritage. The colonists may have taken much from us, but they have also given us much, and have never withheld the benefits they gained by living here. In fact, for the most part, they honor us. We're content."

"Well, that sounds different from what I know of natives in other countries, and I'm glad. But are you expected to integrate with the White culture, or what?"

Mike gave his perspective. "No one demands that of us. My family, for example, has always intermarried with the other First Nations, and sometimes kinsfolk on the mainland. We pretty much keep to our own community and we're comfortable with that. But lots of families intermingle with the colonist culture, and we don't think less of them for it. It just works better in their situation. What's it like in America?"

Allie blushed a bit as she said, "I don't know. We avoid one another, the Whites and the Indians, as we call them. I've never experienced any open animosity, but we're at least indifferent toward one another. Anytime I see some display of Indian culture, it feels to me like we're still exploiting them."

"Well, I sure don't feel that way," Mike said. "The only difference between us and the Whites in my mind is that we have a different way of life, established as far back as anyone can remember. But I can imagine what it would be like if those who came here treated us badly. I would fight, and I'm sure my people would join me. May it never come to that!"

Allie reached her car with just enough time to drive to Laney's school, unsure what to do with the two crabs and a small salmon she carried in a plastic bag. She dumped them into Laney's big sand pail, propped carefully behind the spare tire. Better not forget to bring that in, Allie thought with a smile. Laney will be ecstatic.

III

Something wasn't adding up. At first, Allie appreciated the free wireless service at her condo and at the library where she expected to find them. None of the cafés and bistros she scouted advertised free Internet, which had led her to think the market was hungry for what her company could offer. But one day at an espresso bar far out of town, she went to the counter and asked if it was the café's signal she was accessing. The young barista gave her a strange look. "What do you mean?" she asked.

Allie wasn't sure how else to put it. "Well, I can access the Internet here, and I'm wondering if you have free wireless or what?"

"Where are you from?" Her question was edged with suspicion.

"New York. I'm doing research here."

"And you don't have Wi-Fi everywhere in New York?"

"Well, probably. But you can't access it just anywhere. Most places, you have to pay or have permission to use someone's connection." Allie paused. "Are you saying it's not like that here?"

The girl wiped the clean counter with a rag. "I've never heard of having to pay to use the Internet. That would be like having to pay to use the phone. I don't mean to be rude, but I'm not sure if I believe you."

Allie was stunned. She sat back at her laptop as the girl interspersed her cleaning with doubtful glances at her. Free Internet! If that was true, why the hell was she here? Pearson, Boyle and Fitch's line of Wi-Fi café franchises was a little redundant in a place with more cafés than she could visit in a year and wireless access everywhere. It couldn't be true.

It was. After several frustrating phone conversations with puzzled officials, she reached a man named Nigel who had the knowledge and patience to answer her questions. "So, you can access the Internet anywhere on this island, for free?"

"Almost," he replied. "We have a few isolated dead zones in the north and the interior, as with cell phone coverage. But no one lives there. You sound like this isn't a good thing. Why?"

"Because I'm here doing research on introducing a line of Internet cafés on the island and I feel like a fool. No one told me." Allie explained her line of work and the unexpected invitation from the VI Directorate.

A puzzled silence followed. "The Internet came to the island in the mid-eighties," explained Nigel, "and wireless connection after the Y2K crisis that never was. We immediately recognized the Internet as an essential service and made it universal—and free— within years of its introduction. I have a feeling you're misinformed."

"I'll say! Someone at my office didn't do his homework, and it wasn't me."

"You said the Directorate granted you a research visa. And they knew what you wanted to do here and still granted the visa. Curious."

That thought hadn't yet occurred to Allie. "I need to find some answers. Any suggestions on where to look?"

"None whatsoever." Nigel paused. "But a word of advice from someone who has lived here all his life. It's okay not to understand everything." Another pause. "It's like the engine in my car—I don't know exactly how it works, but it does work and I use it every day. I'm no mechanic, and it will do me no good to lift the hood and start toying with its parts."

"What are you saying?"

"Allie, do your research, enjoy the island, go home and spend your paycheck. Perhaps it's a gift. It doesn't need to make sense."

"You've gotta be kidding! I should act like my entire project isn't up the creek without a paddle!"

"That's what I would suggest, yes. This is not your fault. Enjoy it while it lasts. Maybe some good will still come of it."

Allie ended the call, incredulous.

After some consideration, Allie decided to heed the man's advice. Surely her Company had something to offer to this paradise, and it would be an interesting challenge to find out what. Not Internet cafés. She thought about calling the office and letting them know what was up. But this place intrigued her and she wasn't ready to leave. And Laney loved it. Home-schooling was ruined for her now as she came home from her new school every day and talked Allie's head off about elaborate science experiments and trips to the marine biology station. Where would she find a school like that in New York? She wondered again what it would be like to live here, and if it could actually happen.

Allie decided to expand the boundaries of her exploration of the island. So far, she had focused on the towns surrounding the hub of Nanaimo (as in "Nanaimo Bars"—she had always wondered where those incredibly rich chocolate and cream things got their name). Parksville, Qualicum Beach and other small towns in the area abounded with tourists and senior citizens, the staple customers of her Company. The largest and oldest city was Victoria, the capital at the island's south tip, and she would get there sometime. This weekend promised blue skies, and she booked a room for her and Laney at a resort on the Pacific Coast, following the advice of a young man they met on a beach in Parksville.

Laney had been trying to lift a large rock on the beach, hoping for bigger crabs. A young man with long golden dreadlocks offered to help her. "Okay, when I count to three, you help me push."

Both were a little red in the face when the big rock flopped over, and crabs small and medium scattered for new shelter. Laney dove for the largest one and expertly picked it up from behind; its claws grappled in vain. And of course, she chased Allie with it all over the beach.

The young man's name was Michael, and he was a marine biology student who recently finished his third year of study. He fascinated Laney with his knowledge of what was under the sand. She bent over to pick up a sand dollar and got a sudden shocked look on her face as something squirted a fine jet of water right up her shorts. "Geoduck!" shouted Michael, and he started digging furiously with his spade. After a desperate struggle with something half a yard underground, he came to the surface holding the ugliest clam Allie had ever seen, with a long siphon sticking out one side. "See? This is what he squirted you with, Laney. Want to take revenge? They taste pretty good in a chowder." Instead, they set the geoduck back in the hole and watched as it quickly dug its way out of sight.

Michael carefully took Laney's sand dollar apart to show her the pieces of a perfect little star inside. "Yeh, this is a cool beach. But if you really want to see beaches, you gotta go to the west coast of the island, around Tofino. A couple hours' drive from here." He gave some careful directions. "I used to live in Ucluelet, south of there. Population of a couple thousand in the winter and ten times that in the summer. You should go check it out now before the crowds arrive."

They had lunch together, sitting on the beach. "Michael, you're a young, bright guy. Why are you still living on this little island?" Allie baited him, with the expected result.

"I hope to be a marine biologist! Where else would I live but on an island?" he laughed. "Besides, I've been to other places." He dug his spade bitterly into the sand and looked to see that Laney was preoccupied with her sandcastle. "Last year, I went to attend a concert in Seattle. At the border, they treated me like a criminal, maybe because of my hair, I don't know. They hassled me and questioned me for two hours, made me and my friends miss the concert, and let me go with no apology."

He hesitated, remembering. "We drove back into Vancouver and stopped at a pub—nothing like the pubs here, but we didn't realize that until we got inside. My friend looked a little too long at someone's girl and ended up with a knife in his side. He's okay now, but it scared the crap out of us. I don't have much desire to go back, or go anywhere."

"Couldn't that happen here as well, Michael?" Allie was trying to understand his fear.

Michael looked at her blankly. "Did you know we don't even have a prison on the island? I've read about them, but living here I will never experience one. No one I know has ever been the victim of crime, not on the island anyway."

"Nobody's perfect! People must break the law here sometimes!"

"Yes, but when they do, they have to fix it. Steal something, you pay back double. Hurt someone, and you go work for their family or create a vacation for them. Be stupid with your car, and lose your car for a while. Do something really serious—something that makes you a danger to everyone—and you find yourself deported, with no nation at all. Nobody wants that."

Allie had a hard time wrapping her mind around this. A crimeless society was too good to be true; too rich, like Nanaimo bars. No man is an island, entire of itself. There was also something wrong with an island being an island.

"Michael, the world isn't as dangerous as you think. Some experiences are worth a reasonable risk."

Michael laughed. He had a good laugh—honest, innocent. "I'll go. There are many, many places I want to see. I've learned pretty much everything I need to know about marine life in these waters. But I'll always come back here. This will always be my home."

Home. Despite Allie's enthusiasm for travel, she wished she had a place like that. She hadn't thought about New York once, except when that rotten phone rang. She had no one back there, really.

During this short time on the island, she had enjoyed more pleasant conversations than in the past year. Michael's talk of "home" sounded awfully good.

Friday afternoon, Allie picked her daughter up from school and they set off for the west coast. She was becoming more comfortable driving on the left side of the road, another British throwback. It was an easier transition than she expected; the trickiest part was that whenever she went to use her turning signal, she turned on the windshield wipers instead. Laney was delighted to find that the narrow, winding highway across the island took them through the snow and mountains she had been eying. What does this island not have, wondered Allie at a rest stop as she easily dodged Laney's misguided snowball. I love it, love it, love it. I don't want to leave. She felt the contentment of these colonists and understood more of Nigel's advice to not rock the boat.

The largest trees she had ever seen, towering like skyscrapers right beside the road, turning it into an emerald canyon. Blue and green water thundering through and over a snarl of rocks and boulders, detonating into white in the sunlight. Three eagles, a flock of geese, a doe and fawn, four squirrels (one dead) and two bears—that was Laney's account of their road trip. It was all too marvelous.

"Oh Mom! Oh Mom!" Allie had seen larger beaches—what came to her memory was an astounding 60-mile-an-hour drive down 90 Mile Beach at the north tip of New Zealand, and that was after Thailand, and she was carrying Laney then and didn't know it. But to Laney, Long Beach was her favorite thing in the world, super-sized. The temperature had moderated as they came down from the mountains to the coast, and the breeze was light. Off came their shoes, and they ran barefoot with rolled-up pants to the tide that panned out across incredibly level sand. It was icy cold, painful really, and they quickly understood why the surfers in the water wore wetsuits head to toe.

The waves were huge, the horizon massive. After seeing all the signs that warned what the waves could do with logs and bodies at high water, Allie was thankful the tide was out. Most of the surfers were obvious beginners, but the ones who sat waiting on their boards further out occasionally ripped down and along a green curl, disappeared for a moment in the breaking wave, and flew up and over it to try again. Laney clapped for them all and jumped up and down in the shallow ripples until her feet and legs were red with cold.

Allie had stayed in enough hotels to know that Wickaninnish Inn was world-class. She carried a shivering Laney wrapped up in a warm fleece blanket that the valet brought her when he saw Laney's blue legs. Natural cedar predominated the décor, and as much glass as architecturally possible welcomed in the view but not the cold. It was early season, the desk clerk explained as she offered Allie a room upgrade at no extra charge. It had a jacuzzi, she explained, smiling warmly at Laney in her blanket.

She hadn't told them the hot tub overlooked a curving beach much like the one they had walked on, with only a large plate-glass window between them and the panorama. Mom and daughter slid gratefully into the steaming water. Laney lasted only five minutes, then wrapped up in an enormous towel, grabbed her teddy bear and dropped right off to sleep in a cushioned wicker chair. Even Allie found herself dozing by the time she was ready to get out. What did her Company have to offer this place? Nothing, really. She couldn't think of a thing—and didn't care.

They went to dinner late, long after children's menus, which made Allie a little self-conscious. She relaxed when she noticed the kindly glances toward Laney from the largely older clientele, and blushed but was pleased at a few glances for herself from the not-elderly gents. She choked a bit on the price list, wondering how to rationalize this on her expense claim. Laney had a broiled Pacific octopus appetizer so she could say she ate one, and shared Allie's decorative but ample serving of seared West Coast ahi tuna. Another perfect day in paradise.

Tofino was quaint and touristy. She took note that nearly everyone on the island descended on this little town as a favored destination once or twice a year. Allie had no intention of surfing, but the rustic little surf shop overlooking an inlet and snowy mountains drew her eye, and they went in. Something smelled good, like a berry farm, and she realized it was a barrel full of cakes of surf wax by the door. Laney wanted to buy one—"Only a dollar, Mom!"—but a young shop worker satisfied her with a neon bright surf decal.

"Going surfing today?" He was evidently the owner, and as rustic as his shop: long, graying hair and beard, and bright eyes behind John Lennon glasses.

"No, no, I don't surf. Just looking."

"Heck, anyone can surf! We can rent you a board and suit, and the girls in the shop across the road give great lessons." Allie hesitated too long. "C'mon, let's find you a suit. What size are your feet?"

"Are you really going surfing, Mommy?" Laney pulled her head out of the wax cake barrel in surprise. "Do it, Mommy, you'll be good!"

"Does this beautiful lady belong to you? What's your name?" The Lennon glasses went down on one knee to Laney's level. To Allie's bemusement, Laney carried on a five-minute conversation with him, covering everything from favorite music to favorite Bible characters (Laney didn't know any) to why seals poop on the docks instead of in the water.

But Ted, as his name turned out to be, hadn't given up on getting Allie into the waves. "Hey, why don't I rent you a couple of wetsuits and boogie boards and you can play on the beach in comfort?" Laney squealed. Allie threw up her hands and gave in to the man's contagious enthusiasm. Laney looked terribly cute wrapped in neoprene head to foot, somewhat like a daddy long-legs spider. The surf was small that day, Ted explained as he showed them North Chesterman Beach on the map, but he warned Allie to keep her daughter close and stay in the break.

Glorious, glorious day! Endless waves, jade-green, foaming brilliant white. As they approached the water, Allie was less than convinced that the thin covering outlining the exact shape of her body could lessen the frigidity of the North Pacific. So it surprised her when she hardly felt a thing, only a momentary cooling when the first moisture soaked through, soon forgotten as the sun and the waves overtook all awareness.

"Mommy, Mommy, Mommy, this is the best ever!" Laney was small enough to sit on her boogie board, and even a relatively small breaking wave sent her flying toward the beach until she fell off, usually on purpose. Allie, on the other hand, couldn't catch a wave in the shallow water and caught herself instead watching nearby surfers with envy. One day she would try it.

Sandcastle building led to the equivalent of mud wrestling as the fine sand liquefied in the pools they made. A young boy showed them how to dribble liquid sand into tall columns, like trees with snow on them. Of course, the occasional larger wave destroyed everything they built as it swept farther up the beach, and then they started over again. The best part was that the waves washed the sand off them in a moment, without the usual shock of cold. It was indeed the best ever. Allie couldn't remember ever having more fun with her daughter, and her heart ached when it was time to take the suits and boards back.

Laney was asleep in the five-minute drive back to the board shop, but Ted's enthusiasm woke her. "How was it? Did you catch some waves?" To his surprise, Laney rolled out of the car, gave him a big, wet hug and pattered over to a wicker chair where she fell asleep again. "That good, eh? You're gonna have a job getting the wetsuit off her asleep." It was.

"What are you doing for dinner? I make a mean fettuccine."

Allie looked at him squarely. "Are you trying to pick me up?"

"No… well, yes, but fat chance of that." Ted looked at Laney, who was back on the wicker chair with a blanket over her, unfortunately with her thumb in her mouth. "C'mon, what can happen? Do you like crab and scallops?"

"Love 'em." Allie's defenses seemed to be at an all-time low as she relaxed into the pace of another world. But she had been there before, and alarm bells were ringing deep within her. Careful, Allie, let him know what's what. "But just dinner, thank you, and then I need to give Laney a bath and an early bedtime."

Dinner was even better than promised—no token seafood in this pasta, but heaps of crab, shrimp, smoked salmon, scallops, and even abalone. "Don't tell anyone about the abalone; a diver friend gets it for me and it's not exactly legal." Her daughter ate ravenously at first, then slower and slower until she finally got up, laid her head against Ted's scruffy old border collie sleeping in the corner, and went to sleep. So much for that bath. Ted assured Allie that Barkley didn't have fleas, and a little saltwater never hurt anyone.

They talked—over too many mugs of coffee—long after Laney should have been in bed, though she looked comfortable, wrapped up in a down blanket on the sofa. They had much in common. Both were born in New York and raised in Manhattan. They each had their horror stories of parents splitting up, weekends at dad's apartment, frustration and anger and bad choices in school. Ted had the misfortune of turning old enough just in time to get drafted near the end of the Vietnam war. But he didn't go. He told the story of a wild ride across the border into Quebec, stuffed into the empty spare tire compartment of a truck. He headed west and didn't stop until he saw the waves, and never left. "It was a bit easier back then to immigrate to the island, and the Directorate was especially sympathetic to draft dodgers. But it was a lot of hoops to go through. And They still watch me, I know it."

As the alarm bells beating in her brain quieted, Allie told this stranger things about herself that hadn't come to mind in years. This guy wasn't after her body; he was intelligent and interested, and it was good to talk and know she was heard and understood. Time passed timelessly.

"Mmmm… I can't believe we have to go back to Parksville tomorrow," complained Allie. "I'm not even sure why. My research is up the creek." She told Ted about her assignment and the redundancy of Internet cafés in a place that had everything.

"Hmm, I don't get that one," Ted mused. "Something about your invitation to come to the island creeps me out. They want something from you; I don't know what, but there's no other explanation."

"What do you mean?"

"I mean, I don't trust what I can't see. And neither I nor anyone else in this Nirvana has ever seen the people who run this show. Oh, you see officials and stuff on TV, but never the Directorate. Something about impartiality and security is what they tell us, but you never see Them. They stay behind closed doors, never reveal Their identity. Why?"

"They don't exist?"

"Well, I thought that once, but I don't anymore." Ted looked at her intensely. "Can I trust you?"

"You can see me."

"Touché. But seriously, if I tell you what I think, what some other people here think, will you keep it yourself? You won't write this in your report, or tell someone that—I don't know… could do something about it?"

"Now you're creeping me out. Okay, I solemnly promise not to breathe a word to a soul. Pinkie swear."

She said it too playfully; Ted glared. "Seriously. You have no idea what kind of trouble this could get me and others into. I shouldn't have said anything. I'm sorry." He moved to clear up the mugs, and she placed her hand on his arm.

"No, I'm sorry. For not taking you seriously." Not the last time she would think that. "What is it? I won't tell anyone, I promise." A faintly ringing alarm bell made her withdraw her hand.

He got up and put their mugs in the sink. "I don't know what I was thinking. Not only could others get hurt—so could you. I should say nothing." He absently rinsed their mugs; Laney stirred on the couch but didn't wake up. "Only this: the more I think about your situation… you, uh, better get out. Now. Something's not right about Them inviting you to come on a useless mission. I don't know what They want from you, but I'm pretty sure it's not in your best interest to stay on this island." He looked at her pointedly, almost desperately.

"You're saying I should go? I don't want to leave! I don't care about my project anymore; in fact, I'm looking into what it would take to immigrate."

"That is something I totally understand and totally do not recommend. You don't know what you're getting into, Allie. This place is hypnotizing, but the snake exists. I don't want to see you swallowed up."

"You're scaring me. I didn't expect you to scare me."

"Believe me, right now the feeling is mutual. Leave, Allie. Leave soon."

They bundled Laney into the car without speaking. Ted was clearly upset; for whatever reason, Allie wasn't. Before she got in the car, she hugged Ted, whom she had only met that afternoon.

"What was that for?"

"Ted, thank you. I don't know what this is about, or if I even believe you. But I'm sure your advice didn't come easy and comes from a caring heart. So thank you. I hope… we'll talk again. And you do make a mean fettuccine."

Somehow, Laney didn't wake up as Allie brought her to the suite and tucked her into bed. But Allie sat long into the night, watching the outline of the waves in the moonlight until she fell asleep curled up on Laney's wicker chair.

IV

Monday morning. Six o'clock. Who calls at 6 AM on a Monday? "Rebecca Young, I should have known. Do you know what time it is here?" Allie rubbed her eyes and hoped to God the phone didn't wake Laney.

"All I know is, it's 9 AM here and I haven't heard from you in nearly a week. What's going on?"

"Nice to talk with you too, Rebecca. How about if I call you back in a few hours, like right after breakfast?"

"Allie, I'm under a lot of pressure." Sure, thought Allie. "I need something from you—now! I'm meeting with your team at lunch and we have nothing to talk about." Allie pictured her fellow workers rolling their eyes at having to spend lunch listening to Rebecca. That's what the call was about: Rebecca Young with nothing to say was a national crisis.

"That's simple. Reschedule your meeting for tomorrow. This afternoon I'll send you a summary of what I've got so far and you can spend your next lunch break ooing and awing over it together."

Rebecca spoke incessantly for the next six minutes and forty seconds as Allie watched a wall clock with glazed eyes. She didn't even try to interrupt her supervisor. "Allie, are you still there? If you've hung up on me, so help me…"

"I'm here, I'm here. Are you done? Good. Watch for my email." Allie hung up, a little too smugly for someone who in all reality couldn't afford to lose her job. She rolled over, tucked the down comforter around her and went back to sleep.

Several hours later, with Laney off to school, she sat in bed, laptop on a pillow, highlighting the word "They" and musing over the special nuances given it by each new font. Who are They? Who runs this place? How do you find out? Do you walk up to the front door of the Parliament Building and ask? Well, why not? Maybe it was time for that trip to the big city, Victoria. Allie sighed. *I have so liked not being in a city.*

That evening, Laney came into her bedroom, toast dripping with peanut butter in hand. "Don't even think about climbing on this bed with me until you wash your hands." The little girl obediently sucked her fingers and used Allie's en suite to wash them clean. Then she snuggled under the covers. "Want to go see the big city, honey?" Violent shaking of her whole little body under the comforter. "I have to say I agree: I'm not much into cities these days. But I bet we could find some fun stuff to do there. I think they have an aquarium."

Laney's head shot out of the covers. "With dolphins?" Dolphins were her favorite thing in the world.

"I don't know, but you know how to find out." She had taught her daughter the computer since she was tiny, and she could get herself around Google like a pro. Laney took over the laptop, searching the Internet courtesy of the Vancouver Island Directorate, and—with a little help in spelling—soon found her dolphins. Allie got ready for an early night's sleep and wondered what Rebecca Young did on Monday evenings. *She's probably tearing apart my report,* Allie thought with a smile.

Victoria. Certainly all the island had a British feel, but this city was a microcosm of London on the Thames with Dover in its back yard. Elegant architecture covered in ivy, double-decker buses, a tiny harbor filled with luxury yachts and sailboats, Madame Tussaud's wax museum, and a downtown with not one practical shop (though an entire street of used bookstores). They should have had a wonderful day. But Laney insisted on a two-scoop cone full of chocolate bits, which ended up on Allie's lap not long after she ate it. Something about the smell of little girl vomit lingers no matter how much you try to wash it out in the bathroom. For the first time in a long time, Allie wistfully watched young couples walk by the buskers on the quay, young couples zip past on mopeds, young couples pose with live mannequins on the street corners. Laney lost interest after the first hour of her downtown Victoria experience. The dolphins were calling.

"We'll go see the dolphins after lunch, okay honey? One more stop and we'll find something to eat. I want to go see those big, old buildings across the water. That's where the people work who are in charge of this island, the government." Laney's nose wrinkled, but she didn't say anything, so Allie grabbed her hand and led them along the crowded waterfront, passing through jugglers, native artisans, spray paint artists, musicians of every genre and a man on a tall unicycle who Allie thought must have the best view of anybody.

A polite security guard/tour guide informed her that the massive wooden door she was standing before wasn't the front door of the Parliament Building—which was on the far side—but was actually the rear entrance, though it opened to all the beauty and bustle of the Inner Harbor. Next to it was the Ceremonial Entrance, but since Allie and Laney couldn't claim to be queen and princess of any country they could think of, they had to settle for the back door. Tours were over for the morning, but they were welcome to look around inside, and they slipped into the cool, naturally lit silence of a massive round lobby with a breathtaking rotunda a hundred feet above.

"Does their president live here, Mommy?" Laney's shrill voice parted the silence and echoed off ornately carved stone walls, turning the heads of tourists and security personnel.

"They don't have a president, honey. They run things different here." Allie looked down the long, dimly lit corridors branching in every direction. "And no one lives here, as far as I know." Her notion of finding answers was fading fast. Anyone connected with running the country was buried deep in this maze of hallways. She had seen much older buildings even in New York, but this place reeked of tradition and protocol. One got the impression that nothing surprising ever happened here. "Hungry? Me too. But no pizza this time, okay? I want some real food. Let's go check out the restaurant that overlooks the Harbor."

The real food was a little too Old Country and gourmet for both their tastes, and prohibitively expensive. Even the aquarium was disappointingly non-American. No performing seals and beautiful handlers. Everything was designed to exhibit the marine animals' natural habitat as closely—even religiously—as possible. Half the tanks appeared empty as octopi and other sea life hid away in crevices. Even the dolphins looked like nothing more than dolphins. Laney yawning at an aquarium wasn't a good sign. "Had enough 'big city,' Laney? Ready to head home?"

As they drove the winding highway out of the city, Allie realized with a start that her work project hadn't come to mind once all day. Nor yesterday as far as she could remember. My project's dead, Allie thought to herself. Dead before I ever got here. Why am I still on this island? What's more, how much longer can I get away with it?

The voice at the other end of the phone was polite but firm. "Really, her arm is practically better," Allie responded. "The bruise is nearly gone, and she says it's itchy. She has a small bandage on it to keep her from scratching. It doesn't seem worthwhile to come in…"

"Miss Simpson…"

"Ms., thank you." Allie's pet peeve.

"Ms. Simpson, we're concerned that the vaccination may not have been successful, and it is required by law. If we had the opportunity to examine your daughter, we could ascertain…"

"Look, I wasn't happy about the vaccination in the first place. I won't allow her to have another shot because you're not sure."

"That may not be necessary. But in any case, if another vaccination attempt is necessary, and you refuse, you may have to end your stay prematurely."

"You've got to be kidding! You would... I have a living to make, you know! I have a research contract to complete! I've barely started!" She wasn't about to let this person know that she had little reason to stay. Some remote but alert part of her brain expressed amazement at the panic she felt about being forced to leave.

"We will give you two days to set up an appointment." She gave her the name and phone number of the clinic. "If we haven't seen you by Thursday, I'm sorry to say I will need to hand your case over to the authorities. My apologies, Ms. Simpson. See you soon."

Allie set the phone down and watched Laney on the window seat, playing with Barbies. What in the name of...? What kind of place is this? Up to now, her experience on the island had felt like paradise, but this phone call—especially after her conversation with Ted the other day—left her with a cold feeling in her stomach. Let the doctor see Laney, she told herself. The shot hasn't hurt me at all, so Laney will be fine. What am I afraid of?

But she was afraid.

Laney came over and hugged her middle. Such a sensitive child. "What are we going to do today, Mommy? It's so nice out. We're not gonna stay home, are we? Do we have to visit more cafés today? Can we go for a drive? I want to see those mountains again, up closer. They still have snow on them, Mommy! Snow!"

Allie put her fear on the back burner and crouched down to Laney's level. "Let Mommy see your arm, darling. Does it still hurt at all?"

"Nope, it's just itchy and kinda scratchy." Allie gently pulled the pink pajama top down from Laney's shoulder and tugged at the bandaid. Laney tugged back, and between them, it came free. To Allie's consternation, the place where Laney's arm was injected was red and sore, and when she went to touch it, Laney pulled away. "Laney, it does hurt you, doesn't it?"

"Not much, Mommy, but whenever I touch it something pokes me, and I don't like it."

"What do you mean, honey? Let me see—I won't touch it." She brought the little girl under the light of a lamp and looked closely, and could see nothing. But as she started to look up at Laney's face, she caught out of the corner of her eye a glint of something in the sore spot. Again she looked closely. Nothing. If she had a magnifying glass…

"Hold still, Laney. I'll only be a minute." She went to her camera bag and pulled out her 55mm lens. With lots of light and held at the right distance close to Laney's arm, the magnification was quite good. Still, Allie had to strain her eyes to perceive a tiny something sticking out of her daughter's arm. It seemed to be glass, but not a fragment; it had a smooth, round end, and it wasn't clear all the way through. Allie sat back, astounded.

"What do you see, Mommy? What is it?"

"I don't know, honey. I don't know what it is."

"Let's go see the doctor, 'kay?" Laney was suddenly on the verge of tears. Her mom always knew what to do.

"Darling, you'll be okay. Do you hear me? Give Mommy a chance to think. I want to make sure I'm doing the right thing." She carefully put the bandaid back on, and of course it didn't stick. A little digging in her purse produced another one, crumpled up but sealed, but all she wanted to do was to take her little girl in her arms, which she did the moment the bandaid was in place.

"Mommy!" came Laney's muffled voice. "Mommy, you're squishing me!"

"Sorry, dearest." Allie let go. Laney sniffed and wiped her nose on her other sleeve, and Allie's heart melted helplessly. "Hey, should we make some cinnamon toast? Mommy could use some cinnamon toast right now."

"Okay."

"You go get everything ready, and I'll be there in a minute." Laney ran to the kitchen, and suddenly Allie's breaths heaved in panic. Something is wrong. Ted was right and something is really wrong.

"Mommy, I don't think we have any cinnamon."

She caught her breath and squeaked, "In the drawer with all my spices, honey…" She sat back on the couch and tried desperately to compose herself. Was she overreacting because of what Ted told her? *What did They put in my little girl's arm?* She had to find out.

Allie barely constrained her emotions as she watched Laney create cinnamon toast, practically one grain of sugar at a time. Her mind raced. *Where on this island could she find any help? If the vaccination contained something They didn't want her to know about… Is this Ted's paranoia talking? There must be a perfectly logical explanation. Which is what they always say on TV when there isn't.*

"Laney, I want to look at your arm again."

"No, Mommy. No. Can I go to the Daycare? Or the hospital? I want to be okay. I'm scared."

"You don't need to be scared, honey…"

"You're scared! I can tell. You saw something in my arm and now you're scared." Her big eyes welled up.

Allie took a deep breath and put on her professional voice. "Laney, I want to look again because I think you have a sliver in your arm that is making it stay sore. I've taken out your slivers before, haven't I? Can I look and see if I can find this one?"

She sniffed. "How did it get there?"

"I don't know. But if we can pull it out, maybe we can tell."

"Okay," she said, barely convinced. "Will it hurt?" Her question brought to Allie's mind an image of the woman who gave Laney the injection. *Surely she wouldn't have knowingly injected a young girl with something harmful. Let's get real.*

"Gonna have to hold real still, honey, like with your other slivers. You know how careful I am not to hurt you." They sat close to the lamp, with the camera lens in Allie's left hand and her eyebrow tweezers in the other. On her first try, Allie could get no grip on the tiny rounded surface, especially when she inadvertently touched Laney's skin with the cold metal and made her jump. "It's okay, darling, let's try once more. You all right?"

Laney nodded. Before applying the tweezers again, Allie pressed lightly on either side of the sore spot, and through the lens she saw the glass projectile protrude slightly. This would take more than two hands. "Laney, you get to hold the lens. Careful, 'kay? Hold it as still as you can." Laney's version of holding still required much head bobbing on Allie's part, but she saw the edges of the tweezers grip a little lower on the projectile and she gently pulled… and dropped whatever it was on the carpet.

"Laney, don't move. I dropped it, right by your big toe, but it's too small to see without the lens." Allie couldn't keep the panic out of her voice, but the little girl innocently interpreted it as excitement.

"You can do it, Mom! Find it! You can find anything!" Allie turned on the LED light in her phone, and with her nose centimeters from the carpet, she used the lens to scan the area around her daughter's little feet. Nothing. It could be anywhere, could have bounced…

Or it could be stuck to Laney's sweaty big toe. Which it was.

"Hold super still, Laney. It's on your toe. Carefully hand me the book on the side table, and I'll put it under your foot. There. Okay, I've got it with the tweezers. Move your foot. Gotcha, you little whatever-you-are."

Allie set the book carefully on the table and looked closely through the lens. "Come see, honey."

"No! Gross, I don't want to see it." She strained to look at her arm. "Mommy, I'm bleeding." The smallest drop of blood oozed from where she had pulled the projectile, and Allie took no chances. She cleaned Laney's arm with an antiseptic pad, applied antibiotic cream and yet another princess bandaid.

It was well that Laney had no desire to see it. The thing her mom had taken out of her arm wasn't a sliver. It was a rounded cylinder of glass. It was the diameter of the period it rested beside on the book and shorter than the letter i. Allie pulled out her larger camera lens, but not enough light passed through it to see the tiny object any better. Not wanting to risk losing the thing, she cut a small piece from the black cleaning cloth for her lens and pressed it into the bottom of a spare contact lens case, then carefully placed the cylinder on the fabric. She screwed on the cover and sat back, thinking hard.

V

"Hi, could I speak with Ted, please?"

"You've got him. What can I do for you?"

"Ted, it's Allie." After a moment's silence, she explained, "You made me and my daughter a great seafood pasta a while back, remember?"

A longer hesitation. "Um... actually, I don't. Sorry! You sure you have the right person? I don't remember anyone named Allie."

"Hey, do you have dementia? It can't have been more than two weeks ago. You rented us wetsuits, and Laney fell asleep before I could get it back off her..."

"Listen, I'm sure I would have remembered you. But I'm pretty certain you haven't been in our shop. Can I give you the numbers of the other surf stores?"

"Um... this is really weird. I recognize your voice and everything. How come...?"

"Sorry I can't help you, lady. Gotta run. Surf's up." The call beeped and was gone.

Allie sat back on the sofa in consternation. What the...? Is it me or has the world gone mad? She remembered Ted becoming serious, even afraid, when she told him about her project. And as she remembered, her phone rang. Ted's voice. "Hey, don't say anything. I'm on my way to Port Alberni. Can you meet me at Cathedral Grove? You passed it on your way here before—the gigantic trees next to the road. Be there in one hour, near the biggest tree. You will see signs. See you soon."

Another click. Allie wanted to cry. She never asked to be part of someone's messy life; she only wanted to work and raise her daughter and enjoy some adult conversation once in a while. Not this. Not again.

Laney's artwork was all over the living room floor, along with indications that not all the glue stayed on the paper. She mistook her mom's serious face for serious trouble and employed some frantic dabbing, making a bigger mess. "Laney, it's okay. We can get it out easier when it's dry." Allie didn't even care if that was true. "We need to go for a drive. Remember the enormous trees? Do you want to go back and see them again?"

Laney looked out the french doors at a grey sky threatening cloudbursts. "Now? You want to go now? Why, Mommy?"

"We're going to meet Ted. Remember him?" Head shake. "The guy who rented us wetsuits and gave us dinner?"

Head nod. "Okay. And I don't have to clean up first?"

"No time, honey. We need to go now. Grab your sweater and rubber boots, all right? We'll be back soon and I'll help you clean up."

A drizzle hazed the windshield as they left town heading for the mountains. Allie was still on the verge of tears, frustrated and angry. *Men! Why do they have to involve us in their stupid problems? What does this have to do with me? What did it have to do with me in Thailand, and Justin gets through security with no problem and I'm interrogated like a criminal for two hours and miss my flight, and I never see him again…*

"Mommy!"

Allie's eyes focused and didn't recognize the road ahead of her.

"Mommy, I think you missed the turn! The sign said Pacific Rim Park, and that's the way we went last time."

"Sorry, Laney, you're right. Where will we find the next exit, I wonder, so we can turn around?" Seeing a gravel bed between the divided highway, she signaled to move into the right lane, bringing on the blare of a car horn as a black SUV whipped past her like she was standing still.

Allie swore. "Sorry honey. Plug your ears. I shouldn't have said that, but some guy went by me like a hundred miles an hour." She didn't add, *and I nearly killed us.* Her nerves were shot. Allie needed coffee. She needed to go back to the condo. Or get on a plane and go back to innocuous New York. But around the next curve was an exit sign for a U-turn route. *I guess I'm not the only one who misses the turnoff,* she sighed. And froze. The black SUV was in the exit, angled across the road, red and blue lights flashing inside. It was too late to turn back onto the highway, and a police officer held his hand up for her to stop.

She had no choice. He stood in front of her car and typed the license number into a handheld device, paused and came to her window. "My apologies." Something in his voice didn't sound apologetic. He was young but confident, and his slight British colonist accent sounded so articulate. "I think I must have startled you, passing you back there. Your signal startled me too."

"You didn't have your lights or siren on," Allie countered.

He didn't answer but typed some more. "Driver's license, please?" He glanced at it, murmuring an absent, "New York, eh?" He didn't hand it back. "Where are you going?"

The unexpected question annoyed her. "Are you trying to be helpful, or do I have to answer that?"

"Let's start with 'helpful'."

"Tofino." Laney in the back seat squealed with delight. *Why am I lying, and to a police officer?* Allie scolded herself. *And why the heck did I choose Tofino?*

"Did you know you missed your turn?"

"That's why I'm using the U-turn route. Or trying to."

Two more vehicles were now stopped behind her, but this guy was in no hurry. He stepped back into his truck and talked with someone on his radio for several minutes. When he came back to the window, he seemed angry. "Follow me until we're back on the highway and I'll show you the correct exit. Then you can continue."

Allie was fuming now, but followed him through the U-turn route back onto the highway. He soon slowed and signaled toward her exit. She took the corner at what was a daring speed in the presence of an officer, but out of the corner of her eye, she saw him continue down the main highway. She eased off the gas pedal and heaved a sigh. What on earth was that about? She suddenly remembered Ted and realized she might be late now to meet him. What might this have to do with Ted and his veiled apprehensions? Was she putting him in danger?

They found the biggest tree at Cathedral Grove with no trouble, but no Ted. It was raining, and Allie hadn't thought to grab raincoats before they left. Laney, clambering up an enormous log, was filthy and wet in minutes. It didn't make sense to wait around. They sat in the parking lot for fifteen minutes, rain pounding on the roof and splatting on the windshield, but no Ted. Allie started the car, said nothing in answer to Laney's questions and started back the way they came.

Twenty minutes later, Allie came out of her daze and realized that Laney was no longer complaining but sitting in a huff, curled up in her car seat. "Sorry, honey, I don't know what happened with Ted, and I know you're wet. Hot chocolate?" The little café off the highway looked deserted but cozy, and the waitress kindly put them at a table by a small gas fireplace and turned it on. Allie stared out the window and said nothing. Laney stood before the fire and sipped her chocolate, so she didn't see Ted walk through the café door and directly to their table. But she nearly spilled her drink when he pulled out a chair and sat down.

Allie looked at him, stricken. "Ted, what the...? Can you tell me what on earth is going on?"

Ted returned Laney's hug while carefully taking her cup from her and setting it on the table. "Good to see you, Allie. I'm sorry to scare you again." Laney returned to the fire. Ted sat down and leaned close. "I think you found something. Do you have it with you?"

Allie looked at him incredulously. "How can you know...?"

"If I had a nickel for every person who has called me out of the blue with that tone in their voice, I would have a lot of nickels."

He put his face in his hands, elbows on the table, and sighed. "Is it here?"

The white lab coat with the official VI insignia wouldn't be enough clearance to get Alistair Hopkins onto this elevator. He held still for the retina scan and spoke his full name, "Alistair James Hopkins," but he knew They knew who he was without it. He enjoyed the moment of weightlessness as the rapid car dropped beneath him, the slight g-force as it came to stop on the fifth floor. It was the lowest floor he could go to by pushing a button. He was aware of two more floors below this one, and he wondered if and how he would ever see them.

The doors opened to a hallway cut through grey sandstone streaked with beige, contrasting with concrete reinforcement that looked cold in comparison. A second retina scan brought him into a small control center filled with rows of monitors and a large screen in front, currently displaying a satellite image of the Pacific Rim. His fellow workers barely glanced at him as he went to a monitor and signed in.

His assigned task today was to complete his report on some local effects of the massive earthquakes in Japan several years ago, based on information provided by sensors placed along one mountain corridor north of central Vancouver Island. Minimal effect, which was troubling. The world moved ten centimeters off its axis on the day of the big Japan earthquake. But some giant fist held Vancouver Island, allowing little movement in the past many years, despite the shifting of continental plates in both northern and southern hemispheres on the far side of the Pacific. I wouldn't want to be in this room when the Big One hits, he mused to himself once again. God, let me be safe with my family in a wood-frame house. He doubted that the offices and hallways above him, cut out of seemingly solid bedrock, could withstand a 9.0+ quake, despite measures taken every year to make this underground labyrinth "safe."

His unofficial but no less assigned task involved risks far more dangerous to him than the quake they expected within the next 100 years. So far, no technology here had detected the relatively tiny partition he had created on the mainframe, which daily searched and analyzed terabytes of highly encrypted communications that flowed on this system. He had limited access to this information for milliseconds a day, and it felt like trying to understand an entire new civilization by reading a few of its text messages in an unknown language. But he was at least aware of something large that existed here, an establishment—no, more like an organism—far beyond the scope of any ordinary government bureaucracy. And he was picking up clues that kept him awake at night.

Alistair recalled his training as he pressed the device on his keychain that would in a moment upload by Bluetooth last night's cache of information. If he were to get caught, it would be in the seconds needed to access the software on his partition. He and others had worked hard to reduce this window to a minimum, and it wouldn't help if his nervousness coincided with unauthorized usage of the system. Though he didn't know how closely They monitored this room, he couldn't take the chance. He slowed his breathing and turned his inner eye to a familiar scene, a favorite waterfall near his home in East Sooke. Four, three, two, one. Complete. His attention returned to the geographical chart on his screen. But his armpits were too damp. How long could he do this?

Afternoon became dusk, twilight became moonless dark, but only the large digital display on the wall told the white-coated men and women in the room that their ten-hour shift drew to a close. They left in twos and threes over a twenty-minute span, as per policy, ascended the elevator and walked a hallway that took them from the twenty-first century to the nineteenth, in architecture at least. As he approached his car, a fellow white-coat grabbed his arm. "Hey, you're out in Sooke, right? Can I get a lift to Colwood?

Wife has the car."

Alistair nodded assent, though with some reluctance—this had never happened before. His car alarm bleeped off as he opened the doors with the remote.

"CR-Z. Very nice, Alistair! Are they paying you more than they're paying me?" He played his hand along the contours of the roofline. "You wouldn't let me drive, would you? I always wanted to try one of these. Wife would never let me get one, though. Two-seater isn't practical when I never take her anywhere," he laughed.

Alistair stiffened. "Sorry. Not that I don't trust you. I don't lend my wheels, not to anyone."

"Hey, you'll be in the seat right next to me! What's the deal? Man, you're more stuck-up than I thought! I mean, it's one thing that you're the only one who never goes to the pub with us. Forget it, I'll ask someone else."

Alistair called him back. "Okay, okay. But only in town. Pull over before we reach the highway." He laughed awkwardly. "This baby might get away on you." The man sneered as he took the keys—with the device attached. It would draw too much attention to take it off now, but Alistair's heartbeat increased.

"Maybe I am stuck up—I can't recall your name." He needed to go with it, make conversation, not draw attention... where the heck were they going?

"Paul. Geothermics. Up the other side of the Gorge is always faster to Colwood this time of night. And no highway! Pretty sneaky, eh?" He was a skillful driver, quick but smooth. A person who could drive a car like this one to its full potential and not hurt it. That didn't help Alistair relax. He slid his hand into his coat pocket and prayed he could find the panic button on his phone to reach Fletch, plus turn the volume off at the same time. He heard no sound, but he couldn't tell if he had connected.

"So Paul, what's your last name? You look a lot like someone I know."

"You know we don't do last names in our business, man! Who

do I look like?" Alistair invented a name and hoped it didn't sound too corny. "Nah, never heard of him. No relation of mine. You have kids, Alistair?"

"One and a half." Paul's eyes questioned. "A three-year-old and one on the way. You?"

"Nah, wife teaches at the university 24/7. If she got pregnant, I would be suspicious. I'm okay with it. Kids complicate things."

"I guess. I like it, though. There's nothing like a little person falling asleep in your arms as you read them a story."

Paul said nothing. Drove more aggressively. And this didn't look like Colwood or any other part of Victoria that Alistair knew. Maybe Metchosin?

"You're a good guy, Alistair. I hate to do this." Alistair turned and found the cold barrel of a handgun in his face. "Get out, or I'll blow your head off. I'm giving you a chance—you might survive hitting the ditch. Go. Now!"

They were doing at least 80 km/h, not a house in sight. Alistair unbuckled his seatbelt and opened the door.

"It's old technology, really, which shows how long it's been in place." Ted toyed with her contact case as he talked. "It's an improvement on what's called an RFID tag—Radio Frequency ID tag—used in livestock and pets for identification. Normally a tag this small would be 'passive'—with no power source of its own—and readable a meter or so away at the most. In the late 1980s, someone here on the island discovered a way to make a small RFID like this one 'active,' so it's readable up to 100 meters away. They encase it in glass and inject it into a muscle, and it slowly moves around over the years to a spot where the body finally ignores it. Of course, they never inject it into the bloodstream, as that would cause clotting and a possible stroke."

Allie sighed at this explanation and watched Laney, asleep in her chair with her little body contorted in a way that seemed impossible. "Why do they want to ID everyone, Ted? I don't get this. And why is it such a big deal?"

"At first, I think ID-ing everyone was all they meant to do. We have a limited population and stiff immigration rules. It's useful to verify who everyone is who stands in line at the post office or poses for the photo on their driver's license. But we suspect that the less innocuous uses of an active RFID became apparent quickly. As the number of monitoring stations increased, They began to know not only who you are; They know where you are, all the time. Small electronic monitors are now more closely distributed on this island than sheep in New Zealand. They monitor all your spending, the coffee shops you frequent, and whether you were at the scene of the crime at 11:08 on Saturday night. They know."

"Okay, who's 'we'? Who are 'They'? And aren't you concerned about being here in my condo? Don't They know that you're with me? Are They listening to us?" Allie involuntarily glanced around the room and shuddered.

"Of course not. Like I said, it's old technology. Perhaps RFID version two might attempt to pick up conversations, but this one sure couldn't. And the reason I can be here with you is that I'm not really here. I am right now lying on my bed in Tofino, and tomorrow morning—after a pee break—I probably won't get up before noon."

She looked at Ted incredulously. "You're so full of...!"

"Listen, I found my RFID. It was accidental—I was helping a friend shape a surfboard, and I managed to gash my forearm deeply with the wicked little handsaw I was using. To my surprise, along with the blood and bits of meat that came gushing out, I spotted a glint of something shiny, which proved to be a glass tube like the one in your lens case. Did my homework, found out what it was, and didn't have a clue what to do about it. I realized it might be prudent to hide my discovery from the people who implanted it in me, so I kept it on me always—even surfing—which drove me nuts because now I wondered what the damned little thing was telling

Them, and who the hell 'They' were, anyway.

"Then more than a year later, I was talking one day with a guy in my shop who came to do a bit of surfing, and he said, 'Hey, take a look at this. Have you ever seen anything like it?' And he pulled out a magnifying glass and showed me his RFID. He discovered it as a small, irritating bump under his skin. Being a doctor, he did some self-surgery and found the tiny glass tube inside a small cyst that had formed around it. I have no idea why he thought to ask me about it, except that he had discovered it the day before. I suggested that he not show it to anyone else and that we sit down and talk about it after his day of surfing.

"That was the beginning of several years of building a core of people who knew they were being monitored. A few had discovered their RFID in one way or another, and we found them or they found us. Others we carefully brought into our circle, often because they were people who might help us discover what was going on—government employees, technicians, even a few police." Allie's eyes widened. "No, not the one who stopped you. I suspect he was under orders by people tipped off by your phone call to trail you to Cathedral Grove. That would explain his frustration—he probably got chewed out for stopping you at the exit.

"We also discovered that someone or something was aware of us; that as much as we thought we had been careful, we were being watched. At first, we thought we were being paranoid, and that it was unreasonable to feel we were being followed or our phones listened to. But Tofino is pretty quiet in January, and you notice when strangers show up and hang around, acting like out-of-place tourists. It's obvious to us now. I was at the Cathedral Grove parking lot, watched you get out in the rain and saw a man and woman—also without raincoats—follow you into the woods."

Allie shivered. "So, is that why you said you're not really here? Did you leave your RF...—whatever—in Tofino?"

"Yes, but it wouldn't do to leave it stationary. My dog Barkley is wearing it in his collar in the shop. He follows my staff around all day, impersonating me. But I can't risk doing this for long.

They're constantly watching for people who walk by and don't show up on their monitors, who are separate from their RFID. That's why I asked right away if you had Laney's with you."

"Well, what are they up to? What have you discovered?"

Ted hesitated before answering. "Allie, I don't want to draw you into this any more than I have already. Let's get you off this island and back to safe little New York."

"No, Ted. I know it makes sense to leave, but I'm mad as hell about this. It's the investigative instinct in me—I want to know. I… I want to help…"

Ted rose from the sofa and put on his jacket. "People have died, Allie. At least we're pretty sure they're dead. They simply disappear; we haven't seen or heard from them since. I can't risk you and your daughter's lives. Yep, They wouldn't hesitate to take the life of even a little girl. I'll make arrangements tonight to get you to the mainland as soon as possible, probably within a day or two. Please don't call me; in fact, avoid using the phone, answering the phone, texts, emails. Stay here in the condo except to do ordinary things like picking up groceries. No trips anywhere. Okay? I can only help you if you cooperate." Ted stifled Allie's attempted protest with a raised hand. "Please. You have no idea what we're dealing with. I appreciate your offer of help, but I can't accept it. Good night, Allie." And he left.

Allie sat for a long time with the lights out, processing dark thoughts. She was mad as hell all right, as mad at Ted as anyone. *I'm dragged into this, but I'm not in. I'm going home.* That thought made her even angrier. *I love it here! I have nothing back home except a job I hate. Laney loves it. Why can't we find a way to stay? What's so bad about someone knowing where I am all the time? What have I got to hide?* But she remembered the call from the clinic about getting Laney's shot checked out, and a deep, cold fear that she couldn't name washed over her. She kept replaying her conversation with the nurse on the phone, and then she was with Laney, and they were dragging her through a door with a small glass window into a bright white room, and Laney was screaming and reaching out her hands to her…

She jolted awake to the darkness of her living room, breathing hard, shivering cold. Dragging her wool blanket over, she fell into a fitful sleep on the couch. Ted sighed, pulled away from the window where he had been watching, and walked ten long blocks to his waiting car.

As he opened the car door, his phone rang. Alistair. He answered, but heard no reply, only a murmur of voices, hard to hear… Ted sat in his car, straining to hear the words and identify who was speaking. After several minutes, a louder, unfamiliar voice: "…blow your head off…" He heard a loud bang! and screech of tires, then nothing… Ted could hardly breathe, the phone still connected, sounds of struggle, walking, dragging, grunting. Someone running, a door slammed hard, and another, the sound of a motor starting up, the shushing of tires on wet pavement… Ted listened in horror, the phone still connected, but there were no more voices at the other end.

VI

Morning came but brought no relief to Allie. She groaned. Gotta stop falling asleep on this couch. I'm not like Laney, who can sleep anywhere. Laney—is she up? Allie rolled over onto the floor and went to her daughter's room. The tousled bed was empty. Not in the bathroom either, and the panic surged irrationally, irrepressibly, in Allie's heart. She rushed into the kitchen; no Laney dripping peanut butter, she's nowhere, not in the den, she is... sitting up in my bed, reading the Archie comic she had begged for in the grocery store the other day, days ago, years ago, why would Archie comics attract a six-year-old, she fell on the bed, shaking, weeping, holding her startled daughter far too tightly. I can't take this anymore. It's time to go home.

"Mom?"

"It's... I'm... okay, honey." She sat up, shaking her head. "Had a bad dream, dearest, and didn't know where you were. Sorry for frightening you."

"You slept on the couch last night, Mommy!" Laney said disapprovingly. "Did Ted stay here too? Do you like him, Mom?"

The thought was so far off Allie's radar screen it hardly registered. "No, Laney. Why would you think that? Ted is our friend, and he left last night after we talked for a while." She picked up the Archie comic, which didn't look like what she remembered as a girl. "I don't think you should be reading these." Her daughter had started reading books suddenly at the age of four.

Allie lay on her back, pulling the covers over them both, and sighed deeply. "You like it here, don't you, Laney?"

"Yes, I want to stay forever."

"What about grandma? Don't you miss her?" Laney sucked her breath in through her teeth and wore a loud pout. "Oh, I forgot.

You're still mad at grandma, aren't you. Okay, I understand, but be nice to her; she's extremely busy, and she wanted to come to your birthday."

"I will never have my sixth birthday again. And she missed it."

What can I say to that? thought Allie. Miserable old...! I don't miss her either.

"We'll stick around here today, okay? Maybe get an ice cream and some groceries later? Mommy needs a day at home."

"Okay." They snuggled comfortably silent for several minutes. Laney tickled her mom and got tickled back, and they laughed, and finally Laney managed to slowly, slowly push her mom right out of bed.

She thought about booking a flight home but realized someone might be watching or listening or whatever. We will get off the island, that's all that matters, and then we can worry about getting home. And life will return to normal urbanity, banality, bland nothingness. It will be like coming home from Disneyland and everything suddenly looks so... ordinary. Ted will carry on this war, and I guess I care more about him than I thought. Did he reach home okay, or did some quasi-policeman/Nazi stop him too? And why do I care so much, when not long ago I hardly knew this place existed, and I was okay. But really not. That's it—something about being here has filled up a part of the void in my cold, hurried world. I don't want to leave. Ever.

The phone rang. No number she recognized, and she remembered Ted's warning not to use the phone, but it was so hard to hear it ring and not answer it. On the fourth ring, she picked it up. "Hello, who is this?" Who answers the phone that way? What was she thinking? "Sorry, this is Allie. Who am I speaking to?" Worse.

"This is the Qualicum Medical Centre. We talked the other day about Laney's shot? Anyway, since we haven't heard from you, I've booked you in to inspect Laney's shot at 2:00 this afternoon. As I told you before, this is extremely important, and I strongly suggest

58

rearranging your schedule to attend to this, Miss Simpson…"

"It's Ms., thanks. And I don't think… um, yeah, okay. We'll come." And she hung up. Now what? This was unexpected. Should she go? Of course not, since they were leaving anyway. But would that raise suspicions? Would they actually call the authorities, call Them? She didn't know what to do. She picked up her phone and was about to call Ted when she remembered he said not to. Her head hurt. Needed more coffee.

"Who was that, Mommy?"

"It was… it's okay, Laney, it was nobody. Don't worry about it."

"Are you okay, Mom? You don't look so good. Maybe you should go see a doctor, Mom. Can I be your doctor? I can help you practice seeing him!"

She was so enthusiastic that Allie gave in to her offer. "Okay, doc, I feel terrible! What's the matter with me?" Allie coughed and snorted and tried to look as awful as she could. Laney took charge like a true professional.

"Say aaahhhhhh, please?" Laney screwed her face up in disgust. "Mom… I mean, lady, I don't think you brushed your teeth this morning. Your breath is awful. I quit being your doctor!"

"Oh, but you're the only doctor for me!" Allie chased her around the table, breathing and coughing at her as Laney screamed and laughed. How I love this little girl, Allie thought as she caught her daughter and marched them both off to the bathroom. Ted's right; I can't risk endangering her. I hope we leave today.

The Columbian black-tailed deer that are found on every part of the island, including most neighborhoods, are not much bigger than a large dog. But a mature buck on the side of the road is big enough to slam shut a car door opened at 80 km per hour. Wham! Both airbags went off as the impact threw Alistair's little CR-Z into a spin on the wet pavement; the car lurched a few times but didn't roll, and stalled in the middle of the road. After a few moments of complete silence, his body assessed that—though his wrist hurt—the explosion of the airbag into his face had hardly dazed him. But to his amazement, Paul was out cold. He soon saw why as blood poured from Paul's nose. The airbag had used the handgun to punch him senseless, a perfect uppercut that slammed the cartilage of his nose against his brain.

It took seconds for Alistair to shake himself into action. He dragged Paul across the road where he propped him against the deer, which was quite dead. He was very tempted to use the handgun, but instead picked it up with two sticks and dropped it in the murky water in the ditch. The dented passenger door groaned as he shut it. He kicked it closed and climbed in the other side, panting. He had to get to his family before... He dropped the accelerator to the floor and ripped up the dark, deserted street.

In years long past, when the crust of the earth was more in motion than it is today, Vancouver Island was part of a large, moving mass of rock under the Pacific Ocean near Mexico. Its name is Wrangellia, and today it also forms the panhandle of Alaska, Haida Gwai and part of the coastal mountains of the mainland. It consists of lava deposits formed underwater and the accumulation of billions of sea creatures that calcified into limestone. At the end of its long journey up the Pacific, Wrangellia collided with the west coast of North America north of the 49th parallel and welded itself there, pushing up mountain ranges and eroding softer layers to expose hard outcrops. Like cars at rush hour, one after the other two smaller masses rear-ended Wrangellia along its southwest coast. The Pacific Rim Terrane pushed up underneath what is now the coastline as far as Tofino and formed the rugged headlands and beaches loved by touring colonists. The Crescent Terrain fused itself to present-day Victoria, occasioning a spurt of magma that appears as granite bones sticking out of the parks, lawns and headlands of the city.

To keep things interesting, Wrangellia and the other terrains came to rest near the interface of the North American continental plate and the much smaller Juan de Fuca and Explorer oceanic plates tucked in beneath it. The Cascadia fault line runs between these plates a hundred kilometers or so offshore all the way to California. But the fault line isn't vertical; it slopes down toward the mainland, so the west coast is like the edge of a dinner plate. And Wrangellia—including Vancouver Island—is a chip on the edge of the plate, one that hasn't fallen off. Yet.

None of it has stopped moving.

The movements are now infrequent, rarely noticed by anyone on the street, recorded only by instruments able to measure the millimeters and centimeters that are the shiftings and groanings of these massive chunks of plate and crust. But once in a while, something gets stuck. For as many as several hundred years, tension builds as plates continue to shift, except for this one section. It's like cracking a stubborn walnut—you apply more pressure and squint your eyes, because you know something has to give eventually and suddenly. When the stuck section of these tectonic plates finally gives, everyone knows it, and the shaking up of our little world is devastating.

The last Big One on Vancouver Island was in 1700, before seismographs and careful recording. If it were not for the accurate time-keeping of the Japanese, who suffered from the resulting tsunami, we would know this earthquake only from the stories passed down by the First Nations people of the island. They tell how the shaking was so powerful that their ancestors couldn't stand and lasted so long they became sick. The quake knocked down massive trees and caused many landslides. Tsunamis destroyed coastal villages and threw driftwood thirty meters up into the headlands. The entire rim of the Pacific Ocean felt the effect.

As Alistair drove his SUV through the night, with the children asleep on the back seat and his wife sitting beside him in tears, he felt like the next Big One had hit him. They had this comfortable life together in a place they loved, and in a moment, it was gone. A shaken Ted had told him cryptically on the phone—once Alistair remembered that the phone in his pocket was still connected—that everything was in motion to get him and his family off the island at their secret disembarking point. Alistair resisted at first. "Fletch, I know what it costs to move a package. We can lie low for a while, find another way."

"No way. Too risky. Besides, I have another couple of units I need to move right away too." He paused. "I'm this far from getting all of u… our units… out of here, tonight. I'm done. Some things aren't worth saving or fighting for."

"I never thought we were doing this for us, Fletch," Alistair reproved gently. "I'm forced out for now, but it doesn't mean I'll stop. This is no time to bail on three-quarters of a million people."

"Okay. Look, we need to get off the phone. Text when you arrive. Bye."

Alistair set the phone down, wincing under his wife's reproachful glare. "Right now," she said in a quiet, forced voice, "Right now, I'm not thinking about three-quarters of a million people. I'm thinking about the four of us. With no home, no place to go. You could have told me what you were doing."

He had nothing to say in reply. They settled into an uncomfortable silence as the headlights ate a tunnel through the trees that drew close on either side of the highway. We would have lost our home eventually anyway, he brooded. If I knew then what I know now, I would never have bought waterfront property, no matter how good the sunsets are. For all our complacency, I feel tension on this island—under this island—more every day. For months now, the slightest shiver on the graphs made us all stop and look when for years we would hardly pay attention. Something's gotta give, and soon. The whole Pacific Rim says so. I'm not sad about leaving.

VII

The phone vibrated again and again. Allie slept the exhausted sleep of a mom pushed too far, and Laney concentrated on coloring princesses in a fat book from the world of Disney. The doorbell had a different effect since they had never heard it before. "Laney! Don't! Let me get it." Allie tumbled off the couch, then walked with leaden legs to the door, rubbing her eyes furiously. She looked through the peephole in the door and stopped breathing. Police.

It was too late to not answer—Laney made sure of that with her loud questions. She took a deep breath and opened the door.

"Miss Simpson?"

Whatever. "Can I help you?"

"No need for alarm. I'm here to escort you to your 2 PM appointment for your daughter—at the clinic, remember? It's 1:30 now, so you have a few minutes to get ready." His glance said that getting ready was an obvious necessity.

"Seriously. I need a police escort for a doctor's appointment. What the hell is this about?"

He remained polite, but his voice was decidedly firmer. "The clinic was concerned that you were resistant to attending this appointment, which is required by law. I'm afraid you will have to come with me. I can drive you to the clinic and back, if you like."

"I do not like. I will drive us myself, and you can follow, if you like. Give us a few minutes." And she closed the door.

Laney was silent, but tears were welling in the corners of her eyes. She threw herself into her mom's arms and sobbed. Allie stood and carried her to the French doors in the back of the condo. She saw a head duck down behind the fence of their tiny back yard as she approached. Trapped. She could think of no way out of this. What would happen now? Allie grabbed the phone, sat with Laney on her lap and jabbed Ted's number. Voice mail, right away. "Ted, it's Allie. I have unexpected company. I'm headed to the clinic right now to see about Laney. Call you soon."

Doorbell again. She set Laney on the couch, still shaking, and went to the door. "What?"

The policeman backed off, apologetic. "Sorry, just checking. We need to go soon." He looked askance at her unchanged appearance, but she closed the door on him again. She took Laney in her arms and held her close.

"Honey, it's okay. We're going to the clinic to get this over with…" Violent shaking of her head against her mom's shoulder. "Yes, Laney, we have to." The stricken look on her daughter's face was too much to bear. Allie took charge, changed them both, took her keys and phone and went to the door with Laney in hand.

At the door, Laney pulled back. "Mom, wait!" She pulled her hand out of her mom's and dashed into her bedroom, returning with her bear. They opened the door, and the officer didn't look pleased. "Sorry, my daughter's upset. Well, let's go." She said it as coldly as she had ever spoken to anyone.

The police car led the way. Allie parked, got out of her car and took her time collecting Laney from her car seat. The cop remained in the car, watching as they entered the clinic. Allie was sure he would still be there when she came out. Maybe they had the whole place surrounded. She was ready to give someone a piece of her mind, but when she arrived at the desk, it seemed ludicrous to start in on someone who probably knew nothing about what she had been through. The receptionist told her that a Dr. Johnson would see her. She sat down and started absently reading out loud a book Laney was looking at until Laney indignantly pulled the book up close and began reading it to herself. Allie's hands were shaking, and she tried to will them to stop.

"Allie? Laney?" They followed a nurse with long blonde hair through a maze of corridors, and she indicated a small examination room to her left. "Allie, have a seat. I'll take Laney to the bathroom to get a urine sample. We will be right back."

"Well, I'm coming too—I can…"

"We'll be fine, Allie. This is what I do. You don't mind coming with me, do you, Laney? Is your bear coming along?" Laney looked like she minded very much, but didn't say anything. She hugged the bear and gave her mom an "I-thought-you-would-be-on-my-side" kind of look as Allie silently watched them walk down the hall. With a small lump in her throat, she sat down in the examining room.

It looked exactly like any examining room she had ever been in. A large poster on one wall outlined the dangers of UV exposure and the difference between sunblock and sunscreen. Get a grip, Allie! She reproved herself for her anxiety. No big deal, even if they give Laney another shot. We'll be out of here soon, and then it won't matter. I need to stop looking suspicious. Cooperate, and we can disappear off this God-forsaken island.

Several minutes passed and Allie wondered what kind of battle might be raging in the bathroom. Laney wasn't the type to pee on command. She remembered when they were traveling somewhere and Laney wouldn't or couldn't pee before they left, and inevitably they had to stop at a gas station 15 minutes down the road. Maybe she likes gas stations or something… What on earth; where are they? It's been more than five minutes.

She stood and looked down the corridor. No one there. She sat down, got up again and walked down the hall in the direction they had gone. Allie saw nothing that looked like a bathroom. So she sat down in the examination room again and was about to get up and go to the front desk when a doctor entered the room. Her world came tumbling down in a crumpled heap.

"Allie?" He looked exactly the same: the dark, tousled hair; the straight lines of a face deeply tanned in contrast to his white shirt, opened at the collar a little too much for a doctor but fine for impressing any young nurses. Allie had once been jealous of other women's glances at him. Still athletic and ruggedly handsome.

Justin. She couldn't breathe.

"Allie, are you okay? It is you, isn't it? Allie Simpson? It's been years." He looked around the otherwise-unoccupied room with a frown.

"Seven, to be exact. Where is Laney?"

"Who?" He pivoted his attention back to her.

"My daughter. My six-year-old daughter. She went with the nurse for a urine sample several minutes ago and hasn't returned. Where is she?" Rage was building. This is so surreal, she thought. I'm losing my mind.

"Daughter? Where…" He regrouped himself and stared at her. "No way! You don't mean…"

"That I could say, where is your daughter? Yes, I could say that. But I'm so mad right now, at any moment I will make a scene."

He looked at her like she was mad in more ways than one. "One moment. Stay there. I'll find out what's going on."

When he left, her mind reeled. She put her head in her hands and pulled her hair in an attempt to regain reality. What was he doing here, of all places? The last time she saw him, he was leaving the security lineup in Bangkok, shrugging his shoulders with her laptop bag in hand as she was led away to an interrogation room. She remembered the day she first met him in the marketplace, his intriguing and informed explanations of the items she was looking at, the handsomeness of his day-old beard, his skill in driving a good bargain. What he looked like with his shirt off at the beach, and how she had practically thrown herself at him…

She startled as he walked back in, leaving the door slightly ajar. "Allie, it's so good to see you—I can't believe you're here! But I am concerned. They tell me you're here because of some abnormality with your vaccination…"

"Not my vaccination, Laney's. My daughter." Her grip on the arm of her chair was becoming painful. "Where is she? Where is my daughter?"

Justin studied her silently. "Allie, we have no record of a

66

daughter…" Allie rose in a panic and shoved her way past Justin, who stood back with his arms up. She ran through the corridors to the nurse's desk. The nurse who had taken Laney wasn't there.

"I want to know what's going on," she demanded of the receptionist. "Where is my daughter?" Her breath was heaving. She looked like a crazy person.

"I…? Did your daughter come in here with you? I don't remember… What's your name?"

"Allie Simpson. My daughter's name is Laney and a nurse with blonde hair—long blonde hair—took her to get a urine sample and never came back with her."

"That's impossible! We would never take a urine sample here, only at the lab. And we don't have any nurses here with long blonde hair." She glanced around as if seeking help with the crazy lady and consulted her appointment book. "We have an appointment at 2 PM for Allie Simpson. No mention of anyone with you."

Allie staggered back into the arms of Dr. Justin, who had followed her. He walked her back down the corridor, and when Allie started to resist, he gripped her arm—painfully—and led her firmly past concerned nurses back to the examination room. This time, he closed the door. She was frantic now and nearly incoherent. "Bring me my daughter! What have you done with her?! You animal!!" she screamed. "You can't have her; she's mine!"

He gripped her shoulders firmly and shook her. "Allie, I will count to three, and when I get to three, you will stop."

She stopped, glared at him and said with teeth clenched and a voice full of hatred, "Find my daughter and bring her to me—now!"

He let her go, stood up and sat down in a chair on the opposite side of the room. "What proof do you have of your daughter? Show me."

"This is such…" She dug furiously in her purse, then realized that both of their passports were in her laptop case at home. Birth certificate. Her own was in her wallet, but not Laney's… yeah, that was in the laptop case too. Stupid. Immunization records too—all in that bloody case. Never again. No photos… Phone! She had photos of Laney on her phone. Allie pulled it out and fumbled around on it like she had frozen fingers. Scrolled furiously—yes, Laney! She held up her phone in triumph.

He looked closely, took the phone and scrolled through more photos. "Cute kid, Allie, but this isn't proof. She could be anyone, a niece maybe. Doesn't look anything like me. Sorry."

"Look, I don't know what you're trying to pull, but it's stupid. Lots of people here have seen me with my daughter, all I gotta do is go to my apartment and get her ID…" She stopped. "You don't believe me!" She stood up. "I'm out of here. A cop out front escorted me…" He gaped at her. "Let's go ask him." She put her hand on the door handle. It was locked. "Open this door! Since when does an examination room door lock from the outside? Let me out, damn you!" She wrenched on the door, uselessly. He pushed her firmly away from the door, took a key from his pocket and opened it. In the doorway was a nurse, looking frightened, and Justin shoved past her and closed the door behind him, leaving Allie inside.

She went ballistic. Slammed her fists on the door, threw a chair at the tiny window near the ceiling and missed, screamed and swore, upset a tray of instruments, and finally fell to the floor and sat with her back against the wall, sobbing and shaking. Several minutes passed. One hand was bleeding where her fingernails had pierced the skin. She wiped it on her jeans and got up to pound on the door again, and as she stood up the door opened. Many people arrived—nurses, paramedics, police and a maintenance man. Not Justin. Many hands, many voices, talking to her, giving orders. Someone gave her an injection that turned her to rubber; they put her on a stretcher, tightened straps, and she descended into oblivion.

Ted arrived at her condo and sat low in his car, watching as several police officers entered—he couldn't tell if someone answered the door or if they broke in—and left again moments later. He didn't want to use his phone and didn't want to go to the door, but after 15 minutes of inactivity, he got out and pressed the doorbell with his knuckle. No one came. Allie's message on his phone was more than two hours ago. Something was up. He tried the door handle with his sleeve and to his surprise it was open, and he realized that if the cops broke in, they wouldn't have a key to relock the deadbolt in the door. He entered and shut the door behind him.

Nothing looked disturbed except a laptop case lying on the table, open, with papers and various cords and accessories stuffed inside as if in haste. Careful to not leave fingerprints, he leafed through the papers, and a passport slipped out. Allie's. No sign of Laney's. That's strange, he thought. Why would they take the one but not the other? He found nothing else of consequence: some bills and junk mail. He looked around the room and wondered if it was now bugged, and what They would think of rustling noises and no RFID to associate them with. He could do nothing here, and left. He suddenly had too many places to be at one time.

Allie came to consciousness as if pushing through heavy curtains toward a lighted stage and an audience gazing at her. Two police officers and a nurse came to attention, ready for anything, as she groaned and tried desperately to keep her eyes open. She woke to the tight feeling in her stomach that something bad had happened or was about to happen. She couldn't remember what it was. An image flashed into her mind of Laney walking down a white hallway, holding someone's hand and looking back at her…

"Laney!" She jerked herself up and fell back, too weak to push past the blanket tightly restraining her. Couldn't move her arms. Lay insensible for several moments and turned toward the blurry faces by her bed and pleaded, "Please, please help… my daughter. Tell me where she is. I don't know…"

The officers looked at one another. One of them held something close to her face—too close, so she pulled back her head—and focused on a passport. Laney's photo. "Is this your daughter?"

"Yes, where did you… You were in my house. Why? Where is…?" Darkness tried to limit her vision and darken her mind. She desperately pushed it back. The nurse made a suggestion that was briskly ignored.

"We had to confirm that you have a daughter and that she was with you at the clinic, which we have done. And that she is now… missing."

Allie gasped. Said in a strained, compliant voice, "Missing? What do you mean? You don't know where she is? You don't know where Laney is?" The surrounding faces were blank. She crumpled back into the sheets and started to cry. The nurse rose and dabbed at her face and put her hand soothingly on Allie's forehead.

The officers sat watching, silent and awkward, for several minutes. Finally, one spoke up. "Allie, we need to ask you some questions. Time is critical for finding your daughter. Can you answer some questions?" Allie nodded, eyes closed. "Who was with you in the examining room before we found you? A nurse? Doctor?"

Her eyes shot open. "You don't know? The clinic…" With effort, she pulled her arms out from under the tight sheets and rubbed her face, seeking rational thought. "A nurse took me to a room. Long blonde hair…" She gripped the officer's arm. "The receptionist, she said they had no nurse with hair like that. Who could she have been? Was I wrong? My mind is…"

"It's okay, Allie. You've been through a traumatic experience. Try to remember—was the nurse the only one with you?"

"No…" Panic mounted as memory returned. "Justin… he has her! It's his daughter! I told him he can't have her… Abandoned us, never tried to find me…"

The officers glanced at one another.

"Hey!" Allie's voice firmed, regained some of the rage. "I'm not crazy, okay? A doctor… walked in the room…" She was having trouble catching her breath. "I knew him from… before. Justin. I had a daughter by him six years ago… Laney. I don't know what he was doing… there. Haven't seen him… in more than six years. Must have taken…"

"It's okay, Allie. We believe you. This nurse told us she saw you with a doctor she didn't know. He's disappeared. And I'm afraid no one noticed the blonde nurse. They may have been working together. I'm sorry."

"Bloody let me out of these sheets. I'll behave, I promise." The nurse helped her and Allie sat up, swayed a bit and focused her attention on the officer who had been doing the talking. "You said time is of the essence. What are you doing to find her?"

"What is this doctor—Justin—what's his last name?"

"Forget it. Do you think I haven't tried to find him these past seven years? I don't even know if his first name is Justin. He called himself Justin Farnworth. Pretty hokey name, huh."

"Description, then." She gave him every detail she could, and he typed everything on his phone, not fast. "Sorry, new phone, hate this keypad." He kept typing. "Did he say anything, like was he surprised to see you?"

Allie thought. "You know, he seemed way less surprised than me. I was in total shock to see him, but Justin—it was like he was only trying to act surprised."

The officer nodded and typed. "Anything else?"

"Same when I asked him where my daughter was. I would have expected a guy to be flabbergasted to find out he has a daughter.

He didn't believe me; he wanted proof. I showed him photos…"

He glanced at her sharply. "You had photos on you?"

"On my phone." She looked around the bed. "My bag, where's my bag?"

"No bag came with you to the hospital." He motioned to the other officer. "We'll check with the clinic and see if it's still in the room."

"I'm in a hospital?"

The nurse spoke up. "Am I still needed? Can I go back to the clinic now?"

"Yes, but we'll be in touch with more questions." He motioned to the other officer. "Get the nurse's info, okay?" They left the room. "Leave the door open. Thanks." He looked at Allie. "You okay?"

"Yeah, but why the hospital? What are you going to do?"

"Calm down, Allie. I'm asking a few questions and other people are already looking. Your information will help them." Allie glanced around the room, taking in where she was. "Psych ward. Sorry. You were acting a bit crazy at the clinic when we entered the room, which was locked, by the way. The clinic said that no lock was on that door previously." He typed some more. "You won't have to stay here. We'll take you home soon. We're doing everything we can, okay Allie?"

She felt very alone. The kitchen grew darker, and she made no move to turn on lights or find something for dinner. Life had come to a standstill. Breathing was enough to occupy her; her throat was tight and painful. Where was Laney? She had never spent a night away from her since she was born. Tears squeezed themselves free of the corners of her eyes and ran unchecked down her cheeks. The only thing that made any sense at all was that Justin—or whatever his name was—had found out about Laney and pulled an elaborate scheme to take her for himself. Why, though? He had never seen her, never contacted them, never showed any interest before. And why here? She put her face in her arms on the table, shoulders shaking with sobs.

Allie heard a sharp rap on the glass of the sliding door next to the table. She jerked to her feet, nearly passing out, and sat quickly again. A face at the window, finger to lips. It was Ted, motioning her outside. As she opened the door, he slid away into the shadow of a hedge. She followed, fell into his arms and gripped him hard. "Shhh. Gotta stay quiet. They're watching your place and may be listening too."

"He has… Laney," she managed, struggling to control her voice, which broke anyway. "Justin, this guy—he took her. I met him years ago, had Laney by him, never heard from him again."

"Allie," he whispered, "I don't think it was him." She raised her startled face to his. "I can't tell you why, but I'm certain I'm right." He sighed. "I wish I could tell you more, but I can't. Right now, all that matters is getting you off this island."

She pushed back from him. "I'm not leaving without Laney!"

"I hear you, Allie, but we need you to go. They're using you to get to us, and it's not only my skin at risk—lots of people." She shook her head into his shoulder. "Please, Allie, I can't stay. I'll find you soon and move you someplace safe. We'll do everything we can to reunite you with Laney."

She sagged in his arms. "That's what the cops said too. If Justin doesn't have her, and They don't have her, who does?"

"That's the question." He held her at arm's length. "Please, Allie, trust me. The safety of many, many people rests on you doing nothing right now. Stay home as much as possible, cooperate with the police, wait for me, and don't call me. If I can't get to you, the person who does will ask you if you know where you can buy abalone. Your answer is, 'Only from the back of a truck,' and you'll go with that person wherever they take you. You will remember? Trust me?" She nodded. "Okay, back in the house. We'll all be together soon, I promise."

She kissed him on the cheek and walked across the tiny lawn to her kitchen door, not looking back. Long into the night, she sat at the table with her back to the sliding door, not daring to look toward where he was or might still be, but wanting to be as close as possible to the comfort of his presence. She finally staggered to the couch, wrapped herself tightly in the old wool blanket, and slept badly.

Only a few of Alistair's fellow technicians noticed his absence in the seismic lab, and only one cared. Like everyone in his department, Eric Phillips saw many people come and go, but Alistair's sudden and unexplained disappearance troubled him. They were practically neighbors. The day Alistair didn't show up for work, Eric noticed that his stylish cedar home down the street also seemed deserted—no lights on, no kids playing in the yard, and Alistair's little sports car left in the driveway with the passenger door inexplicably caved in.

Even so, Eric might not have paid much attention, but someone else in his life had disappeared in the past year. His son Trevor gave them trouble from the day he was born, culminating in his being recently charged as an adult with kidnapping and rape. He pled not guilty—though it wouldn't surprise Eric if he had done it—and was convicted and sentenced to lifetime deportation, destination Taiwan, where a second offense could bring him the death penalty. Eric hadn't heard from him since the day he was permitted to see him off at the airport, and though he had searched extensively for him online, he found no trace of his name, address or circumstances. He was planning a trip to Taiwan next month, which was both risky and illegal—he would use a false ID that cost a good deal more than the flight. As much as his son exasperated him, the thought of not knowing where he was and if he was okay was slowly driving him mad.

The other strange thing about Alistair's absence was that instead of planting a new technician at his desk, they had removed his terminal—for "refit and upgrade" the repair guy told him. But why only one terminal? And why Alistair's? It all set off alarm bells for a guy like Eric, who already doubted his government's actions enough to take the law into his own hands.

Real alarms sounded as a mild motion in the heated rock floor indicated a tremor. The large screen on the wall flashed red three times, technicians scrambled into alert attention to their monitors, and several made quick phone calls to various sites around the Pacific Rim. Results came quickly: the US was already rating the earthquake a 5.6, located 145 kilometers west of Pachena Point, 43 kilometers below sea level. Eric and his team were reading it at 5.4, a number the US conceded to twenty minutes later. Not big, not small, no serious damage expected, certainly no tsunami threat, though they issued a warning anyway. It was rare for Eric's lab to feel one of the several tremors they recorded every day, so once status was established, a general excitement buzzed in the room for about twenty minutes. Then silence and diligence ruled once again, a tedium pleasant to a handful of complete nerds.

And one rebel.

Eric replayed in his mind for the thousandth time the instructions he received with his false ID: how to dress; how to pack; how to remain cool and calm at every checkpoint. His son was the only person left in the world that he cared about. He would find him, dead or alive, if he had to die himself in the attempt.

Routinely, Eric ran the several checks and analyses for which he was responsible, taking into consideration the data on this newest quake. It was of the highest magnitude in its vicinity in several years. Eric noted that though the magnitude was immediately intense, the duration of fault rupture was very short, only 2.4 seconds, followed by 7.8 seconds of reverberation. It was like a large object violently set in motion but immediately hitting a wall, so the shock waves created by the collision were greater than those of the motion that caused it. What magnitude would the quake have reached if it had more time and space to gain momentum? It was an important question and would take a week or more to answer satisfactorily.

Except he was leaving for Taiwan tomorrow.

The question would have to wait.

VIII

Allie woke, cursing herself for sleeping on the couch again, which was about two inches too short for her long legs. She squinted at the clock on the wall through blurry eyes: 9:30 and Laney still wasn't awake…

She bolted up, was immediately nauseous and collapsed back onto the couch. Laney. No Laney! Where…? No one had called, they would call if they had found her, she had to call, find out. She fumbled with her phone, found no new calls and struggled to locate the number the police officer had given her when he returned her handbag. It rang nine excruciating times before a recording came on—useless! She thought of calling Ted and remembered not to. Allie called the police officer again and left a message, and she could do nothing more. Do nothing, Ted had told her. Easier said than done, or not done. No diversions interested her, nothing else mattered and therefore she couldn't read a magazine or turn on the TV. So she sat on the couch, mind numb and straining for the ring of the phone or something to end her nightmare. For the first time in her life, she wished she knew how to pray.

At some point in the afternoon, she must have fallen asleep; the ringing phone dragged her from a great depth. It was Laney's school. She tried desperately to sound awake and alert but wasn't sure if her words were making any sense. "Everything is fine—no, it's… Listen, we don't know where Laney is, she's gone mis… No, I haven't been drinking; you woke me up! Damn it, you have no idea…! Forget this!" She ended the call and threw her phone across the room, then realized how much it was her lifeline right now and crawled over and picked it up and it still worked, but the screen had cracked across one corner, and she held it in both hands and the sobs came and the ache and her body shook until no more tears would fall.

And surprisingly, when she had nothing left, reason came to her like soft rain after a squall.

"Allie, what are you doing here? What are you waiting for? Will you sit in this condo until you're deranged and useless to your daughter? She isn't here; she's somewhere out there, and if you leave the finding of her to other people, what kind of mother are you? Pull yourself together, Allie. Do this."

Allie got up off the floor, took a shower, put on her most sensible clothes and filled her handbag with a change of clothing for her and Laney, their toiletries and some granola bars. When she stepped outside, her car wasn't in its spot. She stood for several moments, staring at the spot where it should be and forcing her mind to race through the last 24 hours so she could determine where she misplaced it. The clinic. It was still at the clinic, unless it was towed away. Allie called for a cab, which arrived in minutes, and knew the entire time that her car would still be in its parking spot, that it had to be if she was to not lose her mind, if she was to find her daughter. It was. She got in, started the engine and had no idea which direction to back out because she had no idea where she was going. When you don't know where you're going, any road will get you there, at least in Alice's Wonderland. This was feeling very like it.

She soon found herself on the Island Highway, heading south. That surprised her because if she were looking for Ted, he would likely be west, not south. She didn't know what day it was, nor the time. Groping for her phone to find out, she discovered she had left her handbag at the house. No matter. She needed no one now, not Ted, not the police, and the car was taking her south. So south she would go. She passed an LED sign that informed her it was 4:08 PM and the temperature was 16 degrees Celsius, and her brain—which was now in charge—automatically doubled the number and added 30 to make it approximately 62 degrees Fahrenheit. She swore under her breath because she had brought no coat and it was starting to rain.

On the highway north of Nanaimo, Allie wondered if the black SUV behind her was following her. She slowed down to half the speed limit, and the SUV pulled over. When she sped up, it pulled out again, staying back further than before. Allie turned into the exit that would take her on the old highway through the business district, and the SUV did the same.

This would be fun. She could use some fun.

She exited into a large shopping mall and drove up and down the lanes of cars. The black SUV didn't follow, obviously trying not to be obvious. She kept going—a little too fast—until she found what she was looking for: a parking spot that was open on both sides, so she could drive right through to the next lane. In that lane, she backed into the first slot she could find and flattened herself on the passenger seat so she wasn't visible. She lay there for a long time. She cautiously looked up, startling an older lady who was about to get into the car next to hers. No black SUV in sight. She waited another 20 minutes and returned to the main highway the way she had come, and saw no sign of her follower. As she continued south, with no cars behind her, she allowed her tense shoulders to relax and gave a great sigh. Her game wasn't as fun as she thought it would be. But she had won this round and felt pleased.

She continued south. Ladysmith. Chemainus. Duncan. Mill Bay. People lived in these little towns, busily taking care of their mundane lives, oblivious to the fact that her daughter was missing, that all of their shopping and walking and working were grossly insignificant in comparison. She resented their indifference. She had to pull over several times as a wave of panic hit her, and she willed her breathing to slow, willed her brain to take control and stop being so flighty. It was like being in charge of a young, unruly child who would become compliant if handled firmly, but might run out into traffic at any moment of inattention. At the top of the Malahat, a high mountain pass overlooking a long inlet, she pulled into a viewpoint with her chest heaving, and her concentration kept her from noticing the black SUV until she pulled up and parked right beside it.

They knew where she was. Of course They did. Unlike Ted, and presumably now Laney, whose RFID was in her handbag left behind in the condo, she couldn't go anywhere on this island without Them knowing where she was. How could she be so stupid? Anger boiling over, she opened her door, went around to the driver's side of the SUV and banged on the window, yelling, "What? What do you people want from me? Why can't you leave us alone?"

A startled, older face appeared, and the window opened cautiously a few centimeters. "What on earth? What do you mean?"

A woman's voice from the passenger seat urged him, "Close the window, Kevin! She's drunk, or crazy. We should call the police!"

The window went down another fraction as Allie sagged and turned to go. "Can we help you, young lady? Can we call you a cab, or a relative? You seem distraught! Please don't..."

Allie made no reply. She was far beyond politeness. And yes, she needed a cab—even a relative would be somewhat welcome— and she knew this second accusation of drunkenness was not far off the mark. Rage and desperation had intoxicated her, and she was in no condition to drive. Nevertheless, she started the engine and pulled back onto the highway.

She drove through a narrow, winding piece of highway beside a creek, with signs along it cautioning her not to disturb the spawning salmon, and then she noticed she was nearly out of gas, and remembered that she had given all the cash in her pocket to the taxi driver and her wallet was in her bag along with the phone, back at the condo. So the journey was about to become a footrace, she pondered undisturbed. She would drive until she couldn't and then... She shook her head, trying to clear it. Where was she going again? She must have known at one time, forgot...

In heavy traffic in downtown Victoria, the engine sputtered. As it died, she had to use all her strength to steer to the side of the road into what was clearly not a parking spot. She left the keys in the ignition and started down the street, which looked vaguely familiar. At the first corner she saw the backside of the ostentatious Empress Hotel and knew she was near the Parliament Buildings, the seat of power, and realized all at once that this was her destination. Those grey stone walls held the answers to all her questions, most of which she could no longer remember except that they had to do with finding Laney, and that was all that mattered.

But how to get in? She remembered that the door facing the harbor was the back door, the tourist door, and it offered nothing promising in the way of access to the powers that be. The front door must be on the other side, and she would walk right in and demand to know where her daughter was, because They would know. She suppressed the panic that informed her she was sidestepping the fringes of reason, that she was going mad. Her plan made no sense. It was a long walk to the far side of Parliament, and even then, the Front Door seemed to be still facing away from her. The block seemed endless. She turned down a walkway toward the front entrance, around a fountain, through some trees, and stopped as another wave of panic swept over her and a droning sound started in her head and spots danced in front of her eyes.

Pulled up to the front steps was a black SUV.

Men in suits emerged, surrounded her and caught her as she fell senseless into their arms. They bundled her into the back seat and drove away.

Ted sat back against the log, watching a small boat with no lights disappear into the dusk. Package delivered. Alistair and his wife and family were safely on their way to Canada, then on to England and her family, out of reach of those who were still wondering what he knew and whom he had told. He would miss them, and wanted so much to join them, maybe to go back to New York and sell used cars under a new name. More likely, he would die here—soon—on this island. He would disappear like TJ and Ricki and too many others he had cared about. No trace, ever.

The problem of Allie immediately presented itself. He sensed something new about her case, something of great significance to the Directorate. What were they up to now? Why lure a single American woman and her child to the island, scare her to death with a kidnapping allegedly carried out by the child's father, and now watch her like a hawk? Something had to have gone wrong with their plan; they had botched it and now they were scrambling to fix it. Why would they try to snatch Laney away when they could simply give her a new injection? Did they suspect that Allie knows about her RFID?

And who has Laney?

The local cops were genuinely treating this as a kidnapping. Justin the boyfriend didn't have her. The woman Ted had assigned to watch Allie's house and follow her movements saw Justin come out of the back of the clinic, alone and upset: yelling at someone on his phone; kicking cars in the parking lot; leaving with a screech of tires. Was he the tool of someone higher up? Maybe, but if they got what they wanted, why were they now watching Allie so closely? What if they hadn't intended to separate mother and child? What if a third party stole the child out from under them? But who? It didn't make any sense. He couldn't escape the conviction that somewhere on the island, someone was asking as many questions as he was. He stood and stretched his cold limbs. The cab of his pickup was only slightly warmer, but he sat for two hours before starting the engine.

He drove until the sky turned red in the southeast, pulled into Allie's street and parked two blocks from her condo. Hardly a person was stirring at that hour. No lights were on at Allie's place, and it took him a moment to realize that the blinds were still up, and another one to register that her car wasn't in its parking spot. Damn! He slipped behind the condo, found Allie's patio door and pried until its cheap latch snapped and the door slid open. No one there. Allie's bag was on the kitchen counter; phone and wallet, but no keys. He thought about taking the bag but remembered Allie's contact case with Laney's RFID inside. Digging in the dark, he located the contact case, got the tiny sliver of glass between his finger and thumb and dropped it down the crack between the gas fireplace and the wood flooring. That might eliminate some suspicion, but maybe it was too late. He took the cash from Allie's wallet, scattered the contents of her bag on the floor to mimic a break-in, and fled out the patio door.

Too many missing people! He would have to activate more of his team—more lives at risk—the burden was too much for a person to carry. Things were coming to a crisis, and he hoped it would happen soon.

The man's face was already a mess when they brought him in; they messed it up more. Between groans, the guy with the suit who was asking the questions determined from the man that Alistair Hopkins was still alive, whereabouts unknown. Same with his family. This idiot in front of him screwed up because he wanted Alistair's sports car. Yes, Alistair's key chain had a device, and no, he didn't get it from him. Make the loser disappear, the Suit told his mop-up crew. He had no use for incompetency.

It had been a rotten week, and the Suit wasn't looking forward to his own questioning, which explained his special brutality. Too many people were slipping through their fingers, and now the little kid. And what do these people know? Who will they tell?

He wondered how to explain why he had the woman. That certainly wasn't in the plan! He couldn't believe it when she stumbled right up to the Front Door, and he gave the order to grab her before he could think straight. It looked like she was about to pass out anyway. They probably already knew he had her locked up underground—they seemed to know everything long before the questions started. Trying to trap you with your words. Man, he wanted out, but that was impossible now. He knew only one way out: the way he had sent one of his own men just now. Straight to hell.

He'd better check on her before he went to report. The nurse told him she thought the woman was now conscious but exhausted and deeply asleep. Should she try to wake her? No need. They would question her soon enough, and the more alert she was when that happened, the better. Her vital signs and blood work were okay, a little anemic and showing signs of stress, but otherwise healthy. Whatever, he thought to himself. Her health won't be an asset for long.

Someone was calling her, but not by name. "Mom, Mommy, wake up!" She sighed. So it had all been a dream. She was in the condo, had slept late, and Laney was awake and trying to get her up. She probably wanted waffles for breakfast; good thing it was a Sunday morning. She rolled on her back and stretched, but Laney didn't jump on the bed and cuddle in close like she usually did. Instead, Allie's arms hit cold metal bars on either side of the bed, and her eyes flew open to show her a bare, grey room, harsh lights and a face that was not Laney's.

Allie tried to push herself up, but she felt so weak, and the face coaxed her back down again. "Rest, Allie. You have been through a rough time, but you're okay now. Try to sleep some more."

"No, I… I don't need sleep. Need to find my daughter, Laney. Someone will know… help me find someone who knows where Laney is…" She closed her eyes, trying to find again the young voice she heard calling her to wake up. But Laney was gone, not there, nowhere.

She wept, and a kind, warm hand reached through the rails and held her hands. "It's okay, Allie. It's okay to cry. I can imagine how you feel. If I were you, I'm sure I would cry too. I'm here for you." The warmth took down the last of Allie's defenses, and she gave over to weeping until she couldn't anymore. The nurse was patient and said nothing until her silent sobs stilled. Allie sighed an exhausted sigh and looked up at her.

"Thank you." She rubbed her eyes and tried to focus on the face above her. The nurse had the brightest of golden amber eyes. "Please, what's your name? And where am I?"

"You can call me Sophie, and you're in a hospital. Do you remember anything that happened?"

Allie's face went blank. "No. I have no idea how I got here. I was driving, and I left my car... I don't know where I left my car." She stiffened with tension. "My car! What's going to happen...?"

"Allie, your car is fine; you're safe. Try to relax. I'm certain you will see your daughter soon. They brought you here because you had some kind of breakdown. I don't know all the details, but I do know it will be best if you stay calm and let me take care of you. You can trust me, Allie."

"Trust you..." She sighed. "I would like that. But I don't think I can trust anybody anymore. I feel like the entire world is against me." She looked away. "All I want is my daughter. I want Laney, and I want to go home."

"Tell me about Laney. How old is she? What is she like?"

Allie's tense body relaxed a bit into the hard bed. "Six years old, going on 16. She's so bright, like a little adult sometimes. She says the most discerning things. I wonder if I've been too much of a buddy to her, and not enough a mom. I think I depend on her a lot. But sometimes she's young too, fragile and vulnerable..." She shuddered. Who has Laney right now? Is she okay?

"What do you like to do together?"

Allie looked up and smiled. "Eat. We're both good eaters. She can pack it away for such a tiny thing."

"What's her favorite food?"

"Anything unusual. Pickles dipped in peanut butter. She's the only person I know who likes Brussels sprouts. Once she even ordered octopus and ate the whole critter."

"Mmmm. I love seafood. Especially abalone. You don't know where a person can buy abalone, do you? It's so hard to find."

Allie's eyes opened wide, but the nurse continued to smile benignly down at her. Allie struggled to recall the correct response. "Um, I think… I heard… you can only buy them from the back of a truck."

The nurse laughed. "You're probably right, Allie. Listen, I need to leave you for a bit, and others will come to see you shortly. You will find this to be a tough day. But I will come back as soon as I can. Remember, Allie, you can trust me. I'm here for you. Okay?"

Allie nodded, tense but deeply reassured. She was going to be rescued. I guess I haven't lost my faith in people after all, she thought. Ted knows where I am; he hasn't let me down. But now what?

As if reading her thoughts, the nurse bent over her and said, "I know the human race can be disappointing, Allie. But some people you can trust, all the same. See you soon."

When she left, Allie's thoughts raced. She's the one! Ted said I should go with her, but for some reason I can't go with her now. Where on earth am I? She tried to remember what happened after she drove into Victoria and abandoned her car, but her mind was a fog. She wanted to get up. Her limbs felt heavy, like the last time she ended up in the hospital. Allie wondered if they had drugged her again. She wondered how this would end. She wondered when she would see Laney again. And as the tears came streaming down once more, she slid back into a deep sleep.

When she woke up, she saw several people wearing lab coats and a couple of nurses in the room, talking quietly until they noticed she was awake. They watched her silently. Sophie wasn't among them. It was awkward, and she didn't know what to do. Something about the awkwardness, so unlike her time with Sophie, made her not trust these people. She lay there, staring at the ceiling, waiting for someone to make the first move. The door opened, and a man with a beard walked in, wearing street clothes, greeting everyone and taking charge. The room relaxed, several wrote on clipboards, and the man with the beard came to her bed and introduced himself as Dr. Richards.

"Did you sleep well? Do you feel ready to sit up? Let me help you." He pressed a button to move the bed into a comfortable sitting position with her knees up, but it pinched her until she wriggled free and found her limbs to be dead sausages no longer. She sat looking at him expectantly and without expression.

"Allie, we're all very sorry for the difficult time you have been through." She didn't see much sympathy in the cold faces surrounding her bed. "Do you understand what has happened to you, and why you're here?"

"I don't know where I am."

"Of course, but you can see that you're in a hospital room. And you realize this is the second time in a short while that you have found yourself in such a room? In the psychological wing?" She said nothing, so after a moment of staring at one another, he went on. "I understand that these breakdowns you have experienced have to do with the case of your missing daughter, Laney." He placed a hand on hers. It was cold, in contrast to the warm words. "Most understandable. It's difficult, this not-knowing, wondering where your daughter is and if she's okay." He hesitated and looked meaningfully around at the others in the room. "But I am afraid that what I have to tell you will not be of immediate relief. I must say, regretfully, that your daughter is dead."

IX

She must have fainted, because when she opened her eyes no one was in the room and the bright lights were again dimmed. She was still in a cramped sitting position on the bed, and she couldn't find the button to shift it flat again. So she pulled her feet up under her and half-stood, climbed over the metal railings and down to the floor. She had to pause several times to catch her breath. The floor was warm, not icy like she expected. As she looked around, she saw that the walls were not brick or plaster, but stone, a smooth grey with streaks in it. The room contained nothing but the bed and a chair, which she sat in gratefully; her body was weary of the bed.

So it was over. Laney was gone.

No tears came. No relief to the ache in her throat and heaviness in her chest. She pushed back against the memories of her daughter that flooded her mind; her thoughts suggested no remedy to her pain. She sat numb, blank, cared for nothing, hoped for nothing. Nothingness felt so much better than anything else; she tried to immerse herself deeply in oblivion and void. Instead, irritating objections came to mind. Me! I'm the one who should be dead! Why does Laney get to die and I'm left here? I want to die too; I want to know nothing, have nothing, be nothing.

Darkness filled her mind, her world spun and—with eyes firmly closed—she gripped the arms of the chair to keep from toppling to the floor. It was a typical hospital chair, vinyl green padded seat and curved wooden arms. She felt their smoothness, except in one spot that was damaged, and she pulled a few splinters out of the place and dropped them to the floor. Her bare toe found them and rolled them back and forth underfoot.

They were. Though no longer part of the chair, the splinters still existed. If she were to die, would she still exist too? She didn't want that.

Did Laney still exist?

In the darkness of her mind came a faint warmth and golden amber light, an answer and assurance rising out of the fog, that she would see Laney again, that she hadn't irretrievably lost her. Allie had no category in her mind to place this thing, no shelf to set it on. Such a thought was entirely outside her framework, which was carefully constructed to exclude this type of invasion into her independence and self-sufficiency. Yet it was an alluring thought, and she wanted to entertain it. If she could only find a place in her mind to offer it hospitality.

The complexity of this dilemma kindled anger in her heart. Though she longed for Laney, she didn't want her this way, this pie-in-the-sky way. She wanted to run with Laney on the beach, cuddle with her in bed and make a mess in the kitchen together. A daughter living, not just existing.

Who has taken Laney from me, taken her forever? The little spark of anger fanned into flame and licked at her dry and empty hopes, consuming them. Rage burned its way into her soul; it engulfed her in moments. She was standing now, chair knocked over, fists raised. She swore out loud, cold and deliberate in her meaning: foul words; profane words. Some words she had only heard before and had never used rolled off her tongue and filled the room. She was on her knees, screaming words that were juvenile, crude, brainless and full of venom. She cursed and damned and violated everyone who had ever hurt her and many who had not, but none of it was any good, none of it satisfied her hatred and fury. Her wrath needed more fuel than that; it was a living inferno now, and she raged against the system, against The Man, against the machine that manipulated her and was responsible for her inestimable loss; and even all of that in the end wasn't enough and she fell back against the grey stone wall, exhausted—not in strength, but in coal for her fire.

Who the hell can I swear at now? She was breathing hard, like a boxer between rounds, pushing away the towel wiping at her face, spurning the water bottle placed to her lips. Give me more, let me at him! Only a lack of an opponent held her back, and she searched her mind for one.

Hell—why is hell a swear word? She had a vague memory of telling her mother "Hell, no!" and getting smacked for her emphasis. "Heaven" isn't a swear word; why should "hell" be one? Who decided that? Who indeed! Here was a worthy opponent, or at least a larger One. To her surprise, her mind had automatically given His pronoun a capital letter, and she removed it, demoting him to her equal. You! Allie turned her face upward to the ceiling. You did this! Having a specific target—so universal a target—renewed the flow of her anger and abuse. She called him every foul name she had ever heard and made up some new ones of her own. Told him what she would like to do with him, both violent and obscene. She called on him to do his worst, called curses down on herself to taunt him. She screamed it in his face.

He said nothing in reply, so she gave off infantile cursing and became eloquent. "You... you little-girl-killer! They call you kind and loving and compassionate! But you're nothing but a sadistic butcher, playing chess with us and spending your pawns to mop up your messes. Who put you in charge, huh? What gives you the right to screw up my life, again and again, and I hate it, and I hate you! Do you hear me? I hate you!!"

He seemed to listen but not hear her; he stood there and took her abuse—whether absorbing it or letting it roll off his back, she couldn't tell. None of it seemed to stick or affect him in any way, which was so unfair! Was he without feeling? Did he not care about anything? She wanted him to hurt, an eye for an eye and a tooth for a tooth, to feel her pain, to burn in hell.

She needed to get his attention. Allie rushed him suddenly and shoved him up against the grey stone wall. Ah, he felt that! She saw him crumple, and with his head in close range, she slapped him hard across the face. Again and again, back and forth, loud and satisfying smacks, and she felt him shudder under the impact as his face turned from one side to the other. Allie gloried in the pain in her palms; the strength of her arms had no limit. She went from slapping to punching: nose and eyes, heart and diaphragm. The wind expelled from his lungs in gasps; she kneed him hard in the groin and saw the agony on his face. This was so much better than mere words! His shirt tore under her grasp and she clawed his chest and his back with her fingernails, ripped long strips of flesh from him as effectively as a scourge, blood, blood, blood! More blood! Her hands did astounding things to his flesh, slashed and shredded and lacerated, pummeled and pounded. No instruments of torture were required; her hands and feet did the work, kneading flesh into pulp, kicking when her hands grew tired.

The man still said nothing, did nothing to defend himself, but he evidently felt every blow, every rending of his flesh. He was starting to sag; he fell to his knees, which made him easier to damage for a while but was less satisfying. Allie wrapped her arms around his large and bleeding body, and with every ounce of strength she could find, lifted him back into a standing position against the wall, oblivious to his blood on her face, in her hair, in her mouth. He wouldn't stay upright and kept sagging. For a few moments Allie contemplated this problem, and was relieved to find that yes, she had remembered to bring the mallet and the spikes: they were at her feet. It would have been useful to have one more hand, but somehow she hoisted him by one forearm as high as she could against the wall; she carefully placed a spike against his wrist, took the mallet from her teeth and drove the spike through his arm into the wall. After a few blows she could use both hands, and the blood spurted and covered her like a spring shower and she laughed and cackled and gave voice to guttural ecstasy. She did the same with the other arm and danced in the blood and stood back to admire her handiwork. And she mocked him.

"See? See? This is what it feels like! You put your subjects through this every day, and feel none of it. How do you like it now? Take this—this is for my sister's car accident! Here, this is for making her suffer for weeks until she died anyway. This is for turning my dad into an alcoholic, and here's another one for his liver cancer. And here's for giving me a mother whose idea of raising me was smacking me on the head…" She went on and on, making him feel her pain with every ounce of strength she had left, and he was slippery with blood and she was so tired and he said nothing, only looked at her with puffy eyes when she spoke, and finally she slid down to his feet, wrapped her arms around his knees and kept enumerating to him her pain and grief, then her regrets and mistakes and every stupid thing she had ever done, and by her introspection she saw the dark cloud over every action she had ever taken in life, the self-consciousness or fear or selfishness or vanity that spawned even the things she was most proud of. Her only admirable accomplishment in life was giving birth to Laney—and then the tears poured again, poured down his legs in amazing volume, washing, washing, washing…

They found her lying in a fetal position on the floor near one wall, thumb in her mouth, hospital gown torn, hands, feet, knees and elbows as bruised and bloody as if she had been in battle. Dr. Richards swore at his staff for not securing her to the bed. "Who was watching her? This isn't exactly a room with padded walls, is it? What are we supposed to do now? We can't present her in this condition to… Clean her up! The whole idea was to make her as compliant as possible for questioning, and now we've got this… Hurry up, dammit! I want her bandaged and coherent by morning, whatever it takes, understand?" He stormed out of the room; his staff scrambled into action.

When she woke up, she was still alone in the stone room, stretched out on the flat hard bed surrounded by cold metal bars, with straps across her legs and chest. But that wasn't how she felt. In her mind, she awakened to a bright morning, sun streaming across the sheets of the softest of beds, bundled deep in a down comforter. Allie stretched luxuriously and felt the sleep dissipating and the life flowing through her arms, every burden lifted, every weight thrown down. If she wanted to, she could fly. She lay there for a long time, eyes closed, resting profoundly on the bed and in deep assurance. She slept again, waking to relive the same impression that all was well in her world and, if she wanted to, she could stay in bed all day.

The door opened, and a man walked in and spoke her name. She opened her eyes, a little hesitantly for fear that her euphoria would elude her. Even though it was the bearded face of the doctor—the one who had told her that her daughter was dead— she smiled at him, surprised at his coldness and wishing he could feel like she did. He undid the straps as he talked.

"You're looking well this morning, Allie." She ignored the lie. Allie shifted in her bed; her eyes widened and she groaned. Every part of her body felt raw and searing. No matter. She deserved more than this; it was a small price to pay.

"Allie, I want to tell you how sorry I am for the loss of your daughter…"

To his great consternation, she laughed. What on earth? Was she mad? She laughed with amusement, not with scorn or silliness. "Doctor, doctor, I'm sorry, but I can't help it. The loss of my daughter…" She laughed again, brightly. "I can believe you're sorry you lost her and don't have her anymore!"

"What? What do you mean?"

"I mean, I don't know whether to believe you or not. But I do know this, that whether she's alive or dead, she's entirely out of your grasp. How wonderful! How clever of her, or whoever helped her!"

"Allie, you're…"

"Crazy? Oh good, because if you think I'm crazy, I must be okay. I would be more concerned if you thought I was fine." She laughed again, and her laugh irritated him—so disconcerting! She shifted on the bed again. "Oh, I'm sore this morning. Man, what a night that was! I…"

"Actually, it's evening right now."

"Really? You told me it was morning. You should get out more, doctor." She stifled a giggle.

"It was because you…" This was getting out of hand. It was time for him to take charge of this conversation. "Listen, you're to be interrogated this evening and I expect full cooperation from you. I don't know if you're suffering from delusion or playing some silly game, but you need to understand the seriousness of your situation…" It was no use. At the word "cooperation" she snorted, and at "seriousness" she laughed out loud. He didn't know what to do and stared at her in amazement. "Allie, stop! Stop now. What has gotten into you?"

She stopped and looked at him seriously. "I don't know, exactly." She smiled. "But I like it!" She burst into giggles again, and he watched her helplessly for several moments. "Ah, excuse me. Really, doctor, once again I am sorry, but I feel so good. Sure, I'm up for some questions. I doubt I know the answers anyway, so I may have to make things up…" She smiled brightly at his dismay. "Joke, doc! You should laugh more! Hey, I'll do my best, but I don't think I know what you think I know…" She knit her brow. "Did that make any sense?" Her face relaxed again into perfect ease. "Whatever. I'll do my best, doc, okay? I'm kinda sleepy still," she said, yawning. "You don't mind if I snuggle down and snooze a little more, do you?"

He stalked out of the room, slamming the door harder than his professionalism dictated. In the elevator, he pressed the floor keys like a seven-digit code and spoke his name into the microphone. It took him one floor down and opened to a large, lavishly decorated room, in architecture and design more like the parliament building above him than the other rooms and offices in this underground labyrinth. He strode to an ornamental and slightly elevated dais, and stood in its center with his hands behind his back.

"Well, Dr. Richards?"

His hands and feet were icy cold. He could never get used to talking this way, conversing with someone who had such great power but that one couldn't see, nor ever meet. It was unsettling. "She is… being somewhat difficult, sir. I'm not satisfied she's compliant enough for her questioning. I would like permission to try drug therapy."

"Denied. Is she defiant? Angry?"

"Quite the contrary, sir! I don't know what has got into her. I told her I was sorry for her loss, and she laughed. She wouldn't stop laughing, sir!"

The silence lasted a full minute or more. Sweat ran down the doctor's back, which he knew was detected. The technology had been his own design.

"Curious. I think you should bring her directly to me."

"Sir?"

"You need not concern yourself. We cannot allow her to see the light of day again in any event, which is an unfortunate error. And I require... amusement. I doubt that she has much useful information for us, and what she knows I may be able to coax from her. Bring her. Be sure she is properly attired."

The doctor bowed deeply. "Sir, about her attire, she had an unfortunate..."

"That is all, doctor. Good evening."

He turned and exited the room, closing the door softly behind him and swearing under his breath to relieve his nervous tension.

X

The surf shop was full, with a long line of talkative young adults waiting to rent boards and wetsuits. Normally, Ted would take charge, joke with customers and make each one feel important, but today he was getting in the way. Exasperated, one of his staff went out back, grabbed Ted's board and handed it to him, suggesting he check the conditions at Cox Bay. It sounded like a good idea. He needed some space and time to think, and nothing could be better for it than surfing on a gorgeous day like this. Ted kept driving past Cox Bay—it would have crowds and he didn't want crowds—and continued down the highway. He would for sure find some open water at the north end of Florencia Bay.

Laney's cute little face kept coming to mind, and anxiety made him grip the wheel harder. He hadn't seen this coming, or he would have removed Allie and her daughter from the island the first day he met them. This game had so many big players, and injected into the middle of them all was a little six-year-old girl. If she got hurt, he would never forgive himself. Allie was fragile too in her way, and now he had lost track of both of them, like a surf instructor's worst nightmare.

He took the side road toward the beach and pulled into a busy parking lot, but he knew most of the cars brought hikers, not surfers. He wished he had brought Barkley like he usually did, but it was probably best that They supposed he was working in the shop on a weekend. Putting on his wetsuit, his shoulder twinged as he reached back to pull his head through. Am I getting too old for this? he wondered. Maybe I've outlived my time. Too often lately I've seen and heard things I wish I never knew. It hurts to care this much all the time. His heart was heavy as he padded down the hundred steps to the beach, lifting his board to let a few dogs and hikers by on their way up.

The surf was so clean. Three duckdives and he was past the break, and he sat up on his board to watch for the right wave. He didn't know what to do. None of his team had found any sign of Allie, her car or her daughter. He had put everything else on hold—and didn't even offer assistance to the guy calling from the airport who thought he was being followed and a friend told him Ted could help—but couldn't think of anything else to do. He lay down on the board and let the swell roll under him and slosh cold water on his face.

The sound of barking brought him out of his dark reverie. Not dogs, but sea lions surfacing nearby and drawing closer, about twenty of them. Ted sat up to watch. They were coming directly toward him. He grew nervous—they weren't called lions for nothing—and he was especially edgy when instead of going around him they passed close by on either side. A perfect wave crested twenty meters from him, and a half dozen of the sea lions caught it, some surfing on top of the wave and some inside it but still visible in the cool green curl. Their skill and playfulness fascinated him, and when a dark shadow passed right under his board, he yelled. And he laughed—this was a day when he needed to surf with lions—and caught the next wave, and one gigantic animal surfed on one side of him and two on the other. His smile was so loud, he gagged on a mouthful of seawater at the end of his ride. And they were gone, dark bodies curving and contrasting with the sun on the waves, and he collapsed on his board and laughed until the tears came and mixed with the sea.

No one would ever believe him. He wished someone was with him to share this extraordinary moment, and he thought of Allie and how much he enjoyed her company; that she was too old to be a daughter to him but he was too old to be her lover, and he wondered why he would think about that at a time when love seemed impossible, only desperate acts of survival—or were those desperate acts of love? He longed for her to be okay, for things to be normal again and he would make her his mean fettuccine, maybe teach her how to surf, maybe marry her and make another

Laney with her, have a family, be a family.

He dragged himself out of this happy vision with great effort, paddled to where a wave was forming into the right shape. With practiced ease, he caught it and got his feet on the board, turned hard on the left-hand cut and rode it as far as he could toward the stairs, and when it broke he lay down on the board and let the break carry him all the way in until his dragging hands touched sand. Only then did he realize that his shoulder didn't hurt, though it still crunched a bit when he moved it; that he was surfing again and it was okay and he wasn't too old after all. Oh, but he didn't enjoy getting out of a wetsuit, never had, nor the unfriendly stares of the scandalized old ladies passing by just when his towel proved inadequate. If you don't like it, don't look. He strapped the board down in the back of the truck and saw a notification flash on his phone on the seat of the cab.

Message from a team member. Allie's car was in a police compound in Victoria, near downtown. The search was narrowing, and they requested Ted's presence. He called back. Did anyone inquire about it? Better not, too risky, and it was an unlikely place to find useful clues about the subject's whereabouts. Besides, it was becoming all too obvious who snapped her up. It was more a matter of how many stories she was underground.

He returned to Tofino long enough to drop off the board, grab a bag of clothes and head east and south again. No shower—he would regret that later—but he was anxious to join the hunt. It was such a beautiful day: blue skies, blue waters, blue mountains. How he loved this place! How he didn't want to leave, ever, and he wondered how much of his fight against the system was all about that. Before he reached the pass and the dead zone on the other side, his phone rang and he pulled over. Ted listened for a moment and turned off the truck. After listening for a long time, he managed to say, Okay. Ted put his head down on the wheel and began to cry.

Despite the brightness of the day, the rest of the drive to Victoria was dark and surreal. As he descended the Malahat, he realized he didn't remember passing through Nanaimo or Duncan; his mind was on autopilot and his thoughts far away and out of reach. It couldn't be! Not that beautiful little child.

A team member had infiltrated as far underground as they had ever delved, acting as one of several nurses who cared for the various unfortunates six floors underground who woke up wondering where on earth they were. She was finally off her three-day shift and able to communicate—carefully—her incredible news. The nurse had seen Allie, locked in a "hospital" room, drugged and unconscious. She was with a team of medical staff when Allie awoke. A doctor—the Chief of Staff for the Directorate—talked with Allie briefly and told her that her daughter was dead. Allie had immediately lapsed back into unconsciousness.

It was the only time she saw Allie during her entire shift. Obviously, they didn't want any of the nurses to be with her for long; they wanted Allie quickly forgotten. But Allie's distress for her daughter stirred up sympathy among the medical staff and they talked about her together. One of the male nurses said he had it on good authority that the little girl was abducted, and she escaped her kidnapper and ran out into traffic. The horrified nurses compared notes among themselves about who had been with Allie, but the few who were assigned had no further details.

Ted was ready to give up, fly the coop or turn himself in. It may be okay to die for a just cause; it's never okay for the innocent to die as collateral damage. Tears blurred his vision as he entered the city. What kept him going now was Allie, still underground and in great danger of becoming another chalk mark on the walls of the Directorate. He had to find Allie! Not only find her but also live long enough to save her and get her out of here. He circled a two-lane roundabout with grim determination and drove downtown.

XI

When Allie woke, she wasn't on the hard bed in the hospital room. As her eyes opened, she was immediately and fully awake, but afraid to move as she took in her surroundings. She was reclining on an antique and comfortable chair, or couch, or combination of the two, raised on a circular platform surrounded by a few steps and set with an elaborate pattern of colored stones. This dais was in the center of a large room, dimly lit, richly decorated. Gold was predominant, not garishly as in an eastern temple, but tastefully setting off the stone walls and tapestries and large paintings. The high domed ceiling above her incorporated superb stained glass, glowing in rich blues and reds, suggesting a bright sun shining through from the outside. She raised herself on the couch, then noticed she was wearing a magnificent long dress, like something out of *Pride and Prejudice*, with puffy sleeves and a neckline more revealing than she liked. She looked around the room and saw no one. So she startled when a male voice said, "Good morning, Allie."

She surveyed the room again. It had no other furniture, nowhere that anyone could be hiding. "I am sorry that I must resort to being heard and not seen, my dear," the voice continued. It was a rich, pleasant voice, with a stronger British accent than she heard among the colonists. "Believe me when I say I would prefer meeting with you face to face, but it is not possible. I think what you will find most difficult is not knowing where to look as you talk with me. So I encourage you to get up, walk around and enjoy the artistic quality of this place."

She didn't leave her seat. "Who... who are...?"

"Please," he interrupted, "please do not ask that. In time, I may tell you who and what I am, but let us be content for now with an agreeable conversation between strangers. Perhaps it will make it

101

easier for you if I have a name? You may call me Jim."

"I'm sorry, but you don't sound like a Jim."

He laughed kindly. "I knew we would get along well, Allie. But 'Jim' will have to do for now. Will you humor me with this appellation?"

"All right, Jim." She put her feet on the ground. They were bare, and her right big toe hurt as if she had stubbed it, but the floor was warm and the smooth stone inviting. Her senses registered other hurts that her memory couldn't account for. "Can I ask where I am?"

"You can ask anything you like, but where you are doesn't matter, and so you need not worry about it. Let me assure you that few places on our entire planet are safer than this one, and few are better."

Allie shook her head to dislodge the major cobwebs that had formed inside. She rose, descended the few steps and walked stiffly toward the wall before her, pausing on a rich wool rug that beckoned her bare toes to stay for a while. She had the sense of being watched, and looked over her shoulder again but saw no one.

"Can you see me?"

"Yes."

"That's hardly fair, is it?"

"Fair." The voice considered. "You know, it has been my duty and privilege to determine what is 'fair' for so many years that I am unsure how you might define it. Tell me what you mean by fair."

She focused on a forest painting, with sunshine slanting down into a clearing of small wooden huts, and smoke curling up from a central fire. "Like, equal. You know, like you have an advantage over me because you can see me and I can't see you. No one would think that's fair."

The voice was silent for a few moments. "But what if I knew things that you did not, things that would alter the balance of what is fair and not fair? You might find that by not allowing you to see me, I am doing you a favor."

102

"What, Jim—are you ugly or something?" Cold silence. "Hey, that's it! I've walked onto the set of Beauty and the Beast, and you have to make me fall in love with you to break the spell. Is that what this is about?" She laughed drily and reached to touch a tapestry, then saw what it depicted and withdrew her hand.

"Allie, I can excuse ignorance; I will not tolerate rudeness. I understand that what you have been through in the past couple of days has pushed you to a state of... desperation, or fatalism. But if we are to talk with one another, I ask for respect, and offer you the same." Allie nodded but continued to stare at the tapestry. "The scene depicted on the tapestry offends you?"

"Please tell me this didn't happen."

"It did happen. The depiction resides on these walls as a reminder of what human beings are capable of doing to one another when given too much power. It is something I am working hard to ensure never takes place on this island again."

"This happened here?"

"About two days' march north of here. A native man killed a British citizen, and his village was made an example. It was many, many years ago."

"But the children...!" She turned away, her face in her hands.

"As I said, this must never again happen here. But do you think this has never happened in the world before? That it doesn't happen every day in some sad corner? Have you not read the Psalmist who says to his enemy, 'Happy shall he be, that taketh and dasheth thy little ones against the stones'?"

"No." She felt like she would be sick, and sat on the steps.

"I share your abhorrence. It fuels my work here. I spend hours every day poring over every major news feed from all over the world, not because I enjoy reading every disgusting and malicious thing one man does to another, but to motivate me to seek immunity to the sickness of humanity."

"It's not working," Allie muttered.

"What was that?"

"I said, it's not working. I was told that someone, here on this island, killed my daughter." She hadn't said these words before. They rasped through her voice box like hot sandpaper and tightened her throat.

"We cannot prevent all accidents, Allie. I am sorry."

"You say her death was accidental?"

"That is my information, yes. I understand she pulled away from her escort, that she ran out into the street and was…"

"No!" Allie screamed. "Don't say it! I do not want to hear it! I don't believe you!" She pulled up her hem and stamped back up the steps in bare feet and sat on the chair, gripping it tightly.

They contemplated one another silently for several minutes.

"Are you hungry, Allie? You should be—you have been living on IVs for several days. Would you like some proper food?"

Allie glared, but said, "Yes, please."

"To your left, next to the Emily Carr—no, the next painting—you will find a small cupboard, and your breakfast is waiting inside. It is a light repast, as you will have a reduced appetite, but I think you will find it excellent."

Allie hesitated but opened the cupboard, and a heavenly aroma emerged. She found a tray inside, covered with an ornate silver cloche, which she carried into the room and stopped, looking askance at the lack of a table. "I'm sorry, I cannot abide much furniture in this room. Your lap will have to do."

"I take it you're not joining me for breakfast, Jim?"

He laughed. "No, thank you, Allie. 'I have meat to eat that ye know not of.' I will leave you to your meal, if I can be said to leave you." He paused. "I find you difficult and intriguing. It would please me if we might talk some more later in the day. Until then, this room is at your disposal, and you will find the, uh… ladies' room behind you, through the door next to the large mirror. Till we meet again."

Immediately, classical music lightly filled the room. Allie sat on the steps, set the cover beside her and breathed in the steam from a gorgeous, gold-embossed plate. She had never been so thankful for food before, a thought that comfortably set up shop in her mind. She would never look at eggs benedict the same way again. Especially if she could learn how to make hollandaise sauce like this—and is that smoked salmon? Allie devoured sweet potato nuggets, fresh sourdough toast and a fruit salad containing a few things she had never seen before. But as her host Jim had predicted, she ran out of steam long before she stopped enjoying the food. She reclined back against the steps and sighed, and pondered why she was still alive, if she would stay alive or join her daughter, where this room was located, and what she was meant to do here.

She needed the ladies' room and hoped it was more than a toilet. It certainly was. The room was compact but included a shower and large gilded bath, plush hangings, many gilt mirrors and thick towels and bathrobes. Allie wondered who used this room before her; she also wondered if they monitored it with cameras and discovered that she was beyond caring. She had a long shower while the bath was filling, soaked for half an hour in the tub and took another shower for good measure. The bruises and scrapes on her arms and legs—which the long dress had covered— amazed her. Had she been in a fight? She had a vague impression that she had won, but that didn't seem right, and why was she seemingly captive now? Allie returned in a bathrobe to the chaise lounge in the center of the room, her hair wrapped in a towel. She had found the dress impossible to put on and fasten without help, which made her wonder who had put the dress on her in the first place.

She sat for a while, reclined back and was drifting off when Jim's voice returned. "Ah, Allie, I should have realized. I will have someone come and help you." After several minutes, the bathroom door opened and a beautiful young woman in black and white Victorian maid's clothing beckoned her. Allie wondered out loud how she had gotten into the bathroom, but the maid smiled and didn't answer, didn't say a word the whole time she helped Allie into another sumptuous dress, this one a dark green velvet with gold brocade. She thanked her and stepped out into the room. The maid closed the door behind her. Perhaps a cupboard in the bathroom had a maid in it?

She walked about the room as if to examine the paintings and tapestries, but she was anticipating the Voice and couldn't—or didn't want to—focus on what the walls illustrated. She walked twice around the room, waiting, but still jumped when the voice said, "I am sure you feel refreshed and ready for the day. And you look lovely, Allie."

"Thank you. I have no way to compliment you in return, except to say you keep a charming house."

"I do keep it—and enjoy it—though I have never entered this room. I have several like it, where I can converse with guests like yourself, plus my servants and officers. But I enjoy them all at a distance."

"Guests like myself? Are you saying I'm your guest? What if the guest feels she has outstayed her welcome?"

"Let us cut to the chase, Allie. Surely you realize you cannot leave here. You have found out things—important things—that are secrets of mine. And you have some information we need, and I hope you will give us your cooperation. I am sorry that this has happened—it was not of my choosing, I assure you. You are the one who came to my front door, leaving my men with few options. But I think you might have ended up here in any case. A little knowledge is a dangerous thing."

Allie considered. "If I tell you everything I know, will you let me go?"

"No, Allie."

"Well, how long… and you say I came to your front door. Does that mean I'm in the Parliament Buildings? Do you live here?"

A brooding silence. "Live here. Do I live here? That is a question I have been wrestling with lately. I wonder if I am still alive, or if I simply exist. But yes, you are in a sense within the Parliament Buildings. Only, you are several stories below street level. We are like an iceberg here, with more beneath the surface than above it."

Allie looked up. "But the light coming through the glass…?"

"It is natural sunlight, assisted to this level by many mirrors. It is a way of experiencing night and day here, where otherwise it would be always night; even the seasons are somewhat represented. It is especially interesting on the rare occasion that it snows."

"So, what do you want to know? And why should I tell you?"

"All in good time, Allie. For now, since you have nothing better to do and I appreciate conversation with people who are not terrified of me, let's talk, shall we? I can spare a short time for conversation."

The silence grew awkward. "Um," ventured Allie, "One of us needs to ask questions. In one of my sociology courses, the prof talked about conversation, and she said that when two people are conversing, one of them naturally assumes the role of questioner and prodder, while the other does most of the talking. So, which one do you want to be?"

Sounds of amusement, or bemusement. "You are a most extraordinary person, Allie. I have access to a great deal of information about you, but it would please me to get to know you better. I have not done this in a long while; will you excuse me for blundering in where the more inept would fear to tread?"

"Go for it."

"Tell me, did you enjoy being a single mother?"

Allie turned as if to face him, though the voice came from everywhere. "I see what you mean by blundering in. How can you ask me a question like that? Do you think I enjoyed finding myself pregnant by a man I barely knew and who soon disappeared? Or being forced to drop all my dreams and ambitions and take courses I hated to get a job that I hated more, all so I could work at home and be with my daughter? It wasn't a piece of cake, I'll tell you."

"Hmmm. I see that our conversation will by necessity include emotion. I am not good at conveying my emotions, having to rely solely on my voice. This topic animates you. May I adjust my question, in hope of getting at what piques my interest?"

"Shoot. I can't wait."

"What is it like, to be a mother?"

The question confounded her. The words and feelings that immediately came to mind were in such contrast to her last answer that she felt conflicted. "Why do you want to know? I don't think you're a candidate for becoming a mom."

"Allie, please humor me. It is many years since I have been part of a family, and the memories are fading. I am aware that the reason you came here was in desperate pursuit of your daughter. Such… passion and determination are of great interest to me. I would be obliged if you could tell me what it is to be a mother; tell me about this energy I see in you."

Allie walked up the stairs and sat down. Miles of dress pillowed around her. She sat still for a few moments, looked up and replied, "I've decided that giving birth to Laney is the only pure and holy thing I have ever done."

Pause. "Interesting choice of words. Why do you say them, Allie?"

"I don't know; the words came to me, or came back to me." A brief but violent memory gripped her frame, made her shudder and was gone. "But having Laney, being her mom, is the greatest privilege in the world." She looked down at her bruised hands. "Was the greatest…"

"Because…?"

Allie thought. "Have you ever loved someone so much that everything in your realm of experience gets aligned with that one person? I mean everything, from whether you buy crunchy or smooth peanut butter, to your sudden fresh interest in any animal that's cute and fuzzy. And not because you have to, or like you're spoiling the kid, but because you want to; you feel a great interest in her, you want to see her smile."

"I can't say I have. I'm not sure that what you are describing is even desirable. It seems irrational to me to adjust yourself to the whims of another."

"And that is why you can't understand what it means to be a mom. You don't know what it means to love."

"Not true, Allie. Not true at all. I love the colonists of Vancouver Island! I love every one of them. But I don't love them by pandering to their every desire. I decide what is best for them, and that is what I give them, whether they appreciate it or not. And most often, they appreciate it. Surely you have seen the contentment of the average citizen of this sovereign state! You can't deny they are happy!"

"I've met some who are discontent; it's something to do with the 'whether they appreciate it or not' part, I think." As soon as Allie shut her mouth, she knew she had made an error.

"Really? I would like to hear about these malcontents. Who are they?"

Allie said nothing and sat smoothing out her dress around her, making patterns in the velvet with her fingers.

"Let me get this straight," the Voice continued. "You think that being a mom is like being a... a servant, or more accurately, a bondservant—a willing slave—to your children. Extraordinary!"

Her mind was racing for a way to explain. "Have you ever had a teacher that you didn't like, and they didn't like you?"

"Nearly all of them, as I remember."

"Well, think of one that you did like, one who took an interest in you and cared about you and made you excited about what they were teaching."

"The specifics are hazy at this distance, but yes, I can imagine that."

"How did you do in that class?"

He pondered. "I did well, I think. Yes, here is a memory. I always imagined I hated English history, but then had an instructor like the one you described. He made history come alive; it was all stories of proper places and real people and actual movements, not mere facts and dates. He took us on a Saturday, at his own expense, to museums and historical sites. An incredible man—I am not sure why he did it. I love history to this very day."

"Well, that man was a mom."

"I see what you mean." He paused before going on. "But do you not recognize that this is the very thing I have accomplished on this island? I have bent over backward to make sure this is the very best place on earth for my people to live. They have no one bleeding them for their hard-earned money: no income taxes or goods and services taxes; no water bills, phone bills, data plans. Everyone here can afford to live comfortably, and I don't tolerate entrepreneurs who force up prices needlessly for their own profit. Crime is practically non-existent, and dealt with quickly and fairly. We have the best of medical care, all free…"

Allie cut in. "The medical care is free, but are the people free? Why do you keep tabs on where each person is at any time?"

"Very good, Allie, but I suspect you had help in finding this out. We would like to confirm who has told you this—we have our suspicions."

"There you go—you sound like the Gestapo: 'Vee haff vays to make you talk!' As if I don't know what would happen if I ratted on someone, if I had a 'someone.' Sorry, you have much to learn before I would consider you my favorite teacher."

"This is not helpful. Let me answer your question: why it is that we keep 'tabs,' as you call it. Have you ever heard of a personal locator beacon?" Allie shook her head. "Hikers and back-country skiers use them, so if they get lost or caught in an avalanche, we can find them. Now, imagine a person had such a device, but left it at home—due to carelessness or thinking they wouldn't need it—and they got themselves lost. Would they not wish they had not been so foolish?" He waited for a response, which didn't come. "Allie, the people are indeed foolish. Years ago, I established an elaborate system of personal location, about which they don't have to concern themselves because they are not aware of it. No one becomes lost anymore. I did them a great favor."

"And you gave yourself great power. Tell me, you keep on saying you have done all these things. What about the Directorate? Doesn't a group of people run this place, or do you like taking the credit?"

"I once led a group of men who made up the Directorate." Allie made a noise of disapproval at that. "They are all gone now; I am the only one left. The Directorate—or Director or Governor or whatever you like—is myself. I am the one who runs this place."

"So you're a dictator!"

"A most benevolent one, if that is what I am. But I don't like the term; it carries connotations of a temporary structure in a time of crisis, in which we are not."

"Is your—supremacy or whatever—the reason you don't let anyone see you?"

"It can be useful to rule unseen; greater persons than I have done it. But it is not the only reason. I often think I would prefer to be seen once again. But the reason that I went into seclusion—maybe I will tell you someday."

"What do you think about the proverb, 'Power corrupts'?"

"'And complete power corrupts completely.' It can indeed. Men are morally weak creatures, easily tainted. I am glad to say that I am far out of the reach of corruption. Nothing is wrong with absolute power when the wielder of that power cares about nothing but the good of his people. He simply needs to live forever. But enough of that for now, my dear. I must leave you for a time. I trust you will find enough distraction in this room to amuse you. Later, I have a visitor arriving whom you will treat with courtesy, whether you think him worthy or not. Rest well, madam."

He had dismissed her, but she couldn't leave the room. Allie went to the bathroom and searched every wall and hanging. She found no cupboard with a maid in it, nor any door or opening. When she left, she stormed around the "audience room" for several laps, discovering as she went that the room formed an octagon.

The light coming through the stained glass of the dome above her was fading. Evening, then. Allie tried the magic meal cupboard and found it locked. But as she turned away, she heard a slight noise of cutlery and china, waited a moment and found that the cupboard door opened to her touch. It was disappointing to find awaiting her only a tray of delicate scones, cakes and sandwiches, and a large pot of tea. But it was just as well. It wouldn't do at all, she thought sardonically, if in time she no longer fit these beautiful dresses.

XII

The beautiful day brought out crowds of colonists in the late afternoon sun, strolling along Inner Harbor and around the grounds of the Parliament Buildings. Ted needed the crowds and stayed among the cover of their multiple RFIDs as they sent signals to the myriad of receivers in the area. This is one place where They must never see him alone and signal-less, but it was even more dangerous to carry his own RFID on this mission. As usual, Barkley was impersonating him in Tofino.

Five times, he passed the "Staff Entrance" sign near a parking lot in the southeast quarter of the Parliament Buildings. He was wearing a small pack containing tools and equipment he had thought he would never use. As he drew near for the sixth time, he found his target, a bearded man about his size, wearing a lab coat, lunch bag in hand and leaving the building. He followed the man to the parking lot, close enough to hear all four doors unlock as they neared a grey Nissan SUV. A moment after the man sat in the driver's seat, Ted opened the opposite rear door, jumped in and held a gun to the guy's startled face. "Drive," Ted commanded. The man carefully backed up and left the parking lot.

Ted directed him across a bridge, down several back roads and finally down a rough dirt road to a wooded area near the shore. The man stammered, "Take the truck, I don't have a bit of cash and…"

"Shut up. What's your name?"

"Um, Dave…"

"Try again. I'm about to look in your wallet, and if your name doesn't match up, you're in bigger trouble than you are now. What's your name?"

"Jerry."

"Full name."

"Jerry Davis."

"I'll give you one more chance, okay? Full name, like on your driver's license. I suggest you get it right this time."

"Jeremiah Logan Davis."

"Wallet." Ted glanced at it and threw it back. "Well done. Listen, I have nothing against you, I want little from you, and I suggest you see a doctor as soon as you can. Close your eyes and count to ten."

The man hesitated, and Ted raised the gun. The moment Jerry's eyes were closed, Ted jabbed a hypodermic needle through the man's shirt into his arm. His eyes flew open as he got to the number two, he slurred the number three and before he got to four, he was unconscious. Ted reclined Jerry's seat all the way down, opened his backpack and took out a nylon medical kit.

Part one accomplished: Jerry's name, in his own voice, recorded perfectly on a small device disguised as the barrel of the gun. The retina scan was relatively simple. Ted pulled Jerry's eyelids back with one hand and mounted a small instrument against the man's forehead over his right eye. It took about 45 seconds to do a 3D scan of his eye, which the device could display as an image so perfect that you would swear you were looking at a real eye inside it. Even better, a retina scanner would think so too.

The next step was a good deal more difficult, not so much physically as morally and nauseously. He removed the man's lab coat and shirt and placed a powerful headlamp on his own forehead. Using a calibrated RFID reader, he scanned the man's upper torso at a low setting. As he scanned the man's left shoulder, the needle jumped. Ted narrowed down the location to an area about two centimeters in diameter where he drew an eye-shaped outline in pen above the shoulder blade. Damn! This would be delicate—he didn't want to do any permanent damage.

He rolled Jerry onto his right side into the recovery position as best he could and arranged a thick absorbent pad around the mark on the shoulder, taping it down securely. Gritting his teeth, with gloved hands he swabbed the area with alcohol, took a scalpel from its package and carved as deeply as he dared around the eye-shaped outline, removing a wedge of meat from Jerry's shoulder and stanching the blood with a quick squeeze of another pad that drew the two sides of the wound together. He dropped the slice in a small zip-lock bag in disgust and vowed to never do that again. Quickly, he packaged the wound with butterfly bandages and a large gauze bandage. He scanned the bloody zip-lock bag. Bingo! You're in there all right, you little RFID.

Minutes later, Ted was wearing Jerry's clothes with a nasty, squishy bag in his pocket. Jerry was resting peacefully against a mossy rock, wrapped up in a mummy sleeping bag with only his face showing. He would sleep for at least twelve hours. It was time for Ted to get inside.

No, as she suspected, afternoon tea wouldn't cut it. She wanted some proper food and despaired of getting any, as it was now clearly dark outside. Her mind wandered over the bizarre conversation she had earlier with her host. Who is this person who calls himself Jim? That he's crazy, she had no doubt. Delusional madman—that was the answer to Ted's long-ago question about who runs this show. Ted. Where is Ted? He must think I've disappeared like Laney. I guess I have. I wonder if I'll join her when they finally kill me? She accepted this comforting concept as a fact, without disturbing any of the objections that had been her lifelong practice. But she felt so far from being done with this life; she felt moving within her a desire to survive her daughter, to seek and secure justice for her.

Anger stirred in her heart. Righteous anger. "Out of the reach of corruption"—what kind of statement was that? Was this "Jim" a Brahman attempting to attain divinity and immortality? Did he expect to reign forever? He infuriated her with his charm, so shrewd and convincing. He was a man who could persuade anyone to think as he thought; given enough time, everyone would see things his way. He probably had a toothbrush mustache and a lock of dark hair across his forehead.

She needed to escape. She wasn't helpless, even if she looked the part in her buxomly Victorian dress. Could she overcome the beautiful maid and force her to reveal the secret passage in the bathroom? It all sounded like some romance novel set in nineteenth-century England; how could this be happening to a modern, feminist research consultant from New York? She paced the room again until the dress chafed her, sat once more on the steps, and let tears of frustration roll down her cheeks.

Allie saw movement to her left, and the outline of a door appeared in the wall where she would have never suspected. A man in a dark grey suit emerged, walking backward and pulling a cart or table on wheels after him through the door, which closed silently and invisibly after he entered. He turned, and Allie sucked in her breath. It was Justin.

Neither said anything as he wheeled the table toward her, which was laden with elaborate silver and crystal and tall glasses of dark wine. He sat down beside her and said, "I didn't take her."

"I know." She couldn't look at him.

"You know? How do you know?" He combed his fingers through his gorgeous hair. "I would have been good to you both, but someone snatched her before I arrived. You don't know anything about that, do you?"

"What does it matter?" Allie took a glass of wine and stared into its depths. "She's dead."

Justin said nothing, and they sat for several minutes. He stood, lifted a silver dome off a gold and green plate and gave it to her. "I don't eat red meat," she said. He nodded, returned the steak buried in mushrooms and prawns to the table, and lifted the other dome.

"You're in luck. Halibut, I think. About as white a meat as you can get." She took it from him and tasted the fish, ignoring him on the outside but utterly conscious of him on the inside. Neither said anything for a long while. "Nice dress, by the way," he said. She glanced up and didn't like the way he was looking at her, and blushed like a schoolgirl.

"Why don't you go away? You're very good at it."

"Allie, when they sent me to you, they told me I could tell you anything I know; like, explain things to you."

"That shouldn't take long."

"Very mature, Allie. Look, we're sitting here, acting like a couple of thirteen-year-olds. Neither of us wants to be here." Allie looked at him squarely. "I know you hate me and everything, but I want to tell you what happened, who I am, and what this is all about."

"Is Jim listening in?"

"Who?"

She put her plate down, stood up and walked up the steps. "Jim, are you catching all this?" She turned around as she talked. "If you're listening, say something, okay? Or will you fill in the bits and pieces as he talks?" Silence followed her words.

She sat down again, and he looked at her in amazement. "They told me you were… Listen, if you don't want me here, I can leave." But he glanced toward the now-invisible door as if unsure that was true.

"Yeah, well, I'm sure you don't know as much as you think you do, but go for it," she sighed. "Your version will be interesting, no doubt."

He clearly presumed that he was sitting with a crazy person, and glanced at her awkwardly as he spoke. "My name isn't Justin; it's Brandon, and I'm 33 years old. I've lived on the island all my life, but traveled extensively for the past ten years." He again ran his fingers through his thick chestnut hair as if coming to a confession. "When I met you in Thailand, you didn't know me. But I knew you. I had in my backpack a full report on you, more information than your own government has on file, and I read the whole thing on the plane. You probably thought I was incredible, but I had insider information that made it possible for me to pose as the most romantic guy in Asia. You were my assignment, Allie."

She didn't look up, so he continued. "I don't have much in the way of talents or ambitions. I'm a good-looking guy, and I'm a stud."

She snorted.

"No, you don't get it, Allie. I'm not bragging, not this time anyway. That's my job—I'm a stud. I work for the Directorate in one of their genetic research programs. The Program finds people they want to bring here to add variation to the gene pool on the island. When they choose someone, they send me to close the deal, and later, they come up with some reason to bring mom and child here. And of course, they never want to leave. Especially when I show up again, full of contrition for my lack of self-control, and offer to pay substantial paternity support if they will stay."

She was looking at him now with wide eyes. "And you think I'm crazy! This—this is crazy! How can you...?"

"...Sleep at night?" He smiled. "It's a little tough when I'm on assignment." She incinerated him with her gaze. "Hey Allie, lighten up! Look, I know this whole thing messed up your life for a while, but the fact that it's so messed up right now isn't my fault! It could have turned out so good for you!"

"Like hell..."

"No, listen to me, Allie! You're a young, bright woman with few family connections and not much waiting for you back in New York. Tell me, a month after being on the island, did you want to leave? Or were you wishing you could find some way to stay? Did you and Laney love it here, or what?"

She had nothing to say. It was true. "So what happened? How did she slip through your fingers?" She looked at him searchingly, even desperately.

He stood up and started walking around the room, hands in his pockets. He came back and faced her. "Look, you may think I don't care about my kids, that it's just a job and I have dozens of them out there. But I care, okay? When I realized that Laney had disappeared, I nearly lost it. It took every ounce of energy to not let you know I was upset. And when they told me she had been run over…" He covered his face with his hands.

"Cut the crap, Brandon, or whatever your name is. What you have been doing is evil, and you know it."

He looked up at her in surprise, and his face became cold. "I'm not a liar, Allie. Not now, not with you. I'm sorry things went this way, but it wasn't my fault. You're up shit creek without a paddle, and I don't know what they will do with you. I thought I could help you understand, that you could maybe even forgive me. That's all I got."

She stared at him. "I forgive you. But if I never see you again, it will be too soon."

He gathered their plates onto the table and, without another word, pushed it to the wall where the door opened for him. He disappeared for the last time.

Her composure collapsed, and she sat on the steps and trembled. She remembered Ted's words, way back when she first met him, "They want something from you." That was close, but not on the mark. They had already taken something from her—something so intrinsically and intimately hers—and they lost it. She wrestled with sorrow and fear. Surely I'm of no more use to them, she thought, and the fact that they're willing to tell me so much means I'll never have the opportunity to tell anyone else. Why are they keeping me alive and in this room?

She stood and addressed the walls. "So Jim, is this your idea of torture?"

"What do you mean?" he replied, from everywhere.

"Sending Justin, or Brandon or whatever. Are you trying to soften me up or drive me mad? I feel like a roast being marinated for the oven. Why don't you get rid of me now?"

"I have no desire to get rid of you."

"What, then? More dresses and fine dinners and loathsome conversation and more loathsome visitors? How long, Jim?"

"Did you enjoy your dinner? It is an old—very old—recipe of mine. And if you are tiring of your dress, you have a wardrobe full of them. As for conversation, it seems to me you would make dialogue loathsome no matter whom I sent you. You are bitter in spirit, Allie! Would you rather have a solitary stone cell and stale bread? I could arrange that."

She had no words to respond with and sat on the steps again, seething with rage. It wasn't fair he was so right! She did turn every conversation into an argument. And she was bitter! Had every right to be bitter, to hate, to not trust these people!

Immediately, in her mind she saw the face of the nurse named Sophie, golden amber eyes, kind and compassionate. She precipitated in Allie very different thoughts and feelings than anyone else she encountered here. Bits of memory returned. Sophie knew the passwords. Sophie was her connection to Ted; she was the one to follow, the one who said she was here for her and would come back as soon as she could. "You can trust me, Allie." It wasn't much to cling to, but through the storm raging in her chest, she reached out and held on. Hope steadied her like an anchor, slowed and stilled her trembling, calmed her rage. She heaved a deep breath and lay back against the steps.

"Allie? Are you okay? My words were harsh just now—I am sorry. I find you such an ambiguity. I am afraid I am much too fascinated to let you go, even if the situation allowed. But I regret the unhappy circumstances that brought you here and keep you against your will."

Allie lay still with eyes closed and didn't answer. After many minutes, it must have unnerved her unseen host to see her lack of response. Allie felt someone come and sit on the steps beside her, and a gentle hand smoothed her hair back from her forehead. She opened her eyes and saw a warm and familiar face above her. She smiled and mouthed the words, "Thank you. I so wanted you to come."

Sophie helped her sit up slowly. Her back was stiff and sore. "Are you okay, Allie? Can I do anything for you?"

Allie reached up her arms, placed them around Sophie's neck and held her close. She buried her face in the nurse's hair and whispered, "Take me away from here. Please. Take me with you."

"Soon," Sophie whispered back. "Be patient. Trust me. Don't give in."

Out loud she said, "Let's get you ready for bed, shall we, Allie? I think you're over-tired. Maybe things will look different in the morning." They walked over to the bathroom; the door opened and the beautiful maid took her in. Allie had no energy to fight her, couldn't resist the invitation to a bubble bath already poured, and soaked until she drifted off. When she returned to the couch, Sophie was gone. The maid tucked the down comforter all around her and actually kissed her on the forehead. Allie was asleep before the maid reached the door.

"Jerry's late." The guy who worked beside Jerry carefully folded his lunch bag and tossed his banana peel into the correct bin—green for compostable.

"It's a girl. I've seen them, sitting on a bench outside over dinner break." His co-worker laughed. "He's going to catch hell when…"

A violent shake—only one—was accompanied by a dull thump, like someone had picked up the planet and tried to get the coins out of it. Alarms and flashing lights went off in case anyone missed it. The quake was only seconds in duration, but several monitors toppled to the floor and the room was in chaos. They immediately went to emergency power; fine dust filled the air, and the team of seismologists scrambled to find out what happened from their remaining hardware.

"Dammit! Why were those monitors not mounted to their tables? Jerry, make a note. Where the hell's Jerry? Come on, people, tell me what you've got." Their supervisor was livid. What would happen here when the Big One hit? Heads would roll this time. They weren't ready!

The earthquake registered 6.4 on the Richter scale and was nearby: eight kilometers offshore and six kilometers down northwest of Cape Flattery Lighthouse on Washington's Olympic coast. It had been incredibly short—only 1.5 seconds, followed by 20 seconds of reverberation. Washington State was issuing a tsunami warning for the entire Olympic Peninsula, and they quickly issued one along the west coast of the island, though if a tsunami formed, it would reach the shore moments from now. A technician shouted that Buoy 46206 at La Perouse Bank was registering a 0.6-meter rise, enough to get some tourists wet if they were taking an evening stroll at Long Beach, but not enough to even reach the driftwood at this low tide. The bedlam in the room subsided.

Those monitoring damage reports put them on the screen as they came in: a retaining wall collapsed in Oak Bay; some plate-glass windows shattered downtown; owners of boutiques on Government Street were perturbed. No building damage reported so far—wait, the front arch of Christ Church Cathedral was in ruins; no injuries, but the loss of some fabulous stained glass. Reports would continue all night, but most people wouldn't notice the damage until morning. Jerry's workstation was still empty, but his neighbor was far too busy to bring it to anyone's attention. It would be a long night.

They had returned to dull routine when another alarm sounded but without any shaking. They all looked at one another in surprise. This was new. One tech got up and opened the door to look out, jumped back in alarm and closed the door. "Water!" he said, and everyone jumped to his feet. "Not a lot, but I see five centimeters in the hallway, and it's moving!" A general commotion ensued; everyone shut down their equipment and headed for the door. They—more than anyone—knew the possibilities if the Strait of Juan de Fuca found its way through newly formed cracks in the bedrock above them. Someone had the foresight to make a dam around the door with boxes of paper before they opened it again, and with good reason—water rushed in the moment the door was open. Following their supervisor, they stepped over the dam into bitterly cold water and moved to the elevator, which was on slightly higher ground. They jammed the elevator beyond capacity and the doors closed.

The Suit, standing at the doorway of a flight of stairs, watched them without a word, walked to the lab and reached down to where the water was trickling through the makeshift dam. He smelled and tasted the water, frowning. The Suit closed the lab door, sat on a desk and waited.

XIII

At the time the earthquake hit, Ted was standing at the elevator with a half dozen others who had finished their dinner break, wondering how on earth he had thought this would work. When the shake came, they all caught one another from staggering, looked at each other in alarm and scrambled for the outside exit. Ted stayed, removed the retina and recording devices from his pocket, and held his breath as he tried them. The elevator door opened, and he stepped in. Before he could even think of what button to push, the door closed and the car dropped beneath him, stopping abruptly at the fifth floor down.

The door opened, and he peeked both ways down a dimly lit hallway. No one. Doors opened on either side, each with a pane of reinforced glass. All were empty, except one that was crowded with men in lab coats, too occupied with their computer monitors to notice him. It was all like Alistair's description. He continued to the end of the hall where he found a door marked Maintenance. It was unlocked, and he stepped inside. It contained a sink for rinsing mops and a tap with a short hose on it. He closed the door, pulled the hose out onto the floor, stepped up onto the sides of the sink and turned the water on full blast. The pressure was high, and in a short while, water filled the small room to the level of the top of the sink. When he opened the sealed door, the flood rushed out into the hallway.

After most of the water had escaped, he closed the door, leaving a narrow crack to look through. The end of the hose was still gushing. He heard the alarm and saw the chattering lab-coats leave and splash down the hall. Ted waited a few more minutes, then left his closet, sloshed to the door, scanned the retina device and listened for the click of the lock. He walked into the lab.

❧❧❧❧❧❧❧❧

Something disturbed her deep sleep, and she dreamed of Justin. Not Brandon, not what Justin became, but the guy she met in a market in Thailand seven years ago, the only man to sweep her completely off her feet. Justin knew all the great places to go, and created afternoon adventures that were exactly the Thailand she wanted to see. Evenings were full of great food, moonlit walks on the beach and—soon—long nights of uninhibited passion. She woke with sunlight streaming across the bed, the sound of breakers on the beach and birds she never heard before calling to one another.

He stood on the balcony, leaning against the railing and watching the waves, wearing a long white cotton robe, bare feet. Wind played with his hair—it was getting so long, so beautiful like the rest of him. She sat up, smiled and called him.

He turned, and it wasn't Justin. This man was larger, wilder. His eyes blazed. It was the one she had nailed to the wall. He contemplated her for a long while, composing within her emotions quite different from what she felt for Justin, who was once again gone. She hugged the comforter close around her, feeling more than naked under his gaze, but it was the purity in his eyes that made her feel uncomfortable. With seeming indifference, he walked around the bed to the washroom; she heard the sound of running water. He came back with a white towel around his shoulders and a basin in his hands.

He knelt on the floor in front of her and held out his hands, eyes coaxing. Cautiously, she slipped one foot out from under the covers and gave it to him. He placed it in the warm water and the scent of lavender flooded over her. His hands were rough, but he was gentle, and his touch was so far from sensual that it was nothing but Sensual, chaste in intention and filling her very soul with unadulterated pleasure. He wanted the other foot, and her greater enjoyment of it repeated and improved the sensation. He took his time, and his eyes never left her face but spoke volume after volume to her in inexpressible joy. She pulled her own eyes away for a moment, looking for signs of what she had done to him, but all she could see were the ugly holes penetrating his wrists, slightly healed over. The soft warm towel was as good as the water. He never said a word. Well, none out loud. There was no need. She was undone, forever.

He poured the water out over the side of the balcony, and it was like a torrent, in quantity absurdly more than the basin could hold. The man shook out every drop, laughed and threw the basin as far as he could, which was very far. He hung the towel on the railing, and in one motion leaped over it and climbed down the other side. Pulling the comforter around her she rushed to the rail, but he was already running on the beach, half in the waves, head back, mouth open, arms pumping, hair streaming. She watched him out of sight and sat back to find herself on the hard steps of the lavish audience room, golden light pouring through the stained glass above her. For a long while, she couldn't pull her heart out of the dream and knew she was too light-headed to get up. She pulled the comforter close around her and over her head, and the scent of lavender floated up from her feet.

After a long while, she rose and went to the bathroom. No, she told the maid—a different one this time, and also pretty—she wouldn't require a bath this morning. She might never bathe again, she said, laughing. As she helped with her dress, the maid asked what perfume she was wearing, and it made Allie's heart tremble. This morning's gown was a white muslin, which suited Allie fine, and she went to her meal cupboard in high spirits for one who was both childless and a prisoner.

She was nibbling a bit of breakfast—a nutty-flavored piece of toast with blackberry jam—when he spoke. "Good morning, Allie, I trust you slept well. Are you feeling more yourself today?"

Allie smiled, considering. "You know, Jim, I think I am more myself today. I think I'm more myself than I've ever been before."

"Well now, that is a good beginning! To what do you attribute this good fortune?"

"You have your secrets; I think I'll keep mine too. Ask me something else."

The voice of Jim seemed to delight in this game. "Right, let's see. Tell me, in your limited travels around my island, what would be your favorite place?"

Oh, you're so pathetic at this, she thought to herself. Always fishing for information. What a merry chase I will lead you. Out loud, she said, "I love Victoria. Hands down, that's it. I think it's the bike and walking trails all through the city. And the tea shops."

"Really? I would have thought you would say the beaches were your favorite. Perhaps on the west coast?"

"You know, you've seen one beach, you've seen them all. Now, New Zealand, there's beaches for you if you want them."

"Hmmm… may I show you a beach that is to die for, as they say, right here on our northern coast?"

Allie sat up with interest. A humming noise to her right drew her eye to a white screen lowered near one wall as a projected image came from the ceiling.

"I will not bore you with home movies or slideshows. What you will see is taking place right now, at this very moment." The image resolved itself into what seemed to be the view from an aircraft, maybe a helicopter or small plane. It was flying level with snow-clad peaks rising out of a high skirt of deep green forest, and right ahead sparkled the bluest of oceans on a clear but blustery day, huge breakers fanning toward a grey-white beach that was drawing nearer.

"New Zealand!"

"Not at all. We are over Cape Cook near the northwest end of the island, named after Captain James Cook, who was the first European to land on Vancouver Island and also your New Zealand. But your mistake is most understandable, except for the forests. Surely you must concede that ours are more verdant and extensive than those of our distant southern neighbor?"

She didn't reply, but watched as the small plane—as it appeared to be—skimmed over the waves, turned the world at a sharp angle and came down with a small bounce on the beach itself. The scene was astoundingly beautiful, and the image so clear that Allie wanted to run out into the waves. She clapped her hands and laughed. "Bravo, Jim! This is the most marvelous thing I've ever seen! Do the pictures take you wherever you want to go?"

"This pilot, a videographer, and many others like them." He scrolled through moving images: a quiet cove with a few houseboats and ducks on the water; a high mountain ridge covered on one side in snow cornices over a deep valley; a downtown Victoria sidewalk bistro crowded with coffee sippers. "They believe they are doing it for future tourism, and though we do use much of the footage, foreigners coming here in droves is not my desire. For the most part, their work allows me to be out and about where otherwise I could never go. I hope you are enjoying it. I certainly am."

Allie watched people on bikes descending a winding highway through massive trees, and kiteboarders on a long, narrow lake. "It's marvelous. But it must be enormously expensive to keep this up."

"Oh, it is nothing. Finances have never been a limitation. It employs a good number of people in an occupation they love and affords me both information and pleasure. Why should I not do this?"

She didn't know what to say. Jim continued, "Allie, I have never offered this to anyone, but would you like to share this privilege with me?"

"What do you mean?"

"I will give you an instrument by which you can control the images you want to see. It might help pass the time, and... it would do my heart good, in a manner of speaking, to please you in this way."

Once again, Allie didn't know what to say. "Well, I think I would like that. It would please me more if you let me go, but..."

"Which you know I cannot do. However, I am not a beast. I would like to make your time here as pleasant as possible, and I hope that has been the case."

"Thank you, Jim." She paused, wondering. "You said I'm... hard to understand or something. I can say the same about you. 'Intriguing.' That's the word you used. I find you intriguing, and alarming, and many other things as well."

"I must leave you now—something has come to my attention that I must deal with at once. We will talk again soon, shall we?"

He could trust few men at all, and didn't trust them far. The Suit was an ignorant man in many ways, but shrewd in the ways that he found useful. Everyone in the lab was back at their desks already, though the floor was still damp and the place bitter cold since the in-floor heating wasn't working and the catalytic heaters couldn't keep up. The Suit was efficient at making things happen, like telling him that he had a man in custody.

"Show him to me." The image that came up was a small cell with a human form in a hospital bed. "What did you do to him? How long have you had him?"

"We had a bit of a tussle. I won. Happened last night about nine. They said you weren't to be disturbed, but I figured..."

"Is he conscious?"

"Not yet. I could probably wake him."

"No, send the Doctor in. I want him checked out, in good shape and alert—as soon as possible. Who is he?"

"No idea. No RFID."

"Idiot! Why didn't you say so in the first place? You should have told me last night! Take his photo, blood samples, run

130

whatever checks you can. Identify him, man! Go!"

He remained deep in thought for several minutes, pondering this unfamiliar information. This was most unexpected, unprecedented. Upsetting really, that someone could breach his secure defenses undetected. He needed to take immediate action. Yet he sat at his desk for several hours, not moving, considering the novelty of a new enemy.

Rebecca Young felt a great deal of responsibility for each one of the seven people under her direct supervision. No one gave her trouble like Allie Simpson, and at first she assumed that her second-ranked Market Analyst was being her usual recalcitrant self. But it was now three weeks since she heard anything from her, and she was unsure what to do. She rearranged the pens and paper trays in her cubicle, cleaned up the desktop on her computer and thought about the problem.

Allie wasn't answering her phone. The message now automatically explained that the cellular customer she was trying to reach was not available, and may be out of the service area. What was more, Rebecca had received a call that morning from someone who claimed to be Allie's mother and who asked, Where the hell was Allie? Like Rebecca, she had heard nothing for three weeks. Allie returned no emails, texts or messages. This was a problem entirely out of Rebecca's realm of experience, concerning someone she didn't like, so she initially decided to do nothing except prepare a scathing letter of dismissal to present to Allie upon her return. That endeavor occupied most of one pleasant afternoon.

But now her sense of responsibility—even to one so undeserving—gave her pause. What if there was a real problem? Would it impair her reputation if it turned out that Allie was in trouble and she had done nothing? Could the company deem her negligent? Had she now waited so long that either reporting or not reporting the situation could have disastrous consequences? The debate in her mind cost her most of an unpleasant afternoon, three espressos and an extra dose of a non-prescribed stress medication she had picked up in Mexico. She couldn't wait to deliver her dismissal letter to Allie, especially with the new draft she conjured up at 4 PM.

At 4:30, she finally found the courage to talk with her own supervisor. He gave her a contemptuous glance and immediately went into action, while she slunk back to her desk to await 5:00 PM. But all of his inquiries came up blank. None of her limited family had heard from Allie. Officials on Vancouver Island were less than cooperative and would only say that Allie's visa was still valid for several weeks. He was still at his desk when they called back, saying that no one had responded to the doorbell at her condo, but it was only 3 PM and the car wasn't in its parking spot. They would check again in the evening but saw no reason to list her as missing at this point.

He left it at that. He was a busy man, preoccupied with figuring out how to bring someone who wasn't his wife to a dinner party that evening. If he hadn't heard from Allie by Monday, he would take further steps. He liked Allie and bent over backward to help her maintain her position with the company while homeschooling her daughter. But her lack of communication was overstepping his graciousness. It might be time to cut her loose.

For the first time, Allie was getting bored. She had found virtual freedom through the device that allowed her to view dozens of high-definition webcams, most of them "static" and fixed in key locations, but some labeled "dynamic" that were manned and moving. She liked the roving cameras best because it was like going for a drive or flight or walk, depending on the mode of transportation. But more than anything, she wanted to go for a walk out in the sunshine—at any of the many places she had viewed on the screen. She sought out virtual places where the people were, even though some of the more isolated and scenic images were breathtaking. The only real person she saw all day was the maid in the cupboard, who seemed hardly human since she never said a word. Sophie didn't return. Allie longed for flesh and blood companionship.

This is amazing, she mused. I miss people! She thought a great deal about Ted, wondering if he had any idea where she was, and if and when he would come and rescue her. Allie didn't doubt he would if he could, but along with this new longing for people came a great fear of Ted placing himself in danger. She couldn't handle losing someone else.

Allie switched the screen to one of her favorites, a camera that roamed the more rural places—small farms and cottages and harbors. Today, the scene was from a kayak or canoe; she could hear the swish of a paddle and the camera swayed gently on the calm water. It was passing up a narrow lake with occasional cottages on either side. Sometimes it turned and faced a cottage, zooming in on small docks, gravel paths and front porches of log and cedar cabins. Most of the cottages seemed abandoned for the season, but some had smoke rising from a pipe on the roof. Allie thought about what it would be like to have such a retreat to go to and imagined barbecues and early morning dips in the lake.

As the paddler reached the far end of the lake, the camera turned once more to focus on a small but new-looking log cabin, smoke wisping out of a fieldstone chimney. The lens zoomed close on a wide veranda that reached over the lake, and as it did so, Allie suddenly gripped the edge of the couch with all her strength. On the veranda, pulled up against the tempered glass railing, was a wicker chair with a light blue padded cover. Sitting on the cover was a teddy bear with one ear.

The image was gone in a moment but remained firmly etched in Allie's mind. She discovered that she wasn't breathing. A rush of thoughts stampeded her like a horde of wild animals. It couldn't be! Laney's bear, at a cabin in the woods by a lake! Had she really seen it, and was it actually Laney's? Her heart pounded as thoughts multiplied in her brain. Could it possibly mean Laney is alive? Why else would…? The blood suddenly drained from her face. Why was the camera at that specific lake, zooming in on certain cabins, and the cabin with the bear…? Are they looking for her? And then the awareness—is Jim watching me this very moment? Watching for any small reaction of mine to what I'm seeing?

With great effort, she achieved a level of composure and forced herself to concentrate on every detail the screen could supply on the location of the lake. Really, it could be anywhere. Maybe one could find those three trees sticking up a little higher on a low hill? Could she memorize the curve of the lakeshore shown on the screen? Within five minutes, the screen faded to black and reverted to another channel, a walkway beside a lagoon enclosed by a series of islands. She continued to face the screen, yet her mind saw nothing but an occupied wicker chair.

The last thing she wanted to hear broke her concentration—the sound of Jim's voice. "Allie, is all well? You seem upset."

"I'm… it's nothing. I'm feeling a bit panicky about being here so long. I want to be out in the fresh air and among people again. Please, you need to let me go!" The pleading in her voice was sure to raise suspicion, but she couldn't help it. "Please, I want to go home now."

He did not answer. The silence, the closeness of the room and the pounding of the pulse in her throat were unbearable. If Laney was alive, she had to find her. She had to find a way out of here! Allie paced the room, tried every projection and indentation that might hide a door, knocked on walls. She lay on the steps and wept and shouted and pounded her fists. But no one came, no help appeared, no comfort arrived. Helplessness and hopelessness overcame her senses. She lay in a coma of sleep on the hard steps and dreamed badly.

When they talked next, Jim was not in good humor. "I have something to show you." The screen went blank, then displayed a small stone room with a bed in it, bringing a vague memory to her mind. Someone was in the bed lying asleep on his side, and as the camera zoomed in on his face, Allie gasped and covered her mouth.

"I thought as much. A friend of yours? Tell me about him."

"What have you done to him? His face is a mess! Where is he?"

"Your friend poked his nose where it doesn't belong and ran into trouble. He is close by. Would it please you to see him?"

Allie thought hard. "No, I mean, I've never seen him before. I was upset to see someone hurt..."

"Allie, you are not a good liar, which is most commendable. Now, tell me who he is and what he was doing here." His tone was that of a father coaxing a confession from his child. Allie said nothing, so he continued. "He is no guest of mine, and not under my protection. He is an intruder, and those who caught him have rather nasty plans for him. Should I stop them before it is too late?"

"Yes!"

"Then tell me who he is." A less fatherly tone. "You are trying my patience, Allie. Your own position here is becoming tenuous. Do you want to see your friend again? Have you not lost enough already? Start talking, Allie."

"I don't know him that well. I've seen him only a few times. His name is Ted, and that's all I know about him."

"Where did you meet him?"

Allie knew the questions would keep coming. This man was an experienced interrogator, capable of dragging it all out of her. She dare not reveal anything, for both Ted's and Laney's sake. "I don't know, a coffee shop or something. Really, I don't know him. Only an acquaintance. I can't believe your brutality, Jim! You said you're not a beast!"

"And I told you I love my people, which means I will do what is necessary to protect them from intruders. My understanding is that this man is a foreigner and is on this island illegally. When seized, he resisted arrest and this accounts for his injuries. If you know anything, our government would appreciate your cooperation."

"Our government! You—you are the government! You do what you damn well please!" Allie's anger flared.

"Really, Allie! Your temper tantrums are becoming tedious. I take it you will not help us. No matter, we will find out what we need to know in due time. You would make things easier for your friend if you would tell us about him. I will leave you now. Enjoy the show." The screen reverted to some rolling hills with sheep and blue water beyond.

When Ted came back to consciousness, he was instantly alert, and he felt the blood rushing through his legs and arms with pins and needles. But it was difficult to open his eyes. Hands restrained his attempts to sit up, and he fell weakly back on the bed. "Get the Doc," someone said, and his blurry vision identified the movement around him as several men in white coats. They massaged his arms and legs, which made him take in a breath with a hiss. He slowly opened his eyes, which felt strangely puffy, and took in his surroundings.

He was in a small room with stone walls like the hallway he had infiltrated—how long ago? So he was still underground. He lay in growing and significant awareness of pain on a bed with stainless steel railings, but this was no hospital. Memories returned of a room full of computer monitors and a large screen on one wall, and an unexpected attack from one side, which he had returned unsuccessfully. Nothing more. He was in the enemy's camp and he was in serious trouble, along with the many who depended on his leadership.

The room went quiet, and a man without a white coat brusquely introduced himself as Dr. Richards, then stood and looked at a clipboard. "Do you know why you're here—Ted, is it? Do you remember anything?"

"Name's John, John Smith, Private First Class, nine-four-o-three-six-nine-two-five."

"I see. Well, have it your way. Little good it will do you. Let me tell you about yourself since you have forgotten. Your name is Theodore Allen Burkholder, born in New York City. Joined the Vietnam Day March as a high school student, expelled from Berkeley University for a political disturbance a few years later. Drafted by the US Army in 1973, but evaded authorities, whereabouts unknown. Immigrated to Vancouver Island under a special program for American conscientious objectors. Nothing but two speeding violations since that time. Owner of a surf shop in Tofino, and known to leave town rarely except to surf. And currently a major pain in the ass."

"Sorry."

"I'm sure. Where is your RFID?"

"My what?"

"Stop wasting my time. Your identification chip is scanning in Tofino, and you are here. Why is that?"

"Must have dropped it." Ted leaned up on one elbow, causing several of the white coats to edge closer. He surveyed the doctor and asked, "Tell me, why is a doctor interrogating me? Are all your police sergeants busy chasing dogs or something?"

"Shut up. We will have your cooperation; I will see to that. I'm giving you one chance. You used some highly sophisticated equipment and endangered the health and safety of an employee of the Directorate to get past our security and enter the fifth floor. Why?"

"Will it be drugs or torture, or a happy cocktail of the two?"

Dr. Richards turned and went to a tray with an assortment of bottles and hypodermic needles. Ted watched. "Oh good, I prefer the drugs. Berkeley, you know." The white coats forced him onto his back and tightened straps over his chest, arms and legs. Ted didn't resist. This would be a long day.

The Suit had the audacity to sit on the steps of the audience room; he had been waiting, alone, for 45 minutes before the Voice got around to him. "Get to your feet!" The Suit rose slowly and stood in the middle of the dais.

"A chair would be nice."

"Shut up."

The Voice left him on hold for several minutes before it gave him its attention again. "Well, what did you find out? What did she see that spiked her readings?"

"Just a cabin on a lake. We found no one home, though it looked like people may have been there recently. We saw nothing on the video that should have grabbed her attention. Maybe she's finally losing it."

"Leave the analysis to me. Did you take photos at the cabin?"

"Of course!" He was immediately presented with a slideshow of stills, but he took control and examined each one carefully alongside the footage Allie had seen.

"There, idiot! What do you see in the wicker chair on the deck?"

"Hey, we didn't see no teddy bear when we reached the cabin. See, someone had been there!"

"Yes, and with a child! Organize a search, find her! Find the people who have her! Now!" The Suit started to leave, but it called him back. "Wait, the intruder. You better tell me he's still alive."

"Barely, but yes. We got nothing out of him. Should we snuff him?"

"No, make him well. We will try again. Do you realize what we have found here? It is like discovering a couple of bedbugs in a rooming house. If you don't get on top of this rebellion—and soon!—you will find yourself 'barely' alive. Go!"

A profound silence echoed in the room when he left. Blunders, intruders, earthquakes! The return for all his efforts remained quite disappointing. People disappointed him. The very earth disappointed him. You create the perfect system, place it in the hands of humans and they are no better than monkeys with china plates. Oh, the slow grind of evolution! How endless the labor pains of the planet! If he lived a thousand years, would it make any difference? Live he must, though it cost him everything. Let nothing and no one get in the way; rather, lead the way and the best of them will follow.

Which is why he so wanted this woman! Here was spirit and intelligence, vitality and good genetics! It galled him to have to go so far afield to find the pieces he needed to create his archetype world. You bring them here, give them everything their heart could desire, and they turn on you—and find help in their rebellion! O Jerusalem, Jerusalem, which killest the prophets, and stonest them that are sent unto thee; how often would I have gathered thy children together, as a hen doth gather her brood under her wings, and ye would not!

XIV

She was awake when the blue and red stained glass overhead glowed with morning, and watched as its intensity increased. Another day, then. Allie hadn't slept but spent the entire night yearning for her daughter, weeping for Ted, full of supplication. A stillness held her now. She accepted the reality that she could do nothing more; but instead of helplessness, she found herself wrapped in serenity. It wasn't fatalism; it was hope. The sensation was still strange to her, like new clothing, but it felt pleasant and even appropriate. Something will happen beyond her control, and everything will change. Justice will have its way. This had become for her a non-negotiable truth, another anchor in the storm.

Jim found her hours later, breakfast uneaten, nightclothes unchanged. "I didn't think you were the type to sleep in, my dear!"

She pulled the comforter around her and sat up, feet tucked under her. "Good morning, Jim." Her voice should have been bitter, angry. It wasn't.

He contemplated her calm face for some time. "You are a timeless beauty; do you know that, Allie?"

"Thank you."

"It is the fire in your eyes when you are angry that I noticed before, but this... quietude, it becomes you even more." She said nothing and sat, looking at nothing yet taking in everything. "You will be happy to know they have released your friend after medical treatment, with the condition that he leave the island immediately, never to return. He was an illegal, you know."

She smiled, not with gratitude but condescension, even pity. And said nothing. He felt obliged to continue.

"I am afraid that, for the time being, we cannot do the same for you. I hope you are still comfortable here."

"For the time being, yes. Again, thank you."

Her tranquility was both appealing and unnerving at once. He did not know what to make of it. "If you are willing, I would like to talk with you at length this morning. I would like to answer some questions you have not asked. I want to share with you my... vision." Her eyes narrowed at this, but she nodded. "Would you like some time to get ready for the day? Have your breakfast?"

"I'm fine, but if you would prefer..."

"I would, thank you."

She rose and went to the door where the maid was waiting, and he watched her walk across the room with the comforter still wrapped about her. He could watch her bathe and dress if he wanted, but lust was decades behind him and respect had become the higher value. Yet he did not busy himself with the thousand details that sought his attention; he waited for her and watched as she picked her way through a continental breakfast on the tray from the cupboard. She returned the tray and took a turn about the room, then sat and waited expectantly in a dress of blue and gold, with long white gloves covering her still bruised hands.

"A short while ago, I sent to you a young man whom you met in Thailand." Her face clouded for the first time, but he continued. "I hoped his explanation would be sufficient for you, but should have realized he could not satisfy your sophisticated intellect, nor appease your fiery spirit. I am sorry."

"Accepted."

"Thank you." He wondered how she managed to treat him as an equal. He could read—literally read—the stress and tension in all those who stood before him, but in Allie he found none of it. Only the anger, none of the fear. "I want to tell you what the young man did not know, and what we intended when we did to you what must seem the greatest injury and indignity." He paused, watching her response. "We have here a limited population, living in as ideal an environment and community as we can produce. Well aware of the tendency of such populations to multiply their defects rather than their assets, we sought a way to ensure variation in the genetics by introducing new DNA from outside the population.

"The typical method is immigration; however, to open the gates even on a limited basis seemed to us too high a risk. How does one know what one is getting? What are the immigrants' motives for coming here, and having arrived, will they cause more trouble than it is worth? Will they improve the gene pool or pollute it? To adequately screen the heap of applications that would inevitably come our way seemed an insurmountable task and a poor investment of our time and resources.

"So, we found another way. Let me show you." The screen lowered and displayed a database. Allie took in a sudden breath. At the top of the page was a photo of Laney, one she remembered posting online after her fifth birthday party. It made her heart ache on so many levels: the life she lived alone with a young child in a large American city; the mother who couldn't put her social schedule on hold to attend her granddaughter's party; the dreams she had for Laney and had now lost. Next was a profile of herself. It took Allie several moments to take in the complexity of the page on the screen. It was a complete profile, something like what Justin/Brandon must have read on the plane to Thailand. Not only email addresses and phone numbers, but academic and employment records, medical information and a good deal of data that Allie didn't recognize at all.

"Through social networks, dating service websites and a good deal of discreet hacking, we accessed information on potential new colonists. It is astonishing to me the amount of information people have online about themselves, let alone the data collected by governments, health centers and businesses. It was much easier to gain the information we needed through research than to verify information that immigrants would offer about themselves. At first, we had fairly simple criteria—we sought people who were dissatisfied with life, who had big dreams, few family connections—and we arranged ways to get them here. One of the early programs was for draft dodgers during the Vietnam War, and another for disillusioned scientists working in America's nuclear research. Neither program was successful; in fact, many of those dissatisfied people brought their discontent with them and have given us headaches ever since their arrival.

"A breakthrough came to us when we accomplished backdoor access to a series of genetic databases located in various Western cities—mostly American, some Canadian records, and those of many other developed countries. We invited some of the brightest and most progressive thinkers in the world to join us, and we set them free to seek the establishment of a specific genetic protocol within the human race. With remarkable precision, we began to isolate and bring to this island the people we most wanted. No one has ever established such a mechanism before—the opportunity to shape the human race, not only in theory but in practice!"

"Like the Nazis without the gas chambers," Allie interjected.

"I am learning to overlook your crass rudeness. This is worlds apart from what Hitler attempted. He had stupid assumptions about race—his own race, of all things! The perpetuation of any one race is doomed to fail, as proven by all known history. No, what we were seeking was the perfect genetic recipe for a small civilization, drawn from the best of all races. We began with a design for genetic health in our country; we are progressing to genetic perfection."

"You were wrong—you are a beast. I feel sorry for you."

"Whatever do you mean?"

"Where do you get off, running a breeding program for humans? You told me once that you're not a beast and another time that you're beyond corruption. As if you're becoming a god. You're wrong on all counts. You're a man reverting to the habits of a beast."

"Oh Allie, sometimes I would like to remove your head from your shoulders! But you intrigue me. Explain."

"You're talking about the survival of the fittest. It always includes the destruction of the less-than-fit. I see now that some theories I've assumed all my life are inhuman. This competition for the right to live and procreate is an animal state, not a human one. In the realm of human reason and compassion, it's diabolical."

"Please don't moralize your sentiment, Allie. I have run this question through scads of opinions, and have wrestled with minds brighter than yours or mine, ad nauseam. So don't go on as if your opinion is the only one. I have concluded that human genetic engineering is the very epitome of evolution in application, not mere theory. What Darwin lectured, I perform."

"Well, it's noble of you. I don't imagine you'll succeed, and I'm certain you will never see this 'perfection' for yourself. In the meantime, you're messing with people's lives on a large scale. How do you live with yourself?"

When Jim finally spoke, he sounded genuinely sad. "This is most disappointing. I am sorry, Allie. I thought that if I could show you the bigger picture, everything would fall into place for you. I hoped you would join me, as the first person in a long time whose company I enjoyed. I see I was mistaken." He sighed.

"Tell me, Allie, can I say anything that would cause you to understand me? I am not a beast, and I often hate the things I need to do for the sake of my people. You are right—evolution is a bloody, messy business! Those criminals and malcontents that we 'deport' by the hundreds each year never reach other shores. We drug them, take their lives from them painlessly, and remove them from the genetic pool. Within an hour, they are incinerated and never seen or heard from again. It gives me no pleasure to do this; it is essential to my program."

Allie sat with tears streaming down her cheeks. Ted. She had no words.

The Voice continued. "You cannot imagine the horrors I have seen, nor those I have prevented. Oh yes, I have great power, but at a significant cost! You have seen my cameras, both fixed and roving. What you do not know is that I have thousands of them, and even with the enormous resources I employ to process and analyze the data, it is everything I can do to manage it. On top of that, every cell phone and landline on the island is accessible to me, not only the phone conversations but also everything within hearing distance of them, even when they're not being used. Can you conceive of the volume of information? Can you imagine what I have seen and heard and been helpless to prevent? You say I am not a god; oh, would that you were right, but a god is what I have become—a god without omniscience or omnipresence or omnipotence! It is too much for me! I despair of ever getting it right. Can you not see? Do you not care about my impossible position?"

She had covered her face with her hands, put her thumbs in her ears, but the Voice persisted.

"And still you don't know half! I lost your little girl! More precious to me than all the gold in my vaults. Such promise, such beauty and intelligence! Opposing forces took her from me for their own small ends, caring nothing for the fate of human civilization. When I heard it, I knew my heart should break!

"Do you know who I am, Allie? Do you know what I have come to? If I told you, would you understand? If I showed you, would your reason and compassion bring you to comprehend me, appreciate me, even forgive?"

Allie's shoulders were convulsing with sobs. She couldn't answer, couldn't even acknowledge any longer the horror of this audience room. After many minutes, she heard a door open, and into the room came a nervous-looking, middle-aged man in a white coat. He stood ten feet from her, waited, and finally cleared his throat in an awkward attempt to get her attention. Failing that, he spoke. "Miss, if you please…" Startled, she looked up. "Come with me." He turned and walked toward the still-open door.

She was too astonished to move. When the man turned at the door and beckoned to her, she somehow found the strength to rise to her feet and put one in front of the other until she joined him. He was pale and thin—a complete nerd, as she would have called

146

him in high school. He didn't look her in the eye, and failed to avoid looking at her low-cut dress, though he attempted to not be obvious. She followed him through the door and into an elevator. They descended one floor.

The hallway was long and narrow, grey stone marbled with beige, dimly lit with inset lamps. It was cold, particularly to her bare feet, and grew colder as they descended slightly. At the end of the hall, he opened a door to a room with the look and smell of a chemistry lab, empty of people. He motioned her to a small room with an antiseptic smell and a large shower at one end. "You, um, need to change out of all your clothes and seal them in this plastic bag. Here, you may need two. Take a shower and use the soap in the dispenser, on your hair and, um, everything. Use lots of it. Then put on the clothes that are in this other bag. Okay?" He was sweating at the end of this explanation and closed the door on her the moment she was half through, catching her trailing dress, which he pushed through with one clumsy foot.

Allie had hardly any room to move with her gown bunched up around her feet. She didn't know what to make of this. Was she to be executed at once? No trial, no last defense? Was this some necessary preparation of her body for the furnace? Undressing was more a matter of climbing out of the dress than taking it off. She divided its several pieces into the two plastic bags and dutifully sealed them shut. The shower seemed redundant, but she liked a good shower, and it seemed a more fitting prelude to death than a last cigarette. She showered long and hot, wondered for a moment what havoc the yellow disinfectant was playing with her hair and remembered that it didn't matter. She tried hard not to think of Laney. Her daughter was resilient and resourceful, free from the clutches of the enemy and hopefully with powerful friends. Now it was Allie who got to die first. She had little doubt that when Laney's turn came, they would find themselves together. For now, with only a one-eared bear as evidence, she felt a deep assurance that her daughter was in good hands.

But she did regret Ted. Was he still alive? Had he gone through this purification before her? If so, she had no real qualms about following him. But if he had been freed, she would feel cheated. Allie wished she could have one more conversation with him over coffee in his house at the back of the shop. She would have liked to learn to surf. She could imagine a life with him. Allie wondered also about Sophie, who had exuded such confidence but failed to save her. But she wasn't difficult to forgive.

Someone pounded on the door, and she turned off the shower. The clothes left for her were white and sterile—underclothes, pants and blouse—stiff and uncomfortable. The socks and white booties felt strange to feet that had been bare for so long. She opened the door.

Ted was alive. Many times in the past 48 hours, he wished he were not. Even now, he couldn't be sure that he hadn't screamed out names and locations that compromised people he cared about, and this was worse than the torture. They were healing him now, all kindness and soft words, no doubt preparing him for round two, so he must not have spilled all. He knew he could not hold out a second time.

Permanent damage was likely and this he regretted. Despite all odds, he had hoped to live. Early on, they discovered his shoulder injury and worked that arm—dislocating and reducing it again and again—so he knew his surf session with the sea lions was his last. He felt affronted that human beings could do this to the body of another, but he remembered Jerry and the squishy package of flesh he had removed from his shoulder—and was ashamed. So stupid, thinking he could walk in, save the girl and be the hero. Soon he would die, and his little resistance movement would die with him.

Dr. Richards walked into the room, and all the white coats stepped back from the bed. He ordered them out. "I think you have seen better days, Mr. Burkholder!" Since no reply was forced from him, Ted said nothing. "You're going on a field trip! I will try to make the journey as painless as I can, but these hallways can be a bit bumpy." He pulled the bed after him to the door, and Ted groaned as he bounced the bed over the threshold, obviously enjoying Ted's pain.

He continued talking as they entered the elevator. "You will say nothing that is not a response to a direct question. You will be thorough in your replies, and I suggest that honesty will be your best policy. Consider this mercy, and judgment is coming if you refuse to comply!" Leaving the elevator, they passed down a narrow corridor and through a door into a large, dimly lit room. Lying on his back and unwilling to move his aching head, all that Ted could see was a high, domed ceiling. The room itself seemed circular. The Doctor pushed the bed up an incline, and Ted's injured arm rammed against the bed rail as he slid down the bed. He swore—loudly—and Dr. Richards glared down at him.

"Leave us," said a voice that seemed to come from the dome above him. The Doctor's face disappeared, and Ted waited out the silence. "Theodore, do you know why they have brought you to me? What did he tell you?"

Ted was still breathing hard from the excruciating pain running up and down his arm and torso. He gasped, "Mercy!"

"Very good. This is mercy, all that I can afford to give you. Who I am, where I am, what I am, is of no consequence to you. You need only know that I hold for you the keys of life and death, and mercy comes only from me."

"Keep it," Ted replied through clenched teeth. "I want nothing from you."

"Ah, but I want much from you. We could make an exchange."

"Sorry, my soul is not for sale." Clever, but the effort of talking was more than Ted could bear. The Voice replied and continued, but became a buzz or drone he couldn't comprehend. At the same time, a corner of his mind cleared and he perceived things that he had never understood before; as he watched, the corner grew larger.

149

Life, the world, the universe—all of it stood before him with the clarity of a brisk and sunny winter day in the mountains. Profound ideas shaped themselves like those one grasps in the time between sleeping and waking but can never remember. These concepts arranged themselves before his mind and he could turn them about and examine them at will. Some, he didn't like. He discovered that, up to this moment, he hadn't known (to quote Thomas Edison) one-millionth of one percent about anything.

That's when he realized he was dying.

XV

The little girl gave them only one concern. In every way, Laney was a happy and delightful child who had immediately melted their hearts and was in great danger of getting spoiled. Their only worry was her constant vigilance—she was always watching to see if her mom was coming. While they were still at the cabin by the lake, she played the games and read the books to them as if she were doing them a favor, but always returned to the wicker chair on the veranda, pulled up close to the glass and facing down the lake, bear in lap. She was the one who excitedly told them about the approaching kayak, and she wasn't happy when they made her come inside until it was gone. But as always, she was cooperative.

They thought it best she shouldn't know that they were on the run. Today's spontaneous trip by Jeep up the valley behind the cabin was an adventure to an even smaller cabin on a tinier lake, and they might find snow. Laney didn't want to sit in the front of the truck and watch the forests and mountains emerge; she insisted on kneeling on the back seat and watching behind them, with the inevitable result that she was sick. Fortunately, the woman named Lizzy caught it in time with a once-reusable grocery bag, while keeping her own long blonde hair out of the way. Her husband, Jack, had to step out of the Jeep and take a short walk.

For a time they drove along a creek bed, and this adventure Laney enjoyed immensely, especially when the water sprayed right up over the windshield. "Again, again!" and the couple smiled at one another as Jack did his best to find the spots deep enough. They finally pulled up a gravel bank, stones flying, and ascended a steep dirt road. A short while later, the track ended and Jack let them out. He removed some packs and equipment and backed the Jeep carefully into the salal bushes until both he and it disappeared. The bushes shook and something growled. Jack burst out suddenly and Laney screamed. She ran at him, tackling him to the ground for his joke.

Lizzy and Jack arranged their packs and put them on, giving Laney a small daypack to carry. They were grateful for the blue sky, but it meant that the path was slippery with frost and ice in places, and Jack occasionally carried Laney as well as his pack. Lunch was on a big rock in the sun, where a small waterfall splashed beside them and several grey birds about the size of robins came and watched them from the fir branches. "Pigs-On-Wings," Jack called them, and he showed Laney how to hold a peanut in her hand with her thumb on it so the bird would land on her hand and stay a few seconds before nabbing the nut and making its getaway. She learned that these birds were also called whiskey jacks or grey jays, but she liked Pigs-On-Wings better. Jack made her wash her hands before continuing with lunch.

By mid-afternoon, Laney was slowing down despite the frequent carries. Lizzy held her a long while at one point and let her cry, understanding that the tears were more than about tired feet and knees. Half an hour later, they broke out of the trees to the edge of a small lake, and Laney's vitality returned. Not many more beautiful places exist on earth. Towering above them, too near to take in with one glance, immense snow-bound peaks ascended to a long cornice of overhanging snow, from which a dozen waterfalls emerged and threaded their way down a vast vertical slope, disappearing into scree and deep green conifers and feeding the dancing wavelets of the turquoise lake. They let Laney throw stones into the water—occasionally having to duck out of the way—before they coaxed her along the last two kilometers of lakeshore to the cabin.

Completely hidden, the cabin still afforded a gorgeous view of the lake and one snowy peak. And it was the last stand—they had no way out of here except the way they came or straight up those cliffs. So if They discovered them here, it was the end. Lizzy prayed fervently that this time They wouldn't discover them. In any case, their stay in this location was temporary. One couldn't survive here in the winter, which would dump meters of snow until one would have to dig a staircase down to the cabin. Jack and Lizzy had supplies for nine days if they were careful, and if it snowed more than ten centimeters, they would have to leave. They had no idea where to go next.

Lizzy watched Laney watch a squirrel, centimeters from the window, caught in the act of robbing the birdfeeder. She sighed. They had rescued little boys and girls like Laney before, but they had always saved the moms as well. If only Allie hadn't ended up in detention at the hospital! There was no opportunity to snag her, and by the time they figured out how to evade the watchers at her condo, Allie was gone. Jack and Lizzy discovered too late that They really wanted this child and would go to extraordinary measures to get her back. If they didn't find a way off the island soon, They would catch them for sure this time.

The anger that fueled their drive to foil the genetic program of the Directorate was dissipating, Lizzy realized sadly. Eight years ago, they themselves were the scenario—young woman meets charming young man who gets her pregnant and abandons her. Then she gets invited to a paradise padded with hefty child support checks. Unfortunately, Lizzy and Jack truly loved one another and got back together. It made someone angry: their child was taken and never found again. But they decided to fight back. In five years, they had rescued eleven moms and kids and returned them to their homes. Maybe this time the Directorate had given a child back to them. Lizzy was pretty sure they would never find Laney's mom again. She sent up another appeal that the three of them wouldn't get caught. The Directorate had an uncanny sense of smell in tracking them down.

Laney stayed by the window until it was too dark to see the lake. Lizzy persuaded her to sit with them at the table in the chair nearest the stove, which Jack had stoked with wood selected to give off little smoke. As Lizzy tucked her into bed, she asked Laney, "You miss your mom a lot, don't you?" Though Laney never talked about her mom, she nodded her head. "I'm glad you love your mom so much. We're doing our best to find her, but if we can't… we promise to be as good a mom and dad to you as we can. Though I know we could never do as good a job as your mom. Okay, honey?" Laney looked at her a long minute with liquid eyes and slowly nodded her head again. In minutes, she was asleep.

The Nerd was waiting for her. Allie was confused when he held out a hairnet with steel forceps. She started to speak, but he put his finger to his lips. He indicated that she should tie her wet hair back in a bun before securing the hairnet in place. The next items were a pair of latex gloves and a mask that fit closely over her nose and mouth, so she couldn't speak even if she had anything left to say. She put them on, wondering what on earth it was all about. Prepped like surgeons and decked out for chemical warfare, he motioned for her to follow him.

They walked down a short hallway through more grey stone. At the end, she saw a door—not a door you would find in a building—more like something you would find in the bowels of a large freighter or submarine. The Nerd spun a large stainless-steel wheel; she heard a gasp of air as the seal was breached and the pressure equalized. The door opened and Allie followed her guide, stepping into a narrow space with a similar door at the other end. The Nerd closed the first door behind them and fiddled with some instruments on a panel. Bright lights came from the ceiling, the walls, the floor; she could feel their heat like noon in the tropics, rays that would fry your skin in minutes. He motioned for her to spin around several times, eyes closed. The lights dimmed, and he opened the second door without any sound of pressure change. They stepped over the sill into a large room. Allie thought the air was denser, or there was too much of it; and the lighting was strange, as if they had walked out of doors into a forest, sunlight muted by dense foliage. As her eyes adjusted, she stopped walking—and breathing.

"I liked the dresses better, Allie. My technician friend is too cautious—and perhaps not." He sat in a high-backed chair at a desk where he had been writing—she saw ink splotches on his fingers. The glass wall across from him was all one video screen that flickered to black at a motion of his hand. He was ancient beyond years, skin like crumpled parchment that someone had tried to straighten again. Perhaps he had once been handsome, but not enough membrane and flesh covered the finely structured face, the sturdy hands. Though he rose slowly, he stood without trembling. "Welcome, Allie. Welcome to my home, such as it is."

Jim waved his hand to encompass the room, and Allie took in her surroundings. The Nerd had exited again, and they stood alone in a verdant garden. Short, thick grass carpeted the ground, yet seemed never trimmed. In the shrubbery near her feet, every leaf and bloom was perfect, tending toward blue and purple hues accented by crimson blossoms she had never seen before. Above their heads, branches thick with leaves formed the ceiling, punctuated by the pale gold and red of various fruits she couldn't place. Beyond the trees, Allie could see a clearing with a small vegetable garden, lush and green, with areas of rich, fresh-turned loam ready for new planting. Her eyes returned to the man who awaited her appraisal with a look of satisfaction, and found she needed to sit down.

The grass was cool and thick and ever so soft, like the first grass that ever grew on the earth. Jim returned to his seat, looked at her kindly like a great-great-grandfather and spoke in his familiar tone of voice. "Allie, you are a privileged person. Less than half a dozen people before you have entered this room. But you pushed me to it. It may surprise you to hear I regard you highly, and that I hoped you might join my cause. I now believe that is unlikely; however, neither could I have you think ill of me. I want you to know me, and I hope you will come to appreciate me." She couldn't take her eyes from him, though she wanted desperately to look away, look anywhere else. She was afraid she might be sick.

"See? Despite what I told you earlier, I am not a god. I am

human, like you. But I am old—very old—and I am wise. And I must go on living. So I created this veritable Garden of Eden, where no threat of disease and infection exists, so I should go on living indefinitely. I breathe pure and highly oxygenated air. I drink nothing but distilled water and have the joy of growing my own food. The secrets and privileges of Methuselah are mine; along with the responsibility and the age-long regrets.

"I came to this island many years ago and knew the first time I set foot here that this could be the paradise I always longed for. My initial efforts were clumsy and rough, like a new husband with his bride, but in time I learned to live in harmony with this place and its people, whether native or colonist. I became powerful here but did my best to use my power for the good of the people. Many of those who shared power with me did not have the same ideals in mind, and became consumed with lust and greed. I struggled all my life, through times of popularity and contempt, to uphold, guard and defend my principles. And then I became old.

"A person functions as if he will live forever, but a day came when some palpitations of my heart alerted me to my mortality, and I remember thinking, I cannot die! Too much rested on my wisdom and charity. It was all too likely that the one who would follow me in leadership would not have the same moral fiber; power and gold would corrupt his character and throw the country into a tyrannical dictatorship. I determined to live, at all costs, for the sake of my people."

A cold sensation crept up Allie's spine. This was becoming a horror show, and she had a front-row seat to herself. She was afraid she wouldn't retain consciousness and lay down on the grass, eyes still fixed on his. As if anticipating her growing apprehension, Jim elucidated. "Yes, Allie, I am Sir Frederick James Douglas, born in British Guiana in the year of our Lord 1803, once Chief Factor of the Hudson's Bay Company and Governor of Vancouver Island and British Columbia, now an ancient and humbled servant of 726,384 people living on this rock on the edge of the continent."

She closed her eyes and concentrated on breathing.

"In the 1860s, as the colony of British Columbia joined the Canadian confederation and we did not, I selected a group of honest men to form a Directorate and rule in my stead. That is what everyone was told, but I could not entrust my paradise to these men, lest they lose their souls. I remained as their head and mentored them into my ideal as best I could. One by one, they fell into depravity, and we removed them permanently for their own good and the preservation of our society. Finally, only three of us remained, and we trusted one another implicitly. These were noble men, heroes, saints. I loved them with all my heart.

"Together, we created a land where every man, woman and child could sit under his vine and under his fig tree; and none shall make them afraid. It was a nation of freedom and opportunity, flowing with milk and honey! We had none of the restless discontent you find in your own country, Allie! Everyone was in one accord and had every reason for happiness without polluting themselves by pursuing it. Justice was swift, but fear was gone.

"However, we were all getting old. The day that I grasped my mortality, my colleagues and I began investigating ways of extending our life span. Our research included inviting some of those scientists one never hears about, the Dr. Frankensteins of the world. The majority were crazed, evil men, terrified of death and consumed with fanatical theories. Finally, one came to us with extraordinary skills. He could significantly suspend the aging process, though it cost us much, both in resources and our own comfort and mobility. We had always lived incognito, as it were; now we had to be invisible.

"We gained knowledge and wisdom to extraordinary levels. We learned to manage vast amounts of data long before the accursed 'Information Highway' came to be. We perfected our integrity— in the true sense of the word—by making every decision and action part of a coherent pattern. Astounding systems and infrastructures worked in complete harmony toward noble ideals. As technology increased, so did our efforts to stay alive. Most were not successful. Over the decades, my two compatriots succumbed to decay; for the past thirty years I have ruled alone..."

He stopped, noticing that Allie was curled up in a ball on the grass, eyes tightly closed, fists clenched. He made as if to rise to her aid, hesitated and sat again, watching her helplessly. After several minutes of silence, Allie heaved a great sigh, opened her eyes and struggled to sit up. She groaned with the effort as the world tilted and turned. If anyone in the room looked insane, it was her.

"Allie, I know I have overwhelmed you with this revelation. I cannot help it. My loneliness is beyond comprehension; I am entirely without solace, void of affirmation. One kind glance from you will carry me another decade, and will give me the courage to continue my thankless compulsion. Would that I could free you from your mask so you might speak comfort to me! I would offer you tea; we could sit and chat as friends... Ah, why did I bring you here, but to torture myself? Am I become so thoughtless as to not anticipate your reaction to my presence? I am repugnant to you— I can see that I am! What was I thinking? I am but an old fool, Allie. Can you forgive... can you forgive an old fool like me?" He looked at her wildly and breathlessly, eyes full of longing for the companionship that would never again be his.

Allie raised her dull eyes and motioned for paper and pen. He collected and held them down to her, and she crawled across the grass to reach them. She couldn't restrain from shuddering at the imminence of his touch as she took from him several sheets and an ancient fountain pen. Kneeling on the grass before his desk, Allie wrote briefly upon the paper on her lap, then reached up to slip paper and pen back onto his desk. Scrawled on the page were the words, "God have mercy on your soul!" As he looked down to read, Allie launched herself at his throat.

A violent surge of current coursed through her limbs, and she fell senseless to the grass. Sir James Douglas set the Taser back on his desk and considered her with cold regard for several minutes. The door opened, and white-coat arms dragged her bodily from his habitat.

XVI

It was the headache that pushed its way through her unconscious state, demanding attention and remedy. Allie had none. She awoke, not in the elaborate audience room but in a small stone cell on a hospital bed, firmly strapped down. The smell of her own vomit enveloped her. Turning her head slightly, she saw a small open door to a toilet, which she needed badly, and seeing it made her need worse. Finally, half an hour later, she relieved herself. She was very uncomfortable now, embarrassed despite her isolation, and wishing it would all end.

A shudder ran through her body as she remembered her encounter in the garden, remembered him. It couldn't be. Yet she had seen him, nearly touched him: two hundred and... she couldn't work out the number of years, but they were too many. Tears streamed down her face with the aftertaste of her uncontrollable wrath against such an old man... couldn't believe she had tried to... It was perhaps best she had failed. He wasn't physically threatening; his mind was the menace. She burned with a desire to expose him, to see him made accountable, to free his people. But all that she hoped for now was a merciful end to her own life.

She lay thinking on the bed for a long time, reviewing her life in detail, tabulating achievements, noting regrets. Her past seemed surprisingly free of the latter as if someone had wiped the board clean, but she had many regrets for the future, many things she wanted yet to do and see. She felt it was not so much an injustice that her life was to be cut short; it was more like a loss, a vacuum she wished filled. And it wasn't her own life that she longed for, but the lives of others: Laney. Ted. The well-being of those 726-thousand-something islanders. She was sure it was a noble request, and she posted it on the ceiling above her, right next to a vent in the gray stone.

Hours passed. Allie had no concept of time, of day and night. She lay still for an eternity, it seemed, not in the sense of countless minutes but of endless sameness. This wasn't the eternity she wanted. So she pulled her mind out of that dismal morass and decided to wait, because to wait is to expect something to happen. After a very long while, it did.

A door opened behind her. She couldn't see who it was because she faced the wrong direction. Someone laid a hand on hers, and the amber eyes that she most desired in all the world came into her range of vision. Sophie. In her white nurse's uniform. The room lightened like a spring sunrise; birds singing wouldn't have surprised her.

"Allie. I'm here. Thank you for waiting. Somewhere, down deep inside, you knew I would come, didn't you?"

She realized this was true, and nodded.

"It's time to go, Allie. It will be a hard journey, but I will be with you every step of the way. Will you trust me?"

Allie's voice was faint. "I trust you."

Sophie undid the straps, and blood rushed with pins and needles into Allie's feet and hands. The nurse knew where and how to rub to get the circulation flowing. To Allie's distress, she discovered her wet clothing.

"Sorry... I..."

"No worries, Allie. What could one expect? You're so human, aren't you? Let's clean you up and get you dressed."

It was like being a small child again, without the scolding. Or like a rag doll, since Allie seemed unable to help much; her limbs refused to obey her. Sophie removed her clothing, sponge-washed her body and gave her a coarse but warm wool blanket to wrap up in. She returned with new clothing—not cotton whites, but the style of clothing Allie felt most comfortable in, things she was always searching the stores to find. Sophie was doing something with her feet; Allie looked down and laughed. In the weakest voice,

160

she managed, "Hiking boots? Where do you think I'm going? Even if I could walk, I'm sure slippers would do for where They're taking me."

"Well, we've had a change of plans, Allie. Remember, you said you would trust me!" Allie laid her head back again and giggled quietly to herself.

"I'm... so glad... you're here, Sophie." It was all she could manage; her body felt like it belonged to someone else. When Sophie finished and asked her to sit up, she didn't know how to respond. "But, surely you know... I'm far too weak to..."

"Sit up, Allie. I know you can. I'm not helping you!" She lowered the bars on one side of the bed.

Allie didn't move. It seemed impossible to do so. She felt resentment reaching up for her like fingers out of a mist. Remembering her promise to trust, she pushed the feelings down. Her body tensed to rise, and a cool and tickling sensation swept through each part of her body as it moved. She sat on the edge of the bed with her legs dangling, the weight of the boots strange to her feet.

"Well done, Allie! Now come, wrap the blanket around you for warmth, and follow me." Her words brought back Ted's instruction about the abalone password: Go with that person wherever they take you. Ted. The thought of Ted and the likelihood that They had already killed him made her heart bleed. She wondered if she would join him on the other side.

Sophie returned to the bed. "What is it, Allie?" She wanted to tell Sophie about Ted but found she couldn't. Instead, she let Sophie help her off the bed, discovered strength enough in her legs to walk, and followed Sophie to the door.

In the hallway opposite her door, two uniformed security guards or police stood silent and motionless. They looked straight ahead, blinking but otherwise seemingly unaware of their presence. When the door closed behind them with a click, one of the guards glanced down the hallway, but not at Sophie or Allie. The same thing happened further down the hall, where two more guards stood. Sophie passed so close to one guard, Allie saw the hair on his forehead move. But he stood with eyes fixed on the wall across from him, with no acknowledgment of their passing.

They arrived at an open door—it was still opening—and walked into a cell like hers with another bed in it. Allie stopped when she saw a form wrapped in a white blanket and strapped to the bed, knowing it was a corpse and afraid of whose it might be. But Sophie began undoing the straps and motioned to Allie to help her. After a moment, Allie dropped her blanket and started at the feet, which betrayed no movement and seemed lifeless. It felt like her fingers were learning their business for the first time, but eventually the fastening came free. She couldn't help watching Sophie, who was done with straps and was now working to loosen the blanket. Allie didn't want her to, but couldn't find her voice to object. Sophie pulled the blanket back from the figure's face, and a knot rushed to Allie's throat. Ted.

Sophie looked at Allie with deep concern and a sorrow that matched hers. Ted looked quite good, considering. He wasn't as pale as she would have expected; in fact, he looked merely asleep, hands folded on a chest that didn't rise and with something missing in his countenance. Allie looked upon him with deep affection. *Rest, my friend. They can't reach you now.* She leaned over and placed her hand on his shaggy hair—she couldn't bring herself to touch his face. *I would have done life with you, my love. Even if it was fewer years and you left long before me, it would have been worth it. Laney loves you, I love you. I will be with you soon.*

Inexplicably, Sophie loosened more of the blanket, pulling it from beneath the body until it lay lightly on top of him. She looked again at Allie, but this time expectantly. What was she to do? "He's yours, Allie! Bring him back!" Allie looked wondering at her, but couldn't doubt those golden eyes. She clambered up onto the bed and stretched herself out on Ted's senseless body, held his hands in hers and placed her lips to his; she could feel the cold seep up from him, and it was so bitter she thought her tears would freeze, that she too would turn icy and lifeless, but after a while she realized he was cold no longer.

At the same moment, both Allie and Ted opened their eyes and were aware of one another. Allie couldn't move. She looked deep down into the wells of life that represented his spirit, and loved him. She felt his large hands squeeze hers, then release, and he took her face in his hands and drew her in.

"Ted, I was so afraid!"

"Shhh… don't cry." They looked long at one another.

Sophie cleared her throat. "Um, time to go, you two! Come on, Ted, let's get the circulation going, shall we?" Allie moved to her feet and helped her. In a short time, Ted was sitting on the side of the bed, groggy and shaking his head. Sophie went to the door and motioned for them to follow.

"Come, Ted, we need to go," Allie coaxed him. She helped him down, set the blanket over his shoulders and put her arm around him, following Sophie to the hallway. Ted put much weight on her shoulder at first, but soon began to know his strength again and held her hand instead. His other arm hung lifelessly, and he avoided letting it bang into the wall. He finally reached over and stuffed that hand into his pocket, and gave his other hand back to Allie. She smiled up at him.

Sophie was a short distance ahead in the long hallway. They passed the elevators, and at the very end of the hall, a door opened for her automatically. She beckoned, and they picked up their pace and followed her through the door and up a narrow stairway. It went on and on, turning occasionally, dimly lit by inset lighting. At any moment, they expected to come to the end or to another door but never did. Allie could hear Ted's breathing come harder, and her own chest felt constricted. But Sophie was still far ahead, and at the next turning they could no longer see her.

"I have to stop, Allie! This is crazy. Where…?"

"No, Ted, we have to keep going. It must be okay. Trust!" He looked into her eyes and gained strength. "Come, we're getting behind."

He looked at her questioningly but obeyed. It was like ascending from the center of the earth, stair after stair, endless corners, many level passages. Lift, place foot on step, straighten. A thousand times ten thousand times. After what seemed an age, they looked up to see natural light streaming from around the next corner. As they turned, they had to shield their eyes; Ted freed his hand from hers to do so. They stumbled out of the open door into a small clearing among thick woods, through which they could see the ocean far below. Sophie was nowhere in sight. Ted and Allie staggered to a sunny rock outcropping covered in thick moss and collapsed. He held her close with his good arm; Allie pulled the blanket over, and exhaustion swept them away.

Jack watched the helicopter sweep through their valley and away down the stream. The stove was out and the cabin was invisible, yet someone somehow knew they were here. After only two days, it was time to move again. He weighed their options and found the balance heavily in the enemy's favor. It was David against Goliath, and he selected his stones carefully. If whoever was looking for them did a ground search, would they walk up the valley? Likely. But it was their only way out. He whacked the hatchet into the splitting block and went inside to break the news.

Laney, for once, wasn't at the window but coloring a picture Lizzy drew for her. He stood unnoticed in the doorway and watched them. Their heads were close together; his wife's blonde hair mingled with Laney's golden brown. They discussed the merging of different shades of crayon. Lizzy's natural ability to nurture without smothering amazed him; rather than imposing her own choices on the child, she worked with what Laney selected and showed her how to make the most of them. She was designed to be a mom; her rage had stood in the way for far too long. Laney was a gift, and they wouldn't lose her. He sat down with them to explain what they would do.

An hour later, they left the cabin and started down the trail along the lake. Laney, surprisingly, didn't want to go and whined and complained for the first time since they had taken her. They coaxed her with the hope of animal sightings, but it didn't help much. Jack finally picked her up and carried her. But when they reached the thicker woods past the lake, he had Lizzy and Laney walk out of sight behind him. If he encountered anyone, he would give a loud enough greeting to warn the other two to back off and hide in the woods. It was the best they could do.

They passed their previous lunch break place. Laney seemed to regain her playfulness, singing silly songs with Lizzy and counting whiskey jacks. But at a corner on the trail, where the stream ran noisily beside them, they heard voices and Jack's in reply. Lizzy quickly pulled Laney back, went up the trail a bit and crept with her into the thick woods as best they could.

"Good morning!" Jack's voice called heartily. "You scared me! I thought you were a bear!"

Three men dressed in park warden uniforms came up to him. With no preliminaries, one said, "Did you know this is a closed area?"

"No," answered Jack, genuinely surprised. "Since when?"

"Since last summer. It's being designated a preservation area. We received an alert about a couple of people spotted at the lake. How long have you been up here?"

"A couple of days, camping."

"And where is the rest of your party?"

"My wife is, uh, visiting the ladies' room in the woods behind me. Do you mind waiting until she comes down?"

"Fine. Where are you parked?"

Jack's mind raced. "Friends dropped us off. They'll be back later today."

"We can give you a ride down."

"Thanks, but we have no way of contacting them. They'll be worried if we miss them."

The warden looked at him long and hard. Lizzy chose a good time to show up, minus Laney. "Hi, what's all this about?"

"They say the area is closed. Are we in trouble, sir?"

"Well, no, I guess not. But don't come back. Can we escort you down?"

Jack and Lizzy glanced at one another. "Um, my wife has arthritis in one knee. Takes a hell of a long time to get anywhere. We'll be fine." The lies and even the mild profanity tasted strange to him. This is war, he thought. It's okay.

After a long moment of silence, the warden said, "Just the two of you, eh? No kids?"

"Kids? Hell no!" Jack kicked himself. He wasn't very good at this. "Maybe someday. Having too much fun now!"

The other two men chuckled at this. "Okay. Remember, this area is off-limits. Don't come back. Sorry—I know how beautiful it is up here. It will reopen one day. Be safe!" They turned and headed back down the trail.

Lizzy immediately started back toward Laney, but Jack grabbed her arm. He peeked around the corner in time to see the three men take the next turn. "It's okay now. Where did you hide L...?..." Laney walked out from the bush where she was hiding.

"Laney! I told you to stay where you were!" Lizzy caught her up in her arms.

"I heard a noise, and I wanted to see what was going on. I'm a good hider!"

"You are, honey. Everything is okay. Those men wanted to talk with us and we didn't know who they were, so we were being careful."

"You told fibs!" She looked at Jack accusingly.

He laughed. "You caught me, Laney! Don't worry, I won't make it a habit. Should we have a snack? I know a good place up ahead." He helped Lizzy with her pack and realized they were both trembling. "Courage," he whispered to her. "We're not going to lose her. We'll get through this." He squeezed Lizzy's hand and went ahead down the trail.

When they reached the truck, Jack scouted the area carefully before letting the girls into the clearing. A larger vehicle had been there that morning. He walked a short distance down the road but saw no sign of it. The Jeep seemed to be just as he left it. As they drove down the dirt road, he stopped regularly but heard no sound of another motor. At the place where they drove up the creek bed, he took another route out but didn't breathe until the highway appeared ahead of them. He turned and headed for the east coast.

The body count was increasing. The Suit swore under his breath; he couldn't afford to lose trained operatives this way. "I understand your annoyance," the Voice intoned, "but kindly keep it to yourself. I am taking no chances. How else can you explain two prisoners walking out from under your nose? Your men were collaborators!" The Suit shifted his feet uncomfortably on the raised dais. "Who else?"

"No one else, Sir! Maybe your technician…?"

"He's harmless, and entirely under my control. Give me the status of your search."

"Well, finding the guy is practically impossible—no RFID. But as long as they stay together, the girl should be easy enough…"

"Should? Did I hear you say 'should'? Do you mean to say you still have no idea where she is?"

"She's out of range of all our monitors, sir. Unless they found her RFID too and removed it…"

"Idiot! With the condition they must be in, they could not be more than a kilometer from here! It's a miracle they could even walk! You told me Theodore Burkholder was dead! How do you account for this? And Allie—Allie was senseless and strapped to a bed, the last I heard! Fools!! Blundering ninnies! I am weary of your incompetence! If I had even the slightest better option right now…"

The man on the dais closed his eyes, breathed consciously and bowed his head. The sight of him cowering slowed the escalation of the Voice's passion.

"Are you sure no one was with them?"

The man looked up. "The cameras show only the two of them. For some reason, the camera in the girl's room was off. She opens the door, walks down the hall, opens his door, unstraps him, unwraps him, gives him clothes; they both leave and walk right past the guards and the elevators, and… then I don't know. The cameras only go to the elevator, and past that it's nothing but stone walls. It's like they walked right through them or something. Here, I'll show you."

The Suit made a call on his radio and gave instructions. For several minutes, he felt the attention removed from him. He relieved the stiffness in his shoulders and cracked his neck.

"Stop that. Yes, I see what you mean. It makes no sense. You searched the level entirely?"

"Every corner. Besides, the monitors should pick her up. We found nothing." Another pondering silence. The Suit stood waiting for so long that he felt forgotten.

At last, he was told, "Go! Helicopters, ground crew, everything you've got. Don't dare stand before me again without those two in custody. Leave me."

The Suit made his usual sauntering exit. "Wait!" He stopped and turned, though he had no one to look at. "The child—what is the status of your search for Allie's child?"

"Nothing. Every lead has led to nothing. We still don't know who took her, and the one trail we had went cold." When he heard no response, the Suit heaved a sigh of relief and left.

When he was gone, the room was still and empty, but anyone

who entered that space would feel a brooding presence. Bloody incompetence! He reviewed the footage relentlessly, watched every monitoring camera within several kilometers, and wished for more eyes and hands and feet on the ground. He gave long periods to thinking, but rational thought also disappointed him.

In his very, very long life, the inscrutable occasionally happened, and he never knew what to do about it. Sometimes, he wrote it off as impossible and moved on. Or he pleaded ignorance to enough details to fully grasp what had occurred. Neither option seemed practical this time. He was as stumped as a magician's audience, as puzzled as if it were the most difficult riddle. He could properly feel only one emotion anymore, and he was usually adept at keeping it at bay. But the news he had received brought with it an overwhelming new flood of fear. He alone knew that his Castle of Invulnerability was made of sand, and an enigmatic threat like that of Ted and Allie changed everything, like the turning of the tide.

He must find them, at all and any cost. And he wanted that child, plus whoever took her. The problem gripped his full attention, leaving many of his servants scrambling like ants without a queen. The only explanation was intervention—the two could not have saved themselves. A foreign power was at work here, with stolen intelligence and connections. He must uncover and thwart this espionage; in his mind, he declared a state of war. The difficulty was in leading his country to war without its citizens perceiving it. As much as he must obstruct this menace, he must also not disturb the equanimity of the nation. Complete contentment was their strength; enjoyment, their constancy. Keep the people blithely happy and they will serve you forever. He would eradicate this enemy with the clean precision of a sniper.

XVII

Whenever Allie came to consciousness in the hours they lay there, she found it all too surreal. How could she be in the woods on a warm, clear blue day resting in the arms of a man she loved? Her mind couldn't rouse itself enough to give any serious consideration to the question, so she let it go and drifted back to sleep. The final time she woke, it was to a face looking fondly down at her, with a trace of bewilderment. She kissed him, which was very different from the last time. "You're not dead."

"No." Ted's smile was serene and wistful.

"Were you dead?"

He looked around the clearing, up at the sky. Back at her. "Maybe. I don't remember much. I don't think it was any better than this." He kissed her in return.

She sat up, gingerly, surprised at her strength. She expected to have none. "What on earth am I wearing?" Her clothes were attractive and comfortable, but entirely unfamiliar. Recollection came gradually. "Sophie…" She looked around the clearing in expectancy, but they were alone.

"Who?"

"Sophie—you sent her. The one with the password. The abalone lady."

Ted looked at her quizzically, then shook his shaggy head to clear it. "Tell me about her."

Allie told him about the times Sophie came to encourage her, and how she had slipped the passcode into the conversation. "She was the one who came to my cell and set me free. She put these clothes on me and led me to your room. As you were lying on your bed—lifeless—she told me to bring you back. And I did." She blushed slightly as she said it.

Ted looked down at his feet for a long time, wondering where these hiking boots came from, wrestling with her story. "Allie, I don't know anyone named Sophie or anyone with her description." He sighed and plucked a strand of grass beside him. "I gave the passcode to a man named Bruce, who was to pick you up at your condo. He would never have given it to anyone else without my express permission."

Allie looked at him in wonder. "But how…?" She sat up and searched for the doorway that brought them to the clearing. "How did we get here? We came through a door…"

Ted rolled to his knees, tried to stand and thought better of it. He sat back on the rock. "What door? I don't see anything here." It was true. Allie walked the edges of the clearing. She found nothing but grass and trees, nothing to suggest any opening. She returned to Ted, who was watching her with a troubled face.

"Was it a dream, Allie?"

"Dream? How could it have been a dream? We were in a dungeon! You were dead! Now we're here, wherever here is. And what about these clothes?"

Ted looked down at himself. Nice base layer, good quality fleece, great zip-off hiking pants like the ones he decided not to buy at the co-op, and a handsome Gore-Tex jacket. He had never seen any of it before. "I have no idea. Maybe we're both dead." Allie sat down on the rock in front of Ted, and he put his arms around her. Arms. Both of them. Recalling a flash memory of brutality, he wondered how that was possible. "Someone has done this for us, Allie. We couldn't have done it ourselves. I don't understand what's happened, or what we should do next."

"Do you have any idea where we are?"

Ted looked through the trees, trying to identify the shoreline far below them. "Hmmm… not really. It could be East Sooke, maybe. But I've never been to this spot before. It's a long, long way from where I last remember being."

"What happened to you, Ted? How did you end up in a cell?"

"I could ask the same of you." He told her about his botched rescue attempt, leaving out certain squishy details that made him uncomfortable. "I don't know who was preaching to me at the end. I remember losing consciousness, but not. Hard to describe, like everything became suddenly clear. The next thing I remember is waking up and finding you beside me."

"You don't remember how you got here, through the passage and the stairs?"

"No. Doesn't ring a bell at all. I'm clueless how we ended up here."

Allie sat musing over this for a while, then told her own story in detail. Ted's eyes alternately grew wide and narrowed. "Wow, Allie, if I didn't love you so much, I would call this a load of crap. Unbelievable! But it did happen, right? Did you imagine any of it?"

She hesitated, pondering the question. She said firmly, "No. No, I'm sure it wasn't my imagination. Every time something truly weird happened, some token showed that it had actually taken place. Like these clothes. And you heard Jim yourself! Do you think he's Sir James Douglas?"

"I think nothing will surprise me anymore. Whoever he is, he won't be happy we escaped. We know too much, especially you. No place is safe for us here. We need to get off this island."

Allie went suddenly white. "Laney!"

"Allie, I'm so sorry..."

"No, listen, I didn't tell you this part! I think Laney is alive!"

Blood rushed to Ted's head, energizing him. "What? How?" She told him about what she saw on the screen, the teddy bear by the lake. His shoulders slumped again. "It's not much to go on, Allie."

"But don't you see? We can't leave until we know! If she's still here..." She turned and took his face in her hands. "Please, I can't go. Not even to save you. Not if any chance remains that Laney is alive."

He nodded, and kissed her forehead. "We'll find her. If she's still alive, and as long as we stay alive, we'll find her. I promise."

As the sun set, it grew cold and they became hungry. They couldn't spend the night in the clearing, as good as their clothing appeared to be. But neither could they risk Allie's RFID being detected. "I wish I could find it and take it out," she exclaimed. "It's such an indignity!"

"We could find and remove it," Ted said uncomfortably, "but it's a surgical procedure. We can do nothing about it right now. We'll simply need to keep you away from anywhere that has monitors. Which is practically everywhere but here in the woods." He thought a moment as she looked at him expectantly. "Maybe we can find shelter for you, and I can go buy some food."

It was dusk as they finally left the clearing, and it was darker still in the forest. Allie's heart stopped when a deer burst from its cover not three meters from them and bounded away. Spider webs constantly covered their faces; branches and heavy brush impeded their progress. At times, forward progress seemed impossible, though it hardly mattered since they didn't know where they were going. Soon it was not only dark but misty. They didn't see the light shining through the gloom until they were ten meters from it. Bursting out of the bushes, they found themselves on a narrow dirt track.

It was the proverbial little cabin in the woods, hardly more than a shack. Through an amazingly dirty window, they saw a single LED light hanging from the rafters; below it, a derelict old man sat nursing a brown bottle at his elbow and reading a thick hardcover book. A large, ancient radio sat at the other end of the table, playing 50s tunes with much static. Allie gasped as a wet nose nuzzled her hand; in the dim light that came through the window, she saw an elderly border collie with one front leg missing. She looked at Ted, and they went to the door.

The man was not especially hospitable. Ted did his best. "And we saw your light, which was a God-send, since my wife and I got lost, and we're freezing and hungry. Can you spare us a bite to eat and a corner to sleep, and point out the way to the road in the morning?" From the door came the odor of unwashed clothes and burnt spaghetti sauce.

The man looked from one to the other and back again with disbelieving eyes. He looked past them into the dark, his gaze seeming to penetrate the mist. "How d'ya find me? Nobody kin find me." He spoke like someone who didn't get much practice.

Allie spoke up, and he startled as if he hadn't noticed her. "We stumbled upon your light. We have no idea where we are." He considered this for a full minute, looking back and forth at the two of them, and a sly light came into his eyes. He stood out of the way to let them in. Allie's heart dropped—the place was hardly big enough for three people to sit comfortably, let alone lie down. The dog came in too and curled up in what was obviously his spot by a small wood stove, which did double duty in keeping the room a little too warm and leaking enough smoke to be felt in the back of the throat. Newspapers covered the table, some new, some old, all acting as the tablecloth. Since the place had only one chair, they sat on the bed, trying not to think of what might be crawling through it. The man pulled a big can of beef ravioli off a shelf, opened it and set it on the stove to warm. To Allie, it looked strangely appealing.

He stared at them from his chair. Ted tried a few questions, some of which he answered, others he ignored. He stared at them some more. They settled into an awkward silence, punctuated by air bubbling up and escaping with a sloppy sound as the ravioli heated. The man didn't stop staring as he picked up the can with his bare hands, carefully wiped a couple of spoons on his pants and set it all on the newspapers in front of them. As they ate, Allie noticed that he alternated between staring at them and glancing down at the newspaper half-covered by his book. If they happened

175

to look back at him, he immediately took his eyes off the newspaper as if they had caught him at something. Then, out of the corner of her eye, Allie could see him bob his attention up and down again.

Finally, she was too curious. Leaning forward as if to look into the can, she glanced at the newspaper in front of him. He quickly moved his book, covering what he had been looking at; Allie didn't have time to see what it was, except that it appeared to be a photo with a caption. She settled back onto the bed, looked out the window, and with the extremity of her peripheral vision saw him slide the book to the side again and resume his bobbing.

They finished the ravioli, and it wasn't nearly enough. Allie was amazed to find herself looking at the shelf, which boasted many more cans of beef ravioli. None was forthcoming; the man continued his silent distracted vigil. Finally he spoke, an amazing speech that left them baffled. "I, uh, gotter go… find some transpersation for ya. Itsa distance, mind ya. Perty dark and froggy out. Shunt be too long." And with that he rose, took a hat and green raincoat from a nail on the wall and opened the door.

The moment it closed behind him, Allie dove for the newspaper. In full color were two photos side by side with the words, "Detain With Caution!" and an explanation. The photos were less-than-complementary images of Allie and Ted.

Ted lunged for the door. If it were not for the small flashlight the man was using to find his way, they would have never found him in the utter dark outside. Ted pinned the man's arms to his side before he could even turn around, picked him up and carried him back to the door, where Allie was waiting with a huge butcher knife in her hand. Ted threw him onto the narrow bed; he crawled back as far as he could against the wall and cowered. The dog barked but didn't get up from his blanket by the fire. Ted searched him for any kind of weapon while the man murmured, "Hey, hey, no, don't!" repeatedly. He carried nothing but the flashlight and a lighter, which Ted took and set on the table.

"Look at me!" The man wouldn't. "Hey, I won't hurt you."

Ted reached toward him—the man had nowhere to go—and placed his hand on the thin shoulder. "It's okay—I know you think we're bad people who the cops are after. We're not bad people. We have done nothing wrong." Not moving, he pointed to the newspaper, which Allie handed to him. "The stuff it says about us isn't true. Relax." Relaxation wasn't on the man's agenda. The moment Ted took his hand from his shoulder and shrugged at Allie, the man darted for the door. It was sticky and required two pulls, giving Ted time to seize him again.

"Okay, I gave you a chance!" Ted carried him outside to an outhouse that Allie found with the flashlight, pushed the man inside and closed the door. Allie brought him a couple of short logs, which Ted jammed firmly in the dirt and against the door. After a few minutes of rattling from the other side, the outhouse went silent. They returned to the cabin, opened another can of ravioli, and discussed what on earth to do.

"We can't leave him in the outhouse. Like he said, no one will find him." Allie was taking quite a liking to cold beef ravioli; she said it with her mouth full.

Ted was still shaking a bit from his excursions. "And we can't let him go. What does the newspaper say about us?"

Allie reached for the paper, which had fallen to the floor. "'Detain With Caution.' Our names and wonderful photos. Then, 'Two American agents, recently arrested for espionage, are evading capture on Vancouver Island soil. Their unfortunate escape from VI officials may pose a danger to the public and to themselves.' Isn't that nice of them! And a bunch of contact information if anyone spots us. 'Colonists are permitted to detain these agents, but not at the expense of their own safety. Time is of the essence, and the authorities appreciate your cooperation. The VI Directorate.'"

"Espionage! It makes it sound like we're the enemy! An ironic accusation, isn't it!" Ted shook his head.

"James Douglas, at war with the world. He's a megalomaniac!"

exclaimed Allie. "If he lives much longer, ruling this little island won't be enough to satisfy him."

"So now both of us can't enter public areas, with or without an RFID. What do we do? We could live several years on ravioli, but we won't find your daughter that way." Ted sat in troubled silence. "I have to risk getting to a phone. I need to let my team know I'm okay and we need their help."

"Well, you're sure as hell not leaving me with Mr. Ravioli! I'm coming too, as close to the phone as we dare."

Ted nodded. "I guess the best we can do is toss him a bunch of cans, the can opener and a spoon. At least he doesn't have to worry about where to do his business! What more can a guy want? We'll send someone to let him out in a day or so." They settled down to an uneasy sleep under their wool blanket, sitting on the bed; both were awake when the first light came through the window. The cabin contained little that was of any use to them. They each stuffed a can in their pocket, then remembered the single can opener, so they added them to the stack going to the outhouse. They left the dog inside with a huge bowl of dog food, and between them carried a blanket full of cans to the outhouse.

"Okay, I'm about to open the door, and if you know what's good for you, you won't move. Right?" No answer. Allie removed the logs and Ted braced himself as he carefully opened the door.

The outhouse was empty.

"What the…!" Ted looked up at the roof, which was solid, then down the only other route, which was insane. Light came from somewhere below, enough to show some deep and obscene footprints, slowly filling back in. "No, he couldn't have!" Allie pushed past him and quickly exited with her hand over her mouth.

"That is desperation," she managed. They left the tin cans where they were and set off down the narrow track.

"Where are we going, Jack?" They had driven several kilometers in the silence of their relief at making it down the mountain without incident.

"I don't know, Lizzy." Jack looked grimly ahead. "I have some vague notion of finding someone with a boat who might agree to take us to the mainland or one of the islands. I think we'll go north—the mainland is closer and more isolated up-island. We always knew this might happen one day; we should have planned for it."

Lizzy looked in the back seat. Laney was curled up with her bear, fast asleep. "I don't get it. How did they find us? And they even knew to look for a couple with children, yet they didn't know this little girl was with us? I mean, they suspected, but they bought our line about having no kids."

"Seems a bit uncanny, doesn't it? Do you think they have some way of tracking us? Like a locater beacon on the Jeep?"

"I don't know what to think, Jack. I'm scared! I've learned to cope with losing Raylene, though I'll always love and miss her. And Laney is such a gift. I want to be done. I want to have a normal life as a family again."

Jack laughed wryly. "Huh, you think life will be 'normal' on the mainland? Or in Australia or Norway or wherever we end up? You at least know how to live someplace else. I have never filed a tax return or paid a phone bill. We're leaving all our stuff behind, and our bank account isn't much of a cushion. You know we can't count on your family to help us, and it wouldn't be safe to go to them anyway. Life won't be easy."

"Can we stay?"

"We can't stay and keep Laney too. They want her for some reason. We can't keep running and hiding. Even without Laney, I think our time here has come to an end. It scares me too."

"Jack, if you knew then what would happen, where our sense of justice would take us, would you have rescued that first woman and her son?"

He didn't hesitate. "Absolutely. Joceline and her little boy. Do you remember her face when we told her the true story of how she ended up here? No matter how tough it was for her as a single mom in Winnipeg, not even the promise of a cushy life on the island was enough to soothe her. She wasn't even tempted; she was ready to leave."

"I remember hugging Joceline before she got on the boat. I've never seen such a grateful woman. Do you think any of the ones we rescued might help us?"

"We'll need all the help we can find—without being found. You know we'll need to circumvent the law again. We have no paperwork for Laney—where will we buy an identity for her? It might cost everything we have."

They drove for several kilometers, lost in their thoughts. Jack didn't notice the police car go by the other way until it did a U-turn behind them and its lights came on. He pulled over to the side of the highway, and the car pulled up behind him.

"What do we do?" Lizzy's eyes widened.

"We stay calm and pray hard." Jack was far from calm and couldn't squeeze out one word of prayer. The cop sat in his car a long time, typing things into his computer, before coming to the window.

"License and registration, please." He barely glanced at the papers and handed them back. "You have a headlight out. I made a note that you have 24 hours to replace it. After that, if you get pulled over again it will cost you." He glanced in the window at the back seat. "You know, your little girl should be in an approved child seat until she's eight years old or 35 kilos. You've got 24 hours for that too, okay? Have a good day, folks." He went back to his car.

Jack started the Jeep, heart pounding. In his nervousness, he stalled and had to start again, and he saw in his rearview mirror that the cop was watching him. He pulled carefully onto the highway, and to his dismay, the police car followed him. For several kilometers, he could hardly breathe, but then a car going the other way whipped past them and the police car turned and went after it, lights flashing. The hand Lizzy laid on his arm was trembling. "Okay, Jack, it's time to leave the island. I don't care how. Let's find a boat."

XVIII

A short distance from the cabin, Ted stopped. "This is nuts. We have no idea how long the old man has been gone. He could come back up the road with the police any minute." Through the trees he could still see the strait far below; ahead, the narrow road turned in the opposite direction. "It will be rough, but we need to cut through the woods and down to the water. I don't know how else to avoid both the cops and the monitors. Are you up for it?" Allie nodded and they took the first opening they could find toward the water.

The going was rough. The open ridges that angled down the hillside always ended in bluffs; when they descended the gullies instead, they found themselves waist deep in the brush. Ted was especially cautious—his arm felt miraculously good, but he had slipped in the past and knew how blindingly painful it was to land on that arm. The water was more distant than it appeared; it seemed to take forever to reach it. They were scratched, spider-webbed and sweating by the time they came to the last ridge with a steep descent and a rocky beach below them. A well-traveled trail along the ridge paralleled the shore. They turned left and walked the path a short distance, then found a place to rest out of sight of the trail.

"Ted, I'm tired, stressed out and happier than I have ever been in my life. How can that be?" She snuggled in close to him.

Many thoughts occupied his mind as he absentmindedly stroked her hair. "I'm struggling to process everything that has happened here, and the things you told me. Much of it I don't understand." She looked up at him. "Okay, so we have several interest groups at play. We have our pernicious and relentless government and its megalomaniacal ideals. And me and my team, trying to gain the information we need to resist and prevent them.

There's you and Laney, innocent bystanders swept up into some project of theirs to perfect the human race. And some blonde lady—and likely some accomplices—who kidnapped Laney for reasons of their own. And some other mysterious party—represented by this nurse Sophie—that for whatever reason seems to be on our side and far more powerful than any of us."

Allie thought to herself, Plus one more who is even more mysterious, but I'm not ready to tell even Ted about him. "It's a complicated game," is all she offered.

"It's beyond me! I used to enjoy our covert operations, feeling very much in control. It's all done. I'm a pawn now, with no great hope of winning this one." They sat until the cool wind off the water picked up. Allie was thinking about beef ravioli. Ted stood and looked up and down the shoreline. "I may have been here once before. It looks like the trail that runs along the coast between Sooke and Victoria. I'm not sure if we'll meet anyone on the trail this time of year. I don't even know what day of the week it is! And my stomach feels like an empty pit."

They stood to go. "I think we'll walk in the direction of Victoria," Ted decided. "I'm sure we're not monitored here, though maybe at the start of the trail. What we need is a boat, but that would take a miracle." The trail was easy after their bushwhacking, and despite their hunger—or because of it—they made good time. They saw no other people. Other than ravioli, all of Allie's thoughts were on Laney—where she was, who she was with, if she was happy or traumatized. How on earth would they ever find her now?

The day was grey without rain, and the coastline was amazing—all mossy headlands with sprawling green arbutus trees, their paper-like red bark peeling off in big strips, and gold-leafed stubby oak trees that looked ages old. Her hiking boots felt like comfy friends, and she would be content if it were not for the angst that tugged at her every thought. It was tempting to let Ted worry about it all, to take care of everything and be the man. She found herself strangely attracted to that arrangement, but not in a good way. She determined to be neither the helpless princess nor the independent Annie Oakley, but someplace in between.

They walked over another rocky headland and found below them a sandy cove—containing a miracle. A small motorboat rested where the beach met the quiet water, shielded from the wind by the headland. They saw no sign of anyone around. They debated in whispers about the ethics of helping themselves to someone's boat, of likely stranding them. Should they wait for the person to show up and ask nicely? Ted couldn't believe Allie would even make that suggestion, considering the imperative nature of their flight and their quest for her daughter. He wondered about the change in her since they reconnected. But he wasted no time convincing her that their need was critical, and in this case, forgiveness would be more prudent than permission.

No one challenged them as they untied the boat from an overhanging tree, pushed it out and jumped in. It started on the first try, and Ted steered the boat out into the strait before turning toward Victoria. "We'll stay at least a kilometer offshore," he shouted above the noise of the motor and the wind. "No monitor reaches more than a couple hundred meters. You will be fine." They saw no one along the shore as they passed, no irate boat owner waving his arms. The boat had two full containers of gas, and best of all, a large hamper crammed with food. The wind was chilly, but they wrapped up in the precious wool blanket and ate big sub sandwiches with scalding hot coffee poured from a thermos. It was better than anything Allie ever tasted.

After half an hour of roaring past the distant shoreline, Allie saw the tops of the Parliament buildings and shuddered. She had no doubt they were being watched on one or more of Jim's arsenal of cameras and hoped they looked as innocuous as any fisherman on his way to a favorite spot. He was most certainly searching for them. She had spotted three helicopters circling so far, but none came over the water.

"Where are we going?" she shouted into the ear next to her.

"I'm not sure. This much gas should take us past Victoria and into the Gulf Islands, which is still Directorate territory, but I think safe. If we can find more fuel, I'm game to go as far north as we can, closer to my team. I'm concerned about the wind that's following us, though. It could get sketchy if whitecaps form behind us. We need the cover of the islands in this little crate." Streaks of white foam were forming on the choppy water, and further out Allie saw white waves rolling in the same direction they were going.

Digging deeper into the food hamper, she discovered a plastic bag with a phone inside. She unzipped the bag and showed it to Ted. He immediately slowed the boat. "Here, keep us straight. I'll try to reach my team. They must be frantic." He turned it on. "Blast, it's picking up a carrier from the opposite coast—in Washington state. I'm glad I'm not paying the roaming charges!"

Ted typed a number, let it ring once, hung up, dialed again and let it ring three times. Allie could hear a man's voice answer, hesitantly. "Hey, it's Fletch," Ted responded. "Yeah, I'm okay, and I have the package. Yeah, not my phone—if someone calls on mine, don't answer. Listen, rendezvous at Departure Bay; I'll be at least three hours, maybe more. If you can swing it, I need gas— yeah, I'm marine. Pender. No, the other one. What's the date and time?" He swore. "Sorry, a little hard to believe. Guess I spent more time fishing than I thought! Sorry to scare you!" He laughed. "Later."

He took the wheel and opened the throttle; spray flew on either side of the boat. "That's good. We should be able to take this all the way to our concealed departure point—not the Departure Bay where your ferry landed on the island. That's a smoke screen, just in case." Ted seemed in better spirits. She could tell he loved the intrigue. But the word "departure" bothered her.

"We're not leaving until we have Laney, right?"

He couldn't return her gaze. "I want you safe!" He lifted his hand to restrain her protest. "But I won't make you leave. We're in this together. We'll find Laney and go together, or not at all."

Allie suddenly remembered Jim telling her he could listen to every cell phone on the island, even if it wasn't being used. Her face paled as she told Ted. "What if They're listening right now?"

Ted thought. "No, I think the phone is connected to an American cell tower across the water, so we're okay. But what you're telling me answers a few questions I've wrestled with. No wonder they can track my team so easily. Better not take any chances." He tossed the phone overboard, harder than necessary.

The sun broke through the clouds, but the wind behind them increased to the point that it hardly blew in their faces anymore. Ted looked back, and his eyes widened. "Not good," he said. At the same time, a wave picked up the back of the boat and slew them slightly sideways. Ted squeezed a bit more speed out of the motor, which pulled them straight again, racing down the wave. It subsided behind them. "We need to get out of this!" Ted turned the boat toward shore, riding the leading edge of the trough between the waves like a true surfer.

The seas diminished as they neared land—not too near—and were merely choppy by the time they came into the lee of a small group of islands with a lighthouse on one of them. Ted relaxed his grip on the wheel and eased off the throttle, directing them across an open, relatively calm bay. Allie took the wheel while Ted rummaged in the food hamper, finding a can of Coke and a bag of chocolate chip cookies. A few minutes later, the motor coughed a couple of times and stopped.

"I didn't do it, honest!" Allie gasped.

"Relax. The tank is empty. We need to switch to the other one." But as Ted shook the "empty" can, he realized it contained plenty of fuel. "That's funny…" He switched the fuel line to the other tank anyway and tried the ignition. The motor sputtered and coughed, but didn't start. He squeezed the ball in the middle of the fuel line a few more times, sending gas into the motor. When he tried again to start it, they both smelled strong gas fumes. "Nuts, I've flooded it. Nothing we can do now but wait a while."

They were drifting rapidly across the bay, more or less in the direction Ted was heading anyway. Ted tinkered a bit with the outboard motor but admitted he didn't know much about them. "I can hardly do a thing with car engines beyond changing the oil; boat motors are a whole different ball of wax. I don't have a clue." As they drifted, Allie asked about Ted's team. "We're a small active crew with a growing group of supporters. Of course, we have had to be extremely careful about who we let in. The key criterion is a verifiable story of getting screwed by the Directorate, motivating a desire to do something about it. Our supporters send us cases to deal with, and we check them out and take action if the risk is within the limits we set."

"Was rescuing me within your limits?"

"Nope, clear out of the ballpark. Why I thought I could save you is beyond me. I guess my judgment was clouded—I must love you or something."

"Or something." Allie laughed.

"And you end up saving me. Thank you."

"I can hardly take credit for that! Sophie saved us both. Thank you Sophie, whoever and wherever you are!"

Ted tried the motor again. It turned over but wouldn't catch. "I don't think it's firing. I wonder if the boat has any tools." He searched under the bow and in every nook and cranny, and found a rusty screwdriver and an adjustable crescent wrench that would no longer adjust. The boat was drifting a little closer to shore than Ted liked, so he took the single oar from under the bow and started paddling them slightly into the wind, which nosed them out toward open water again. It took a long time.

Allie enjoyed watching him. He looked like a sailor, a rogue. Someone a girl could be romantic over at any age. But he also looked worried. She wished she could share her confidence with him, instill in him a little hope. His life—like hers until recently—was altogether like this boat, drifting in an endless sea with no compass and nowhere to go if he had one. She had an anchor now, but she could only see the end of the chain that was attached to her. The anchor itself was in depths too great for her to fathom. She wondered at the source of her assurance, the object of her trust. Wondering, she turned her head and screamed.

"Ted! Rocks!" Thirty feet away, water surged over black rocks lined with sharp teeth. They were drifting directly toward them.

Lizzy couldn't get enough of Laney. The girl's intelligence and breadth of knowledge amazed her. The playground at the little seaside park held her attention for only minutes. They walked the beach, turning over rock after rock to discover what lived underneath. Jack was on the phone, and she hoped he was being careful. She had no doubt now that someone with authority was tracking their every move, not only because they were under suspicion but because this Power tracked everyone, knew everything that was happening on this island. Her sense of being watched was palpable.

The small seaside town of Port Hardy was sleepier than most she had visited. Two seniors with a wheelbarrow were collecting seaweed for their garden; they piled up a small amount and each took a handle and wheeled it through the parking lot and down the street, returning diligently after ten minutes to do it again. A family of young boys played "grounders" on the slides and monkey bars; across a small cove, boaters carried supplies up and down the wharf. Laney gathered seashells, one of each kind, and entrusted them to another of Lizzy's grocery bags. This is what I want, Lizzy thought. Normal family life. And after Laney is secure, I want another of her, and another and another.

Jack pocketed his phone and joined them. Lizzy's eyes asked the question, and Jack mouthed the word "maybe." When Laney went seagull-chasing down the rocky beach, Jack explained. "I met someone who knows someone who knows people who might be able to help us. Yeah, I know, it's a bit of a stretch. He's checking on it now—it would be a series of boat trips that would take us to the mainland, in exchange for the Jeep." Lizzy's eyes widened. "Hey, we can't take it with us! And we wouldn't get much for it if we sold it. They would also help us sell the cabin after we leave, and that money would be all ours. It's a better situation than I imagined."

"Who are these people?"

"I don't know. The guy I met on the dock was careful, and he instructed me to talk cryptically on the phone with his contact. Sounds like they have done this before, and they fund their activities by selling off things people leave behind."

"Can we trust them?"

"We don't have much choice. I liked the guy I met, and the one on the phone sounded pretty confident and knowledgeable. I think it will be okay."

"So we're leaving with what we can carry on our backs. Oh, Jack!"

"And Laney! And the money from the cabin, hopefully soon. I asked the guy if his contact does IDs and he said he thinks they do. Our own passports will be enough for you and me, but we need something for Laney. So it sounds like we have the help we need."

"I don't know. What's their motivation for breaking the law and putting themselves at risk? Did you ask that? It can't be for the money, or they would take the cabin too and everything we've got." Laney came back with an armful of twisted driftwood; they received her explanation of each piece. Both of them were preoccupied and less than responsive. After a few minutes, Laney left in a huff and joined the boys in the playground.

"Lizzy, we're out of time and options. The longer we stay, the more I feel we're being monitored, that we're not safe! I'm sure the park rangers and the cop were no coincidences. We have to leave as soon as we possibly can."

Lizzy looked at him with tears rolling down her face. "I know. But we're leaving behind our lives, Jack. Your family, our home, our work. What's next for us?"

Jack stretched and stood up. "I know, I know, all right? But I feel strangely okay about it. For one thing, we can stop looking over our shoulders after all these years."

"I hope so, Jack. I hope so."

All their surveillance, all their watching eyes, turned up nothing. Ted and Allie had vanished into thin air. At the same time, the Suit pursued his search for the little girl. The best they had was a conversation from an island cell phone with the keyword "Allie" used twice, but the other phone used an American signal and its location was untraceable. It wasn't much to go on. They also tracked several persons of interest previously connected with the genetic protocol program who might have reason to work against them. But so far, no sign of the girl.

He figured the Voice wouldn't be in a good mood. So it surprised him to only be asked how the search was going and to receive no comment in return. It was a full 15 minutes before the Voice noticed him again. "You—you are still here? Leave me, do something useful. I don't care what you do, just go do it."

The Voice was, to say the least, preoccupied. With every cell in his body, he hunted intensely, scrutinizing every screen, replaying every conversation his search engines selected. To find the people who eluded his clutches had become an obsession. He would not again make the mistake of relying on other human beings. His own superlative resources would serve him. He would solve this mystery and put an end to it.

It was difficult to grapple with an enemy one could not identify. That he had an enemy—and a powerful one—he had no doubt. He was also certain this was a foreign opponent. Undoubtedly some element of American intelligence coming to the aid of the carping Canadians. What do they want now? They are all full of covetousness. He watched their noble causes every day on the news channels, sticking their noses in everyone's business in the name of charity or justice or freedom. What they really want is everyone's stuff, which has become their god.

Well, they can't have my stuff, he mused. Beneath me sits enough gold to threaten their economies—do I pull it out and let them take it? I own enough wood, oil, and mineral resources to vastly enhance their oppression of the world's poor and needy—should I empower them further? No, they will not have my stuff, and they will not alienate me from my people.

What is wrong with giving the people what they need? He remembered Allie's foolish tirade about teachers and leaders who looked to the interests of their students and followers, who listened to them and used their ideas. Interests! What cared he for the interests of the people? They are entirely flawed in their judgments! Some are like ignorant children and others like brute animals, all without any idea of what is in their best interest. Let someone older and wiser show the way! He who has a lifetime of experience is surely more qualified to chart a person's course than the cabin boy born yesterday! He pled with the oblivious crowds who passed his cameras at that moment: Come to me! Learn of me! Find rest for your souls! He longed for them; he was jealous for them. He turned his attention once more to locating the flies in the ointment of his benevolence.

XIX

Ted paddled furiously, but too late. Before he could lift the prop out of the water, it came down with a crunch on hard rock, lifting the motor off its mount and snapping its chain. It disappeared behind them. The next wave swung the boat around, nearly capsizing them and filling the boat to their ankles. Its fiberglass keel came down on the rock with another sickening sound, throwing them off their feet, then lifted again and was free of the reef. Within minutes, the water level was rising. The shore was an unswimmable distance away.

His arm throbbed. He had no more strength to paddle. Allie gave a hand to the oar but gave up after several futile minutes. The water was painfully cold, enough that they would die of hypothermia long before they would drown. Several lifejackets floated up from under the bow and each put one on. They sat on the opposite rails of the boat and looked across at one another in desperate defeat. It wasn't fair to come so far and fail now.

After a while, the boat seemed to have taken on as much water as it could; it sank no lower. But it was a constant battle to keep it upright, like some children's contest with a homemade raft. The food hamper and other equipment floated in the pool that had been their boat. Against all odds, they kept up their game of balance for half an hour, an hour, recovering from the next unexpected wave and correcting for every involuntary repositioning. It was exhausting. Allie could no longer feel her hands or her feet; energy drained from her, but she wouldn't lose hope. All the while, the wind and tide carried them across the bay, no farther or closer to the shore. They spoke little, having nothing to say. About the time that Allie's mind became as numb as her feet, she heard a shout behind her. She almost capsized them as she turned to look.

A boat was bearing down on them under full sail. Swinging past, it pulled sharply into the wind, and all hands pulled frantically to lower the sails. The commotion they caused was too much for their little swamped boat; Allie suddenly found herself in water up to her neck and swimming hard for the sailboat. Someone tossed a life ring to her; she grabbed it and got a good mouthful of seawater as they pulled her to the stern. Two sets of arms hauled her out and wasted no time getting off her lifejacket, peeling off wet clothes and wrapping her in—yes, another wonderful wool blanket. They took her into the small cabin and placed a cup of something warm in her shaking hands. Ted soon followed.

"That better, eh? Seems we reach you only in time!" He was tall, blonde, something Scandinavian. The woman as well, and the young man could only be their son. The man spoke to them from the cabin door, one hand on the wheel.

"Thank you," Allie managed, smiling up at him. "I knew someone would come."

He looked surprised. "How do you know that? Look around; we are the only ones! You are most fortunate you are alive! Your little boat go, bloop, behind you!"

Ted echoed her thanks, and said, "Are you colonists?" The man looked askance at him. "Are you from Vancouver Island?"

He shook his head. "No, no, visiting from Sweden." He laughed, "No, no, we don't sail from there in this little boat. We sail near our 'omeland often, rent this little dinghy in Seattle." He rubbed his blonde beard and looked at Ted. "I think maybe we are not where we should be? Not American waters?"

"No, you're within Vancouver Island marine limits."

"Ach, that's not good, I hear. We go back out into the strait, I think." He put the motor in gear and made two turns of the wheel. The three of them raised the sails again, which snapped to attention. They picked up speed. With the engine turned off, Allie could hear the hull slicing through the waves. "That okay with you? Where we take you?"

Allie looked at Ted with fire in her eyes. He caught it and said, "We're from Vancouver Island and need to get home. But ahead are islands where you could drop us off and not get in trouble. Are you traveling north?"

"Yeah, north. Desolation Sound is our goal, but I am thinking not today. Who is worry about you? Can make a call; 'ere." He handed Ted a phone. While he called, the woman came and sat beside Allie. She indicated she couldn't speak English, nor her son, but she spoke volumes as she rubbed Allie's back and followed up the warm drink with a hot, grainy porridge. With gestures, they introduced themselves. Allie learned that her husband's name was Staffan, but he called down the hatch to call him Steve. Her son was Tomas, and she had the name Anneliese, which Allie thought was the prettiest name she ever heard.

In the meantime, Ted and Steve determined that tomorrow they would set a course for Mitlenatch Island, a bit of rock that was a World Heritage site—and a bit of no-man's-land—in the open straight between Canada and Vancouver Island. Ted's contact would pick them up. They would first spend the night at Stuart Island in American waters. Steve said he would put off checking in at Canada Customs until after he dropped them off, and if he had any trouble, he would revert to Swedish. They gave Ted and Allie clothes to change into and hung theirs out on lines. In the breeze and sun, everything was soon dry again.

That evening, they pulled into a small bay near Stuart Island. Steve wanted to avoid the more crowded harbors where people might ask questions. He and his son dropped anchor like they were one person in two places, each knowing the other's mind. Allie and Ted found themselves alone in the stern, which swung toward shore on the incoming tide. The wind diminished; lights from houses on the shore reflected perfectly in the still bay. Allie sighed. "Right across the water—those are American homes, a dinghy ride away, and we can't go. And if we return to the island, we're in immediate danger; we have a death sentence on our heads."

"Tempted to swim?"

Allie looked at him. "Tempted to make you swim, and leave it to me to find Laney."

"You know that doesn't make any sense. But we could do it the other way around."

"No! No, we can't. I can't." She wrapped her arms over his shoulders and laid her head against his. "I know that if we both go back, I put us in greater danger. But I can't leave without her."

"And if we can't find her?"

"*Can't* is not in my vocabulary."

"I'm serious, Allie. What if she's not to be found?"

Allie unwrapped herself and lay back across the ropes so she could look him in the eye. "Ted, you need some faith. Somebody is helping us." A memory returned to her. "Sophie. Sophie told me, the first time I saw her, 'I'm certain you will see your daughter soon.' Not 'maybe,' not 'if you're lucky.' Certain."

Ted sighed. "I'm sorry, I don't get any of that. I don't know who Sophie is or who her people are. But they're people, and you can't trust people. I know—I am one." He looked her straight in the eyes. "I don't think you should even trust me that much, Allie. I can't promise that you'll ever see Laney again."

She didn't crumple, didn't even get angry. After a few moments, she said, "Well, for now I'll just have to trust for both of us. But one day soon, when we're walking down some country road holding Laney's hands and swinging her off the ground, you better do some hard thinking, young man!" She leaned forward and kissed him.

Their evening in the boat was wonderful. It was so good to laugh again, and Steve kept all of them going with his mix of English and Swedish and his bawdy songs in both languages, which made his son blush and his wife throw biscuits at him. They feasted on marinated prawns caught early that evening, fried and served on a bed of lettuce with heaps of mashed potatoes. Steve and Anneliese insisted on giving them their berth up in the bow, which could have been awkward if they weren't so exhausted. They slept

196

the sleep of the dead until Steve playfully tooted Jingle Bells with the boat's horn to let them know that day was breaking.

The sky was grey, but only because the sun was still below the horizon, creating a red-rimmed yellow glow over a snow-capped mountain to the southeast. Mount Baker, they were told, a volcano down in Washington State. Everyone thought it might blow up years ago, but Mount St. Helens beat it to the punch and relieved the pressure. Steve seemed to know their home country better than they did, at least this end of it. They had a quick meal of the gritty porridge, and then it was all hands on deck to raise anchor, set sail and tuck and tidy. The family treated them as part of the crew and patiently explained how it all worked. By the time the sun broke free of the mountains, they were already cruising under light winds, bow pointed north.

Allie would never forget that day. She had never sailed before, yet proved to be a natural helmsman, keeping a perfect course, or so Steve told her. "'ow you know to do it that way?" he asked as she coiled a rope and secured the coil to a cleat. He looked her straight in the eyes. "That is exactly right!" Allie thrived on the family's affirmation and gained confidence that quickly became exuberant. Unfortunately, Ted couldn't share her enthusiasm. The surfer soon got sick and lost his porridge over the side.

When he had recovered sufficiently, Ted was worried. He couldn't exactly explain to the skipper why they should stay far offshore, and Steve took the more sheltered route through the Gulf Islands. But after an hour of short tacks between islands into an increasing northerly wind, he changed his mind and determined to motor through Active Pass and out into the open Salish Sea, the island's name for the Strait of Georgia. It was the Pass that made Ted nervous—it was narrow and the bluffs were speckled with houses with large windows. He didn't know if the area was monitored. When they reached the pass, the Victoria ferry was entering ahead of them, and they slid in behind it to avoid its wake. Ted found an excuse for Allie to go into the cabin, hoping that would help as they passed close by two ferry slips on the small islands on either side. He didn't breathe until they reached open water again.

Allie didn't share his anxiety and chatted excitedly through the hatchway with the couple in the stern, Steve translating for her and Anneliese. Ted didn't know what to make of the new Allie or the impossible stories she told him. But he couldn't deny something beautifully new about her, something even more attractive than whatever drew him to her in the first place. He could hardly believe the fact that she loved him. The whole thing was so surreal it made his head swim. He couldn't take his eyes off her; yet at the same time, he felt like he was on the outside looking in at something of which he had no part. He hadn't been so distracted from his own cause in many years—his team would laugh at him.

It was a long day; the winds stayed moderate and they made steady progress, but the afternoon passed and they were still a distance from their goal. Allie recognized Nanaimo and Parksville across the water and wondered what was happening with her condo and her stuff, which seemed a world away. The sunset cast ribbons of violent yellow and crimson across the enormous sky, reflecting vividly in the waves below. Steve was reluctant to spend the night at Mitlenatch, as the charts noted that anchorage in the tiny cove wasn't good, plus it would be hard to find in the dark. But they had little choice—the broad expanse of water in front of them left no suitable options to put in at either shore. Steve shrugged, grinned and took up the challenge. Ted got back on the phone.

The wind remained full and steady; the sky cleared entirely. Tomas checked that all their red, green and white lights were working properly. It grew cold, but no one wanted to stay in the cabin; they wrapped up in blankets and watched the dark settle around them. At first, Allie thought something was wrong with her eyes, like she had too much sun or something, but then realized that little lights did glow in the foamy wake behind them. "It's bioluminescence," Ted explained, caused by tiny plankton reacting to the disturbance of the water. As the dark grew deeper, a glowing path formed behind them. Allie trailed her hand in the water and it lit up with blue-white light. She was fascinated until looking down made her queasy. Then she was content to lean back against Ted and revel in the lights in the water and the lights in the sky that looked the same, despite their massive differential.

They sailed on and on. Steve stood confidently at the wheel, consulting the chart on his computer regularly, on which their little ship rode close to a line he had plotted to the east of Mitlenatch. Few other boats passed near them except for an enormous cruise ship that went by like a floating Christmas tree. It had a huge TV screen on the top deck, apparently beside the pool, and for a few moments Allie had the bizarre experience of watching The Office while sailing on a yacht on the open sea. She wondered who on earth paid so much to watch TV on a boat. Finally, Steve pointed out a flashing green light ahead that he said was the island. Even then, it seemed an endless journey; to Allie it was like she had always been sailing, as if this were eternity with ghosts of white sails blotting out a section of brilliant stars.

When they finally came even with the flashing light, the boat was all action: Anneliese pulling sails; Steve barking instructions; Tomas readying the anchor; Ted and Allie mostly getting in the way. They were aware of rocky shores on either side of them only by sound and a faint shimmer—and Steve's enormous spotlight playing on both sides. The bay was utterly calm, but the streamers on the mast above them still flapped and rippled in the white mast light. Steve was less than satisfied with the anchorage and announced a night watch on rotation, two crew at a time for two hours (skipper exempt) until first light, when Ted expected his contact to arrive.

Allie and Anneliese took the first shift, from midnight to 2 AM. They snuggled down in the bow against the stay lines. Allie thought it was unfair of Steve to admonish them not to wake him up with talking, since she and Anneliese couldn't even understand one another. But the two made enough noise anyway that he pounded on the deck. Anneliese showed photos on her iPad— Scandinavian scenery and her family—making Allie laugh with her charades about who was who in the family. She began to sing— soft and contemplative melodies in her own language that made the tears pour down Allie's face. The wind stilled, and the small ship tugged gently at its firm anchor. All the while, brilliant stars wheeled and danced in the utter dark. Two hours was not enough; Allie was reluctant when Ted and Tomas came to the stern to relieve them of their watch.

It felt like her head had barely hit the pillow when she heard a motor and voices up on deck. Daylight diffused through the skylight, and Allie sat up and willed herself awake. Poking her head out of the cabin, she saw Ted and Steve talking with two men in uniform who were maintaining a safe distance in their large rubber boat. She quickly ducked back inside. The conversation continued for ten more minutes, but she couldn't make out any of the words. The motor started up and roared out of the little bay. She went up on deck.

"Conservation officers," Ted explained. "From Vancouver Island. They don't have jurisdiction here, but both they and their Canadian equivalent regularly patrol this little island, making sure that no one except approved naturalists step foot on it." He sipped his coffee, but Allie saw his hand trembling. "We're fine. But they told us not to moor here overnight again. They have no reason to suspect us of anything else. I hope they're out of sight before my team arrives."

The sun rose violently over the water to the southeast. The wind picked up, and Steve started looking frequently and pointedly at his watch. Ted was reluctant to make another phone call. Anneliese brought porridge up on deck and they ate silently, watching, listening. It was Allie who heard the motor first. Steve brought out his binoculars, gazed intently for a moment and said words in Swedish that Allie thought weren't parlor talk. "It is they again, the *myndigheter*. They come back." He put the binoculars back in their case and looked at Ted. "We leave."

Ted and Allie looked at one another. They had no option. Steve didn't want to have to explain to the conservation officers why they hadn't left Mitlenatch yet, but of course, he also didn't understand the desperate nature of Ted and Allie's situation. By the time the rubber boat (Ted called it a "Zodiac") reached the bay, Steve and crew were under sail again, headed north. The officers circled twice, talking with one another but not to them, and sprinted back toward the island. "Eh, is A-OK," Steve assured. "We go Desolation Sound, spend another night, come back tomorrow and meet your friend. You call." He handed Ted the phone. "Meanwhile, we are good friends!" Allie watched as Vancouver Island receded behind them until another island—long and thin with sandy shores like something from the South Pacific—blocked her view. Her heart stretched over the distance until she thought it would break.

Jack regretted the Smarties. A Canadian version of M&M's, Smarties seemed to be the reason Laney couldn't hold still that afternoon. "The blue ones rev kids up," Lizzy explained. They bought her a swimsuit and took her to the hotel pool, where Jack got more exercise than she did, pulling her around on a small yellow inner tube. The weather had been deteriorating all day, and by the time they left the pool, raindrops were streaming down the windows of their room. Fortunately, the TV had a kids' channel, and for a while Laney was content to lie on their bed and soak in cartoon reruns.

"So it's on for sure."

"Well, I think so," Jack sighed. "The guy's name is John, and he seems pretty confident. He said he had to talk with the boss, but he was having trouble reaching him. He thought the answer would be yes, though we may have to delay our crossing."

"Delay why?"

"They try to do as few trips as possible. He thought his boss might have someone else to take, so he wants to wait until he knows."

"And in the meantime?"

"In the meantime, we stay in this hotel. The owner supports their cause and protects the identity of people waiting to leave. We are not to go anywhere."

"And how are we paying for all this? We need every cent we've got! And for how long?"

"Relax, it's all part of the deal. We're not paying anything, except they get our Jeep. We can order room service or eat at the hotel café. I don't think we'll be here a long time." But he said it as if he wasn't sure.

"Jack, let's drive down to Nanaimo and get on the ferry!"

"No, Lizzy, it won't work. They're on to us. Once they realize we're running, they will stop us. If you don't believe they would do that, think back six years."

Lizzy gave him a stricken look, buried her face in her hands and sobbed. Jack tried to hold her, and she pushed him away and sat on the bed. Laney put down the TV remote, crawled over to Lizzy and put her arms as far around her as she could. She didn't ask any questions; she just held her and shared her pain. Laney giggled at something on the TV, and it made Lizzy giggle, and in no time they were laughing until the tears came anyway. Lizzy wondered at her sensitivity; she knew she was holding one special girl.

As she lay with Laney in her arms, her mind wasn't on cartoons. She was thinking about Laney's mom. Had she and Jack done everything they could to find her? She knew that if she were in the mom's situation, she would be frantic. It would be easy to forget about her, to go on as if she were no longer in the picture. But Lizzy knew what it was like to lose a child, and she couldn't let go of the fact that Laney had a mom who might very well be still alive and hurting desperately. She didn't have a clue how to find her, but she knew in her heart that she should try. All the same, she couldn't bring herself to talk with Jack about it that night after Laney went to bed. The overwhelming fear of losing another child kept her conscience at bay.

His phone rang once, stopped and rang again. He answered it, "Zephyr here."

"Hey, it's Fletch."

"Good to hear from you, man. Hey, sorry about earlier this morning. Pickup was blocked by some, um, unexpected red tape."

"Understood. No worries. Change of plans again anyway."

"For sure. What's up?"

"A day's delay on the incoming packages. Can you arrange pickup same place tomorrow but six hours later than previously?"

"You got it. Gonna be a heck of a long day, though. Hey, question for you. We have an inquiry about a delivery, three units, ASAP. Go ahead or wait on combining orders?" After several moments of silence on the other end, he said, "Fletch?"

"Yeah, go ahead. The other order could take a while. Don't wait. Are they cleared?"

"Yep, seems pretty legit. Though I wish you were here; this is more your line of work. Should I wait until you can check it out for yourself?"

"How urgent?"

"Pretty urgent. You know, freaked out customer."

"Yeah, go for it. I trust your judgment."

"Cool. See you soon." He hung up and stuffed the phone in his pocket with a smile on his face. *Trusts my judgment—I like it!* He picked up his grating tool and continued to rough up a spot on a tube of his Zodiac to receive a rubber patch while planning in his head another midnight run.

At noon, John walked over to the hotel and found them in the café, ordering lunch. An older couple was eating on the far side of the room. He walked up to the table and said, "Mind if I join you?"

Both Lizzy and Jack jumped in their seats. "Whoa, John, you scared us! Whew! Yeah, come sit down." He introduced his wife and daughter. The couple was edgy; their little girl looked on curiously.

"Sorry about that. Should have realized." The waitress came back, and John ordered a chickpea burger, yam fries and a ginger beer. "So, about our little boat ride—how would you like to go tonight?"

"Tonight? Really?" Jack and Lizzy looked at one another, and Lizzy put her hand on her husband's arm. "Jack, we should talk about something first…"

Jack uncharacteristically disregarded her. "We'll be ready. Name the time!"

John looked at Lizzy, then back at Jack. "You're sure about this? You need to talk about it together?" Jack shook his head. Lizzy withdrew her arm and said nothing. "You understand the deal, right? You sign your Jeep over to me this afternoon. I take you by Zodiac to my contact—he's on an island up the coast—and he transfers you to an isolated spot on the mainland. My second contact meets you and delivers you to a little coastal village up a long inlet. From that point, you're on your own. Only one road runs out of the place, and no bus. Your best bet will be to buy a cheap car or catch a flight. Do you have enough cash?" Jack nodded, and John shook his head at him. "No, you don't. Because you'll need Canadian cash. How much can you withdraw at an ATM?" Jack told him. "Like I said, a cheap car. Try to find a Honda; they run forever."

Lizzy spoke up. "And what about our cabin? And ID for

Laney?"

She said it a little too loud for John's liking, and he looked around the room. The older couple had left. "I'll give you a way to contact us when you're ready to sell the cabin. You should wait maybe six months. That's a better time of year to sell a place like yours anyway. Can you wait that long?" They nodded. "And the little girl's passport, I can do myself this afternoon. It will be a squeeze, but only because I take great pride in my work. Go get instant passport photos done for her right after lunch—you'll find a photo place down the street toward the water—and drop them off at the front desk before 2:00. Along with name, birth date, place of birth, everything that's on your own passports."

They looked at one another. Neither had thought of that. What name do they use? Is it safe to still call her Laney? Do they fake it all? The questions rolled between them, but they couldn't ask them out loud.

"Look," said John, "I get the impression you two have some homework to do. Give your info to the front desk, and I'll come see you at about 5 PM with the passport. Be ready to go when I arrive. We'll do the transfer of ownership for the Jeep on our way. You bring only one bag each, okay? Like, what you can carry; same for your daughter. See you at 5:00." He picked up the rest of his burger and walked out the door.

Lizzy looked coolly at Jack. "What?" he countered.

"I don't like him. I'm not totally sure he knows what he's doing. Who is his boss, and why can't we deal directly with him?" She glanced at Laney, who was still busy dipping each chicken finger five or more times. "And I've been wondering—have we done everything we can to find…?" She nodded toward Laney and mouthed the word, "Mom."

Laney caught it. She put down her chicken and looked at Lizzy. "When can we go and see my mom?" Though she constantly watched for her mom's return, Laney hadn't asked this question before. Lizzy didn't know how to respond.

Jack stepped in. "Hey Laney, you're a wonderful girl, and you've been very patient. We're looking after you because we don't know where to find your mom. No one seems to know. We have tried to find her and we can't…"

"I know where she is," Laney interjected, picking up her chicken again.

"You do?"

"Yes, she's out looking for me. She will never stop looking for me. I know my mom." She dipped and ate again, and Lizzy looked at her husband with tears in her eyes. Laney munched for a while and stopped again. "But you can keep taking care of me for now if you like. You're doing a good job."

Lizzy opened her mouth in surprise and laughed. "Thank you, Laney. We would be glad to keep looking after you until your mom finds you, or we find her." She glanced at Jack again, who was rubbing his beard in consternation. "We used to have a daughter, a young girl like you, and she got lost. So we know what your mom must be feeling."

"Are you still looking for your little girl?"

Lizzy sat back, barely controlling her emotions. "I guess we are, but it has been a long, long time. We'll keep looking for her, just like your mom."

Laney nodded and focused on her last chicken strip.

When she was done, they took her down the street to get her passport photos, where she made an appropriately serious face. Back at the room, Laney was convinced to take a nap, with the promise of an evening boat ride. When all was quiet, John led Lizzy to the balcony and they watched a tugboat haul a barge down the channel. "No Lizzy. Think about it. We're out of time. If we start looking again, they will find us, and they will take Laney!"

"No, you think about it!" Lizzy's voice was quiet, terse and agitated. "She's right—her mom will never stop looking for her! I will always have this feeling she's out there somewhere, and I have her child. What's more, I can't get Laney's question out of my mind—are we still looking for our little girl?" She stopped and looked him in the face. "Well, have we stopped looking? Have we done everything to find her? Can you leave this island with the possibility that Raylene is still here?"

Jack's overwhelmed emotions neared the breaking point. "Stop! Just stop, will you?" She pulled back, shocked at his tears, his anger.

"I'm sorry." She put her arms around his shoulders. "I'm sorry. Better than anyone, I know how you feel. Oh God, what have we done? What should we do?" They stood that way a long time after the tugboat and its load disappeared around the point.

Jack sighed deeply. "We need to go, Lizzy. I promise you we'll keep searching for Raylene and for Laney's mom. But we have to leave. Remember when we were training to be kayak guides? Safety took priority over every consideration, no matter how beautiful a day it was or what the client wanted. Right now, safety says we get off this island while we still can, and deal with everything else later."

She held him close. "I love you, you know. You always know the right thing to do. You're right—if we stay here, we could lose everything. Laney too. Let's go, Jack. Let's go now while we can."

With all their packing and the vehicle transfer and Laney's restlessness after her nap, 5:00 seemed to come too fast. Someone knocked on their door. Lizzy opened it and faced a total stranger. Surprised, she blurted out, "What do you want?"

"I'm the manager here," he panted. He was an older man, bald and a little stout, and he mopped his forehead with his bandanna. "Listen, I know your whole story and I'm on your side. But a cop downstairs just asked me if you two checked in. I'm glad I had you under different names. They said I'm to let them know if a young couple checks in with a little girl about six years old. They're on to you. I'm betting it was the fellow who took your passport photos—I never liked the guy. Maybe he was told to report on the names of people who get their photos done. Whatever. The cops are here, and they will be watching. We gotta get you out of this place—

now!—down the back stairs. John's waiting."

Jack and Allie stuffed a last few things in their bags, put them on their shoulders and took Laney by the hand. They followed the man down the hall and descended a stairway, moving agonizingly slowly as he seemed to have problems with his knees. At the bottom, he opened a door and saw John with the Jeep, pulled up close. "It has different plates; they won't think it's yours." It was strange to pile into the back seat of their own vehicle. John threw the bags in the back, jumped in and drove down the alley to the street.

Ten minutes later, they were on a dock, throwing everything into the bow of a Zodiac. John covered it all with a tarp. "It's choppy out on the water. I'm afraid you're likely to get a bit wet." He gave them another tarp to ward off the worst of the spray. "Here we go."

It was dusk when they pulled out of the calm water of the marina. Immediately, they were bouncing over waves, sending out sheets of spray on either side of them for every swell. They had Laney tucked in between them, and she shivered with excitement and squealed when they hit the bigger waves. They were running with no lights, and the motor was amazingly quiet. "My own design," John explained, pointing out a housing he had placed over the motor as they set out.

"Where are we going exactly?" Jack yelled through the wind.

"We'll round this point ahead of us and make for the first cluster of islands; then we have a short stretch of open water to another group of islands in the middle of the strait—that will be the bounciest part. We'll transfer you to a bigger boat for the crossing to the mainland. Should take an hour in this thing, since we're pretty fast, 25 to 30 knots if it's not too rough."

The wind was bitterly cold on their faces. Lizzy was glad for all the clothes John had told them to wear, which no longer seemed like overkill. She tried to shield Laney from the wind and spray with the tarp, but Laney pulled it down again so she could see. The

208

dark water contrasted with the white spray. "How come we can see the spray so well?" Lizzy asked John.

"Little bugs in the water—they light up when you disturb them. Look behind you!" Lizzy had to hold Laney as they both turned around. Their wake glowed in the dark with a blue-white light. She remembered walking with Raylene and Jack at night on a beach and stirring up the lights in the water with a stick, but the memory was too painful and she let it go.

An hour of bouncing seemed like forever, though the bouncing was far less when they passed near the islands. John played a bright searchlight along the shoreline. A moment later, it was as if they had tumbled out of a torrent onto a quiet lake. The wind died completely, and a big, bright star near the horizon reflected on the water, a phenomenon Lizzy had never seen before. She asked Jack, who asked John, who said it was Jupiter, not a star. It was reflecting sunlight back to earth, like the moon. To Lizzy, it was just as beautiful. Finally, he switched off his searchlight, slowed and cruised in toward a dim light in a small bay. A dark shape loomed above them, and the Zodiac bumped up against the hull of a commercial fishing boat.

"All good, Zephyr?" a voice called down.

"All good, but I think we took them off just in time. Folks, we call this fellow Trans, and he's the one who will take you to your next port of call. Including into Canadian waters." A ladder lowered to them. Strong hands grasped Lizzy's and helped her up onto the deck as she reached the top.

Trans was a giant of a man in the shielded deck light. He shook Jack's hand—Jack winced a bit—and pecked Lizzy on the cheek. Then he lifted Laney from the Zodiac where John held her up and got down on one knee to ask her name. Laney told him and asked why he was called Trans. She received a short and confusing explanation, and then he said, "You can call me Hans, okay? I never liked nicknames." John—or Zephyr—laughed.

They made a quick transfer of bags from the Zodiac, brief

thanks and farewells. John pushed off and the two boats started up—though they couldn't hear John's next to the roar of Han's engine—and set off into the dark waters. One carried its precious cargo farther east and north and into Canadian waters to meet their final transfer. The other sped west and south, back toward the dock. Then a two-hour drive and another two-hour boat ride to rendezvous at Mitlenatch Island with Ted and Allie at noon. John was entirely unaware of the incongruity he had set in motion.

XX

Desolation Sound was aptly named. Heavy clouds hid the coastal mainland mountains and bucketed rain all day, reflecting Allie's mood. Thankfully, the sky cleared brilliantly an hour before the sun set over the mountains of Vancouver Island. Ted convinced Steve to aim for Teakerne Arm, instead of tacking up the Sound, with the promise of the opportunity to moor beside a waterfall. Plus, a straighter run back to Mitlenatch the next morning. They pulled in as the last light played along tall walls of rock on either side of the boat and a thundering white fall of water at the end of a box canyon. Ted took the dinghy and tied mooring lines to big rings in the rock walls on either side, but Steve insisted on dropping anchor as well. Allie would have been content to stay on board to feed her anxiety, but Ted convinced her to go with him in the dinghy to a small dock and hike up a steep path to a lake right above the falls. She had to admit it was a marvelous place. By the time they got back to the boat, dusk had set in.

As beautiful a night as it was, they ate in the cabin—wind from the waterfall took fine spray and wafted it across the deck, which was okay for a while but got damp quickly. Steve seemed remorseful and apologetic for taking them the extra night away from their home, as he supposed, and tried to make up for it with stories and jokes and even a very good bottle of wine. His goodwill had little effect on Allie, who smiled wanly and tried to be polite but looked often toward the island. She had no idea that, not so far across the water, her daughter was fleeing with strangers out into the wide, unsearchable world.

She dreamed of Laney again that night. It was morning, and Laney crawled up onto her bed and snuggled in under the big white duvet, and they talked about favorite animals and favorite birds and favorite bugs. Laney turned to her and said in a serious, grown-up voice, "Do you still trust me?" And Allie realized it was Sophie's voice, and she said crossly, "No, I don't think I do. You said I would see her soon. I don't call this soon!" And Laney replied, with Sophie's voice, "I call all times soon." Allie went to hug her daughter and suddenly couldn't find her. She searched through all the covers, crawling under them, throwing them all over the room, and Laney wasn't in any of them.

And she heard Ted say, "If you're too warm, toss the covers off yourself, not me!" She felt him roll over in the berth beside her and she was suddenly afraid.

Grabbing his shoulder, she said, "Please, please hold me, just hold me." He rolled over again and held her, and it seemed strange and appropriate that she felt more intimate with this man who had never known her than with the one who had made her pregnant. Fear slipped away, and she slipped away too, into a deep and profound sleep. She woke only once, hearing thunder and remembering it was the falls, and their resonance soon coaxed her back to sleep.

Morning broke clear and windless. The sky glowed at the end of the canyon, but the sun didn't yet reach even the tips of the trees above them. Their clothes felt damp; the deck was dripping. "A fine bath you give my boat, Ted," Steve laughed. "I should get you swabbing decks." Ted set off in the dinghy to untie the lines. Tomas went to the anchor but soon called his father over. They talked briefly in Swedish and Steve's voice took on his non-parlor room tone. Ted pulled up in the dinghy to see what was wrong. "Anchor fouled on something. Not moving. Better tie us again." Ted returned to the walls to do so.

They wrestled with the anchor line for half an hour. The narrow canyon afforded little room to maneuver, and pulling the boat ahead and astern didn't help. "We wait," announced Steve. "When the sun gives enough light, Tomas and I dive. I don't want to pay for new anchor." Anneliese brought out an apple pie she made the afternoon before and they had it for breakfast along with her porridge. Allie wondered why she had never thought of apple pie for breakfast before—it was marvelous.

She talked with Ted about the delay; he shrugged his shoulders. "I don't think we should worry about it. We have to…" He stopped and looked at her with exasperation. "I love you, Allie!"

She hugged his arm. "Yeah, I know."

"So believe me when I say I can't take you back to the island."

She pulled back. "What?"

"The moment you set foot on the island—probably before—They will know exactly where you are. I love you, and I can't let that happen."

"Ted, you promised."

"Yes, because I'm an idiot in love. One of those fools who would do anything for you. But I've come to my senses, and I'm sending you to the mainland when Zephyr picks us up."

"And you'll come with me?"

"No, only until we reach the first transfer point. Then I'll go back and find Laney. I've thought and thought about it, Allie. We lucked out this far—though I'm willing to admit your luck is extraordinary and maybe someone is tweaking it—but the only one who can at all safely go back to the island is me."

"Ted, your photo is all over the papers!"

"I'll shave!" Allie reached up and stroked his beard. "I'll cut my hair short, wear glasses. It can be done."

Allie looked at him for a long time. She said, "It will be okay, Ted. We'll find her. If you think this is the best way, I trust you. But please come after me—both of you. I can't afford to lose anyone else." She kissed him on the cheek and went below to help Anneliese.

It was nine o'clock before Steve decided the light in the canyon was enough to dive safely. "Is not as deep as it looks; only seven fathom or so. We go suit up." He and Tomas went below and came up several minutes later in wetsuits and carrying an oxygen tank each. It looked to Allie like a lot of equipment to keep someone

213

alive underwater—tubes and dials and weights everywhere. When they were ready, each stood on opposite gunnels, and on the count of ett, tva, tre they back-flipped into the water.

It didn't take long. Allie watched with fascination the strings of bubbles they sent up. A sudden torrent of bubbles burst out of their masks and neoprene heads as they surfaced. They were carrying the anchor between them, and Ted quickly hauled in the anchor line. Steve pulled his mask back on and yelled, "We go find lunch!" They came up again five minutes later with five huge abalone. His wife scolded him and Ted laughed. Allie was taken aback that Ted no longer seemed in a hurry to leave. He and Tomas rowed to shore and hammered the abalone into softness with rocks. When they returned to the boat, he told Anneliese it was his turn to cook, and took the shellfish down into the cabin.

"Is a tangle at the bottom!" Steve exclaimed. "Old rusty cable left all over. The Canadians should clean up their act, I think." Tomas untied the lines from the walls and they motored out of the long inlet toward the dark water that indicated wind in the strait. Ted came up with plates and a platter of grilled abalone, which everyone agreed was the best thing they had ever eaten. Or ever will eat, Anneliese demanded in severe Swedish. No more taking protected shellfish!

It was another perfect day for sailing. Once out of the islands, the boat sliced through the whitecaps at full hull speed—the maximum speed the boat could go, Steve explained—which was about seven knots. Allie loved sitting in the lower side of the cockpit with the water flying by behind her, sometimes inches from the gunwale, and looking up at white sails against a cobalt blue sky. The problem was that noon had come and gone, and they were still a long way from Mitlenatch. Ted wondered what Zephyr would do, how long he might wait around. He would call, but Steve's phone got wet while he was changing out of scuba gear, and it was drying out in a bag of rice with the hope that it might still work.

One of the best things that happened on this voyage was the

arrival of a couple of visitors. Allie was dragging one hand in the water and looking forward when a flash of black and white zipped by her. A fin creased the water near the bow and disappeared again. She yelled and jerked her hand away. Was it a shark? A baby killer whale? Steve laughed and said it was a porpoise, and pointed out two of them, one on each side of the bow. In a moment, everyone but Anneliese—who was at the wheel—went forward to watch. Allie could have touched one as it leaped right out of the water and dove down beside the bow. Steve said not to do it—Canadian laws are severe about people touching sea mammals. He read about a lady on a whale-watching boat who got a big fine for touching an orca as it rubbed up against the hull. The porpoises were so fast, so graceful, so beautiful. She longed to have Laney with her to share the experience. The animals stayed with them for several minutes, dove deep and came up again far behind them. The visit was over.

It was three in the afternoon when Mitlenatch finally came into sight, and then—as before—it seemed to take forever to arrive, as fast as they were going. They saw no boats near it, but as they dropped sail and drew close to the cove where they had moored before, a red Zodiac dashed out from between two rocks and swept up to them. Instead of a couple of uniformed conservation officers, this one had a young man with blond hair escaping from under a black toque and skin the color of mahogany. "Hey Fletch! About time!" The man laughed and pulled alongside. "Been dodging uniforms since eleven this morning. Where ya been? Man, I thought you were dead!"

Ted made the introductions. "We call him Zephyr because he's so quiet," Ted explained teasingly. "But his name is John. He knows these waters like nobody's business, after many seasons as a fishing guide." He jumped down into the Zodiac. "How much gas you got?"

"Enough to get you back home, but if we don't move soon we'll be against the tide, and then I don't know—could be tight."

"Well, we're not going home. We need to get Allie to Hans. By water. And you and I will return to the island to find her missing daughter. Do you have your phone?"

John looked at him like he was a fish with two heads. "All the way to Hans? You gotta be kidding! I just came from Hans! And it will take forever by boat! I haven't slept more than two hours…!"

"I'll take the wheel. What do you mean, you just came from Hans? What were you doing up-island?"

"The three units I told you about. Hey, we got a nice Jeep from them. I delivered them last night, drove back down to Oyster Point and boated straight here. Well, almost. I stopped at home for a couple of hours to get some shut-eye."

"Well, we can't help it. She must go to Hans in the Zodiac—she can't set foot on the island—and you and I will return. We have a lot to do."

Steve was anxious to be off. Ted and Allie gave hugs all around, along with many thanks for everything that Steve and Anneliese and Tomas had done for them. "You come to Sweden," invited Steve. "I show you some real sailing then. None of this fishpond and little paper boats."

Anneliese held Allie in her embrace for a long time. "You… sister!" she managed. She made a gift of her wool sweater that Allie had been wearing, and Allie wished she had something to give in return.

"We will never forget you," she told Anneliese, looking to Steve to translate. Allie and Ted boarded the Zodiac as it bobbed about in the waves so that she had to quickly sit down. Anneliese and Tomas raised the sails, and Steve at the wheel was already hard to see before Allie could grasp that they were gone. She sighed. She had no more stomach for people going away. These she would have liked to keep forever.

Ted and John wasted no time; they were soon cruising north at great speed in the red Zodiac. It was a far less comfortable ride than the sailboat—they had to cut diagonally across the waves and the bow climbed and fell with each one, sending up big plumes of spray on either side. Allie soon felt exhausted from the motion and was grateful when they came into the relatively calm water between the islands. "How far?" she yelled to Ted.

"Long way, Allie! We need to find more fuel. It will be a good three or four hours before we drop you off with Hans. You'll like him—a huge teddy bear. He will take you in his big fishing boat to another contact on the mainland way up the coast, a Canadian by the name of Gerry, who will take you the rest of the way to a small town called Bella Coola. He and his wife will help you find a place to stay until we can join you. And then…?"

"Yes, and then what? You can't get rid of me now, you know." Allie moved onto the seat where Ted was at the wheel and snuggled in close, drawing her blanket around both of them. John complained she was messing up the trim of the boat, so Ted sent him up to the bow. He went, grumbling loudly to himself.

"Rid of you? I feel like I've been waiting for you all my life." He looked at her wrapped up in the wool blanket and wondered again at his good fortune. "I don't know what will happen next, or how long my life will be. But whatever I've got left is yours—and Laney's."

"Is this your idea of a proposal?"

"Call it what you like, but you won't get rid of me, either."

Moments later, the boat lurched from side to side, and it felt like they were moving at terrific speed. "Yuculta Rapids," Ted yelled over the roar. "Like a river in the sea, caused by the tide pouring out through the islands toward the open ocean. We'll be out of it in a moment, and then it will be easy going for a while." They navigated three more rough sections, difficult in the twilight. John pointed the searchlight at a vast hole in the water, an enormous whirlpool swirling around utter darkness. Allie would rather have not known about it. They all became quiet. Ted was concentrating on threading his way through the islands.

Hours went by. Allie woke when they stopped at a fishing lodge for fuel but was asleep again before they set out. It seemed like minutes later when she woke again to see the boat slow and arch into a small bay where a rough beach still showed white against the trees. A dark shape in the middle of the bay resolved itself into a sizable boat, with a large cabin in the front and tall poles on either side—a typical west coast fishing troller. Ted brought their craft alongside so smoothly it barely touched, and a huge mountain of a man leaned over the rail and took their rope. They all scrambled up the ladder and were welcomed aboard. Hans gave Allie a hug that took her feet off the deck and nearly did the same with Ted. John, he slapped resoundingly on the shoulder.

"You're keeping us busy, Ted. But I'm happy to see you alive and well. I thought maybe you met your match this time."

"I did, but this amazing lady saved me!"

Allie shook her head. "Don't believe him. I can't explain how we escaped—it was like a dream or something, I don't know—but since then, it's been all Ted."

"Anyway, no time to waste, eh? Kiss her, Ted, and let's get her out of here."

He did. She didn't want to let him go. "I won't ask again to go with you. I know you're right—I would put us both in danger. But please, no heroics this time. Be safe." She turned to John. "You will make sure he doesn't do anything stupid for me, right?" He laughed, but she looked at the two of them with all seriousness. "Both of you—go with all the help we seem to have been given, all the help in heaven and earth. Come after me soon. Bring Laney."

As she looked at him in the fading light, all the color drained suddenly from John's face. "You said what?" he stammered. "Bring who?"

Allie's throat constricted suddenly. "Um, Laney. My little daughter, who was taken. That's why…"

John gave a shout of rage, walked several steps down the deck and kicked a fishing float overboard. "No! No, it can't be. Of all the…"

Ted went to him and grabbed him by the collar. "What, John? What's happened?" John looked at him fearfully and shook his head. Ted seated him bodily on a deck box, squatted down in front of him and seized his shoulders. "Tell me," he said tersely. "Tell me—now!"

John's voice shook. "The three units, the ones I told you about. A man and a woman and they had a little girl with them—and her name was Laney."

Ted grabbed him by the collar again. With great effort and restraint, he slowly released him. The young man was shaking, and Hans came behind him and put his arms gently and firmly around him. "It's okay, John. Tell them everything"

John's story, including the fact that the couple had no passport for the little girl and he had made one for them, eliminated the possibility of mistake. Hans confirmed the girl's description, which easily matched Allie's daughter. Allie stepped in, finding it hard to control her voice. "The woman—describe her to me!"

"Striking, tall. Maybe thirty years old or so. Long blond hair." Allie's face fell, and John began to cry.

"When, John? When would they have arrived in Bella Coola? What were their plans?" Ted's voice was urgent.

John caught his breath. "Early this morning. I told them to buy a car as soon as they could, and…"

"And…?"

"Disappear."

Hans got up and readied his boat. Everyone rushed for the cabin except John, who started lowering a hook to his boat. Ted stopped him. "What are you doing?"

John pled with him. "I gotta come; you can't send me back now!"

Ted looked at his anguished face and relented. "Hans, do you have room to bring John's Zodiac on deck?" Hans nodded, and they soon had it hoisted aboard, leaving little room to navigate the deck. The sound of anchor chain coming in, the growl of a powerful engine, and they were underway.

Allie felt like she was living a nightmare. As they roared over the dark water, she realized that Laney had been in this very boat not twenty-four hours before. Her daughter was with a couple of people who were fleeing and who didn't want to be found. Within the next twenty-four hours, the three of them could be anywhere in the world. The chances of finding Laney now were next to nil. She broke down and sobbed. Ted moved from where he had been standing helplessly, sat beside her and held her. Allie clung to his arms.

His emotions were in as much turmoil as the open water they were passing roughly over at that moment. So much had suddenly changed for him that he didn't know what to do with it all. He had no longer any reason to return to Vancouver Island—ever. He and Allie were moving as fast and safely as possible to refuge on the mainland, and if they were to find Laney, that's where she would be. His heart ached to find her still in Bella Coola. What would he do if they were already gone? His mind raced with all he was leaving behind—the surf shop, his team, the home he best knew and loved—and thrilled with all he had ahead of him: freedom, peace of mind, and a woman whom he loved more and more every minute. He felt flickers of guilt and insecurity related to all the above. He was in as much need of this embrace as she was.

It was a long ride. Hans sat like a small mountain in front of them; his hands on the wheel knew these waters by touch, and his eyes were a secondary device. Allie noticed all at once that she could see mountains far ahead by some ghostly light. Not bugs in the water this time; she glanced behind her and a large yellow moon was rising over the island they had just left. She turned herself around on her seat so she could watch it, and it shrank as it climbed into the sky. At one point Hans swerved to port, and suddenly a large shape rose out of the water ten meters from them, a fin massive and jet-black, and a big spout of fine spray that shone silver in the moonlight. A transient orca, Hans shouted, hungry for seal. Allie saw it once more behind them, its white collar marking it out against the dark. She was glad she wasn't a seal.

Despite John's loud and continuous one-sided conversation

with Ted, Allie must have drifted off to sleep. She woke when the motor went from a loud roar to a putter, and she looked around. The moon was the only visible light. Ted and Hans were talking quietly, and Hans was pointing at something she couldn't see. The water had a swell to it now; she could feel it and could see the mountains rising and falling, though it was really the boat. Hans shut off the motor. A minute later, Allie could hear another boat approaching, and it came up behind them in a blaze of light, moving fast. She couldn't imagine it wouldn't see them, but it went by 300 meters away and didn't slow down or change course. Hans waited until the boat was well ahead of them before starting the motor again. He followed it, lights off.

Ted came and sat beside her. "Canadian Coast Guard," he clarified. "That would have been awkward, trying to explain a fishing boat running with no lights and no lines in the water, and no one has any ID with them. I'm glad they weren't curious."

"What can we do about ID?"

"Well, we've got some time. No one in Canada will ask us for ID until we get pulled over for speeding or we want to cross a border. Let's find Laney—the rest we'll worry about later."

The Coast Guard lights were now far ahead and soon disappeared. They entered a wide channel, its steep sides illuminated by the moon on one side and utterly dark on the other. Allie was getting sleepy again when she heard the sound of rushing water behind her. Something suddenly picked up the back end of the boat and hurled it forward, like Laney in the surf with her boogie board. Hans yelled and wrestled with the wheel to keep them straight, and in a moment it was over, though they seemed to be moving faster than before.

"What was THAT?" John exclaimed. "That was no rip tide!"

"No idea," yelled Ted. "Never experienced anything like it."

Hans was still grimly holding the wheel, finding the current a stranger to his experienced hands. "You know what I think—I think it was a tsunami!"

221

"What? Here?" everyone exclaimed. John laughed, "Kinda small for a tsunami, don't you think?"

"They're not always big. This one was maybe half a meter or so. It will get larger as it travels up the inlet. And it came from the south of us, of all places." Hans' voice was tense. "Somewhere down that way, we've had an earthquake."

"Are we okay out here in a tsunami?" John wasn't laughing anymore.

Hans shrugged. "Can't say I've ever ridden one before. But I'm glad we don't have far to go. The current feels strange. And I don't like how fast we're moving. I would say lifejackets are in order." Ted found them in a locker and handed them around. They had only three, and Hans waved off the one offered him. Allie found hers to be the most awkward thing she had ever worn, and wondered what she would do anyway if she suddenly found herself in the water—at night, in a tsunami.

Twenty minutes later, Hans slowed the motor and cut across the current into a bay that glowed pale in the moonlight. He shook his head as he misjudged the flow of the water, pulled back the accelerator and nosed the boat into the current, angling parallel to the shore. A moment later, a Zodiac sped across the bay and pulled alongside, idling to keep up against the surge of water.

"Man, am I glad to see you! What the hell's happening? Some weird tide's been running by here for ten minutes!" As Allie pulled off her lifejacket, Ted introduced her to Gerry, an older man, judging by the light of his headlamp. He apologized for blinding her with it. They explained to him their theory of an earthquake and tsunami. "Makes sense, I guess. I didn't feel any quake, but I might have been on the water myself when it hit. I was standing on the beach waiting for you when I was suddenly up to my waist in water. Damn glad I tied the boat while I was waiting. The rope saved me." He looked at the water. "I think it's slowing." They all looked, and all gave agreement except Allie, who had no means to evaluate. She wondered if they did either.

By the time they loaded Allie into the Zodiac, the channel did seem calm again. Hans gave her a bear hug before helping her down the ladder. "I'm not coming with you. I'm... um, not welcome in Bella Coola." He kissed her on the forehead. "I'll be thinking strong and hopeful thoughts toward you, Allie. Angels help you." The rest of them piled into Gerry's boat as they pushed off.

It was more of the same—relatively calm water with steep forested slopes on either side rising straight up from the channel. The men talked endlessly about earthquakes and tsunamis. Allie lasted ten minutes and fell dead asleep in her blanket in the stern. When she emerged hours later, the sky was a dull red and the wind was bitterly cold on her face. They wrapped a tarp around her, and the three of them wrapped up in another. Only Gerry was minding where they were going, and even he took frequent breaks behind the tarp. The fjord was red with ripples. On either side, rose-colored snowy peaks commanded their view. She ducked into her shelter again, snuggled down and tried to go back to sleep. But every time she closed her eyes, she found Laney watching her.

XXI

Far beneath Wrangellia, a relatively small deposit of limestone lies between two masses of basalt and granite that make up Juan de Fuca and North American continental plates. Billions of skeletal fragments from marine organisms formed this limestone, and unbelievable pressure has compressed it into marble. This pressure increases every year as the plates shift. It's like one of those hard zits a person gets on their face, the ones they say come from too much stress in our lives. They're too deep to pop, yet the pressure they create is painful to the touch. Sometimes they explode, leaving a bloody mess on the mirror.

At 4:12 AM, the limestone hit the mirror. The two plates, released and lubricated, ground against one another along the fault line, sending powerful shock waves out and up to the surface. Vancouver Island moved 8.3 meters northeast toward the mainland and 1.8 meters down, a journey no colonist would ever forget.

Nor any mainlander. Imagine a grocery store lifted and shaken back and forth a meter or so from side to side. Not one item remained on the shelves. If the quake had happened during business hours, avalanches of baked beans and cereal boxes would have buried every shopping mom. Do the same thing to the soil deposited century after century by the muddy Fraser River, now lying at sea level or below, once agricultural but taken over by office buildings and condos. Within minutes of the quake, water-saturated soil surrounding the Vancouver International Airport liquifacted and oozed up through the cracked basements of houses. Multi-story apartments sank at crazy angles. Water and sewage poured out of the ground; flooded roads hampered emergency vehicles.

Just offshore, where the delta formed by the Fraser River

extends kilometers out under the Strait and drops off into deep water along a steep incline, an enormous section of the delta gave way and slipped into the deep, surging up a wall of water three meters high that raced across the Salish Sea at five hundred kilometers per hour. Homes and towns along the east coast of the islands had no warning when the tsunami forced itself relentlessly over their beaches and headlands to a height of four meters above the high tide line. Then it pulled back into the Strait, grasping and clutching every object and building it wrapped in its powerful arms.

Cities don't realize how much they take communication for granted. Not a cell phone or landline was operational in all of Greater Vancouver. Not that it mattered—incoming calls from frantic relatives had already overwhelmed the lines. No one could access the Internet. Police raided their storerooms for ancient radios, but couldn't charge them up because of power outages. Every major telecommunications provider was offline, and a few small ones that were still working hardly knew what to do with their unexpected audience. Vancouver fell virtually silent, while the real screams and cries of its people went long unnoticed by the dazed and panicking crowds that fled dark streets oozing mud, air choked with a fog of dust and the potent smell of natural gas.

The city of Victoria looked bombed. Fires raged out of control; emergency vehicles couldn't navigate the streets, and people employed buckets in a vain effort to keep fires from spreading. Ornate masonry from nineteenth-century buildings rested on the street, burying cars and making roads impassable. Though the soil didn't liquify, the bedrock underlying the city was not kind to the structures constructed upon it, and many buildings gave way to the stress of the motion. Wood frame buildings fared better, except those not bolted to their foundations; some now lay on their sides. Crowds sat on rubble in the early light and stared, sick to their stomachs and unwilling to get to their feet.

Yet many heroic deeds were in progress at the hands of energetic people. Disregarding their own safety, the colonists of

Victoria climbed and burrowed into rubble where they heard people in distress. Emergency personnel became foremen rather than workers, directing many teams of civilians in rescue operations. Four-wheel drive trucks were the only vehicles able to transport the injured and traumatized to wherever they could find help. Only one of the city's hospitals was still capable of receiving the wounded. Doctors and nurses came from everywhere by foot and on bike, and worked tirelessly. The same scenario presented itself all up the island, scaled back further north where the shaking had been more moderate. Many were dead and dying, but many more survivors displayed astonishing resilience and compassion. Vancouver Island was reeling, but rallying; its colonists were quickly relearning the tenacity of their forebears.

This Invasion landed before dawn, in a form so subversive that most people thought it was a natural phenomenon. But he knew it was not. Sir James Douglas had anticipated an assault of some kind; only its deployment was unexpected.

It was so violent an earthquake that it threw him to the ground—he was not sure at the time if he would live. Jim had weathered the occasional tremor in his lifetime. He had even enjoyed the sensation. But this movement was so expansive and aggressive that several of his trees toppled and crushed the desk where he had been sitting. He lay prostrate on the grass, his fingers clawing at the turf even after the ground ceased to shudder beneath him. Jim remained for a long time, unable to move, sick to his stomach and sick in heart. About the time the alarm sounded, he noticed his clothes were wet under him. With every remaining ounce of energy, he rolled to his side and got to his hands and knees, heart pounding painfully from exertion and terror. His chair was on its side within his reach; he righted it and pulled himself up, and had barely the strength to wave his hand toward the monitor in front of him to turn it on.

Every image he could conjure on the screen was of devastation. Many cameras were not responding, and his wall monitor flickered like an old movie screen. Yet he could see enough to know his people were suffering intensely. The air in downtown Victoria was hazy with dust; colonists walked dazedly in the early morning light past piles of brick and timber lying in the streets. Port Alberni was emptying as rapidly as possible, remembering the tsunami that destroyed the town in the 60s, though the seismic lab above him had not yet issued a warning. He received no response from the lab and he soon gave up trying to reach them. As he surveyed the damage, tears formed in eyes that had not produced them in many decades, flooding into obscurity the war zone depicted before him.

The gold statue of himself that once graced the top of the Parliament Building was lying on the ground in a pile of rubble. When he saw the small crowd clustered around it, his tears hardened into bitter resentment. It was as if his people had thrown him down and were gloating over him. The thought was ludicrous and entirely unfair, but he could not help it. They had no idea that the Original still remained, seven stories beneath their feet. He was a forgotten entity, an excuse for a holiday and party once a year. He was no more than a golden statue on a pile of bricks.

He wanted to do something, make some response, remind his people that their Directorate was standing with them, that he would lead them out of this calamity—that he was still in charge, dammit! Where was his technician? Why had he not checked up on him? No response on any radio channel. All the cameras on his level were nonfunctional. He could see no reason why…

A sound interrupted his complaint, one that he had not heard—except as a recording—in a very long time. It was the gurgle of running water. High above, near a reef offshore, granite had pulled mere centimeters away from limestone. The crack ran deep and direct, and seawater rushed in like a besieging army digging its way beneath the walls of the city, widening the gap on its course. A spring of it gushed from under the rhododendrons in one corner; it dashed among the hostas and other lilies, seeking and ravaging at will. Water ran along the fieldstones near the verge and showed here and there as grassy pools, widening quickly.

He observed it and considered his Enemy, now clearly identified, and realized that this One had been his enemy all his life. It was so ironic. Here were the two of them, each seeking the same goals, yet plotting one another's demise. The thought, "Why can't we get along?" was immediately superseded by, "I will never concede to His ways, His program, His design." Yet he acknowledged his defeat, accomplished by means irrepressible. The strategy was so simple and infallible in its deployment, Odysseus would be envious—he and his big horse.

He could do nothing about it. The system automatically deployed water pumps, but they were hopelessly unable to keep up. The water rose on the lawn by centimeters, irreversibly constant. He composed in his mind things he wanted to say, needed to say. Lacking listeners, he turned on the microphone in the audience room that Allie recently vacated, not caring if it still worked or that no one was listening. His synthetically moderated voice filled the room with the rich tones of a grandfather.

"I am Sir Frederick James Douglas, born in the Year of our…" He paused. "…born August 15, 1803. I am full of years and wisdom, and have done my very best to be a good steward of my many gifts and talents. Let no man call me a coward or narcissist or carnal man. All I have done, I have done for the good of my people, who look to me for guidance and depend upon me to keep the peace, though none knows me. My efforts have been tireless, and all for naught. In much wisdom is much grief: and he that increaseth knowledge increaseth sorrow.

"There is a man whose labor is in wisdom, and in knowledge, and in equity; yet to a man that hath not labored therein shall he leave it for his portion. This also is vanity and a great evil. For what hath man of all his labor, and of the vexation of his heart, wherein he hath labored under the sun? For all his days are sorrows, and his travail grief; yea, his heart taketh not rest in the night. And who will that man be, who takes my place? They are all fools, all corrupt or corruptible. I leave you nothing, sir—fend for yourself! See if you can build what I have built, produce what I have planted—all torn down now, all ravished. None of my doing."

The seawater reached his ankles and poured into his leather shoes, and dread likewise crept up his body. He pushed down the fear but could do nothing about the bitter cold that numbed his feet in moments. "You! What do You want from me? Why persecutest Thou me? Do you not know I am striving for the very thing You desire? That I am doing Your work?" He groaned in anguish. Such an end was so unfair to one who had survived for so long. "Fine. You win. Take this wretched world! Take my wretched life! I hate…!" The amplified sound in the audience room died for the last time, but his tirade continued long, long, as the water continued to rise.

The Suit, standing on the dais in the audience room, listened to the very end. He laughed, looked at the end of the only cigar he had ever dared smoke there, and laughed again. Water was pouring across the intricately tiled floor, and he stepped down and sloshed his Gucci shoes ankle-deep to the door he had left open. His thoughts rested on many tons of gold stored beneath his feet—underwater now, true—but that wouldn't be an unfathomable problem. He would need only a fraction of this depository to go anywhere he wanted, have anything he wanted, be anyone he wanted. This day had been in his dreams for many years, and now he couldn't believe how easy it had turned out.

The hallway was filling rapidly, and he walked past the now-useless elevator toward the only stairwell leading from this level, for which he had the only key. In his pre-occupation, he realized he had somehow walked past the door. He turned, swearing under his breath. A few moments later, he found himself back at the elevator. The Suit stared at it, and carefully retraced his steps down the hall as the water passed his knees. He walked right to the end and could find no door at all.

Still, he didn't panic, even while forging his way through the water back to the elevator, and his legs felt like lead and his breathing was hard when he arrived. He pushed the button, knowing nothing would happen, then pried his thick fingers between the elevator doors and pulled with all his might. His well-toned arms strained with the effort, but he might as well have tried to separate two sections of a sidewalk. The water was now to his waist, and he surged down the hallway and back twice, swearing loudly and slamming fists occasionally on the solid rock walls. The way out, the one he had used a thousand times, wasn't there. A chill reverberated down his neck to the waterline, not only from the cold water. He thought of other recent events that had brought the same response, and he wished now he had paid more attention to the inexplicable.

Death was a familiar companion. He lived under its threat daily, wielded it often. He found it an interesting study to watch the faces of his victims, their varying levels of terror when they realized their mortality was near. It was always so much better than what the boss ordered, but the boss never watched and so the boss never knew that peaceful euthanasia was rarely the scenario. Sometimes he wondered what he would feel when it was his turn, and where he would find himself on the scale of composure to terror. As he thrashed and gasped at the last frothy centimeters of air at the ceiling, he realized he had gravely underestimated the terror.

Dr. Richards hadn't waited for disaster to strike before arranging his escape and securing a comfortable future. A well-padded Singapore account was the result of years of trickled funds that weren't his own, and a sleek yacht awaited him, dry-docked at a marina a half-hour's drive away. A black SUV pulled up in front of his downtown condo right on time; his only consternation was that the chauffeur was a woman. He did not like most women and frowned uncertainly when she reached for his baggage. He sat in the back seat and engaged in no conversation.

She seemed an excellent driver and was skilled at avoiding most of the mayhem on the damaged roads. They passed much destruction, and some mutilation; at times, he closed his eyes. Many people waved and yelled as they went by, seeking assistance and transport. "Should we stop, sir?" the driver inquired once, and didn't ask again after his snarled reply. In places, the road seemed impassible, and the bumps tossed him about in the back seat despite the driver's competence in four-wheel drive. He hated seatbelts but decided it was time to buckle up. It didn't help. After a short time, the roads improved, but when he looked around, he didn't recognize the area through which they were driving.

"I told you to drive to the marina in Sidney. Where is this?" he asked curtly.

"The highway is closed, sir." She turned and looked at him with intense amber eyes. "I'm taking the best alternate route I could locate on the GPS. I'm sorry for the inconvenience."

He looked away with no reply and gave his attention to papers in his briefcase that assured him that he was a very rich and important man. Dr. Richards knew from the start that no Nirvana could last forever, so he had enjoyed creating his own version to succeed this one—someplace far away. Everything was in readiness. His adaptations included pleasures he was constantly denied here, and he couldn't wait to get to the new arena and begin his work.

The SUV's engine was making a strange sound. He looked up and his jaw dropped in horror. They were descending into a deep valley at reckless speed. At the bottom, a great crevasse yawned blackly across the road. He screamed for the driver to stop, then realized she was no longer at the wheel and he was alone in the vehicle. The doctor lunged forward, but the seatbelt prevented him—the release buckle was jammed. He strained to reach the steering wheel, but it was inches from his grasp. As the SUV plunged over the edge, his last thought was that his life had been quite a disappointment, on the whole. In contrast, the earth swallowed him up with great satisfaction.

XXII

Allie struggled with the tarp that the wind glued to her body, and saw they were still passing up the long fjord. Mountain ridges rose for thousands of feet around them. She lay back and watched the never-ending, never-changing panorama of trees and rock. Allie heard the men exclaim and sat up to see why. Logs, branches, debris and every sort of flotsam were flowing toward them, and Gerry had a time of it avoiding collisions or fouling the prop. They assumed it was wreckage grabbed from the shore by the tsunami. Another hour passed. As they cleared yet another headland, she saw a small breakwater and marina near the end of the channel. She left her tarp and joined the guys in theirs. "Is this it?"

"This is Bella Coola," Ted confirmed. "People live here. My hat goes off to them. In the winter, some of the time you can only get here by boat, like us." They bypassed the big wharf with its cluster of fishing boats and landed at a small dock with a gas pump. Gerry started filling up his big red tanks and promised to join the search as soon as he could. His wife Nancy pulled up in a crew cab truck and took them the few kilometers along the river to the center of Bella Coola.

As Ted, John and Allie walked up the main street, Ted wondered where to start. "We need to split up and report back every hour—at that café. I'll check every hotel, motel and bed & breakfast. John, you ask anywhere someone might sell a car—gas station, around the wharf, wherever. Allie, walk everywhere. Don't hesitate to ask anyone if they have seen a young couple and little girl around here. Don't give a full description until you find someone who thinks they have. We sweep wide and narrow down as we have the opportunity. See you at 8 AM."

Allie noticed right away that people seemed pre-occupied. The first two people she tried wouldn't even talk with her, and waved

235

her off. The third was a middle-aged woman coming out of the café with three paper cups in a cardboard tray. "Little girl? Good grief, I don't know. All I can think about is the earthquake! You didn't sleep through it, did you?"

"I guess I must have." Allie thought that was probably true. "Tell me what has happened."

The woman set the tray down on an outside table so she could use her hands. "It was, like, 4 in the morning, and I'm thinking, what's my boyfriend doing, pushing me out of bed? And there I am, lying on the floor, and I can't even stand to my feet for a minute. And Matt—that's my boyfriend—he says, 'It's an earthquake, that's what!' and I go out to the kitchen and that's all my mug collection lying all over the floor, half of them with the handles busted, and if you didn't notice something like that, I don't know how you got up this morning, and that's a fact!"

At this amazing speech, she picked up her tray and set off down the street before Allie could thank her. Other attempts at interviewing people on the street went more or less the same way. No one remembered seeing any young couple with a child, except ones they already knew, and they looked at her like she had three eyes. Everyone chattered together in little clusters all along the street. She returned to the café, where waitresses were still sweeping up broken dishware, and found Ted and John sitting at a booth. Neither had much to report except earthquake news.

"Big quake," John informed them. "They're saying it might even have been 'The Big One' everybody has been expecting all these years. It registered 8.9 on the scale, plus some strong aftershocks, though no one has felt them here. Its epicenter was offshore from Victoria, across from Port Renfrew. News is pretty sketchy, but it hit hard in parts of Vancouver. They say Victoria's a disaster." Allie couldn't believe what she was hearing. She could have been there when it happened. She and Laney.

"And the only road out of here is closed," sighed Ted. "Big landslide; nobody knows how long it will take to rebuild that stretch of highway. The problem is, we don't know if that helps us or hinders. Are they still here, or did they get away before the earthquake hit?" They decided to focus on asking people about vehicles—sold, rented, stolen, inquiries. "Ask everyone. It's a small town. Someone will know. And I'll check the dock and seaplane base." They disbanded again.

Allie started down a residential street and knocked on doors. Most people were home, glued to their television sets; some invited her in to watch. The destruction was incredible: a collapsed overpass in Langford; old buildings on Vancouver's impoverished East Hastings Street with entire brick walls lying on the street; estimated death tolls that rose higher with each house she visited. It was hard enough to get anyone's attention to ask her questions, and the answers were short and always depressing. No one had sold a car, lent a car, or knew anyone who had done so in the past few days. She returned to the café at the appointed time with a heart so heavy it was hard to breathe, let alone talk.

But John had news. "They were here yesterday! I talked with a guy who sold them a car, a beat-up old Honda Accord with no back window. That was yesterday morning, which gave them plenty of time to get out of here before the quake hit last night." Ted asked him many questions, and in the end had no doubt about what John had heard. John touched Allie awkwardly on the shoulder. "I'm sorry, Allie. I think they're gone."

"But we don't know! We have to keep looking here! Maybe we'll find their car. We should…" She stopped, because both Ted and John were looking at her with such sad and helpless faces. She glared at them. "You both think we won't find them! You've lost all hope!" She stood up to leave.

Ted grabbed her arm. "Allie, wait! Let's think about what's best. If it was me, I would have got out of here as soon as I could, which means they're long gone. Do we keep looking here, or do we try to get to where we might intercept them? Gerry can take us south…"

Allie deliberately removed her arm from Ted's grasp. "Do what you want. I'm looking for my daughter—here!" She walked out the door and strode down the street, with no plan except desperation.

"Please, sir, I've lost my daughter, and I think a young couple may have taken her…" Her frantic pleas produced sympathetic looks, but little help. Had she talked with the RCMP? Once she realized they meant the Canadian police, she accepted their directions to the local office, but knew she couldn't go. She moved from desperation to anger and wasted time walking off steam, furious at sympathy, at men, at the whole world. The energy it required soon slowed her down, and she walked back toward the café, wondering how to smooth things over with Ted and John.

It surprised her that she wanted to do this, with so much at stake. She realized Ted was right—the couple and Laney had no reason to still be in town. As much as she admitted the fact, she couldn't accept the alternative, that Laney was gone beyond her grasp. How could they even begin looking for her? The couple wouldn't go to Vancouver, reeling in its calamity. They would go east, and Canada was an enormous country. But Allie would not, could not, let go of hope.

She walked into the café; the men were gone. She sat down in a booth, looking around the room. The place was empty, with not even a waitress, and she gazed at the swinging kitchen door, wondering if the workers were in the back cleaning up or watching the news. Not that she wanted anything more than a place to sit, somewhere to be connected to the earth in case it decided to move again, like her world had been shaking for so long she couldn't remember what it was like to get up, have breakfast, go to work, make dinner, watch TV and go to bed. That kind of life seemed like someone else's life, not hers. She realized the clothes she was wearing hadn't left her body in a long time, and wondered if she smelled to other people. Allie couldn't smell anything, but something was surely wrong with wearing clothes for so long. She couldn't remember what, but the thought pushed her to the edge of panic, as if it was the largest of her many worries. Allie realized she was holding on to the edge of the table with both hands, and willed herself to slow down, calm herself, just breathe.

Breathing, she felt a hand on her shoulder, and the least expected person in the world sat down across from her.

Sophie. Allie sucked in a deep breath and looked at her with wide eyes. "How...? Why are you...?"

"Hey, Allie." Sophie's face was a pool of quiet water, reflecting... something. Serenity. Understanding. Confidence. Absorbing all the cares of the world around her. Exuding peace.

Allie put her head down on the table, and her shoulders shook with sobs. Sophie reached across and grasped both of Allie's hands in hers, and kissed Allie on the top of the head. She didn't say anything, but held Allie like an anchor enabling her to ride out this tempest. The tears passed, the seas calmed, and Allie turned her face up to find Sophie's close, watching her. "I love you, Allie."

She sat up, wiped her eyes fiercely and shook her head.

"You don't believe me?"

Allie sniffed. "I want to believe you. I want to trust you. Just look at you; who could want anything else? You're so perfect. And me—I'm... I'm so disappointed, Sophie."

Sophie sat back, releasing her hands. "Tell me about your disappointment."

Allie felt she had a right to spill a tale of woe with everything she had been through. She talked a long time. "And now—after surviving everything thrown at me and coming so close to finding Laney—she's gone forever! We'll never find her now; they don't want to be found, and by the time she grows up she will have forgotten all about me. I will never see her again! I don't blame you—even though... I mean, you did tell me I would see her soon." Her shoulders slumped. "I'm so tired, Sophie, and it's not fair, and Ted thinks I'm mad at him even though he's doing all he can, and I don't know what to do or where to go..."

She looked up at Sophie, who was drinking it in with an expression that was hard to read—all at once joy and compassion and sorrow and radiance. "Sophie, who are you?"

She laughed, and Allie couldn't help joining her. "Sorry, your question made me think of a favorite line in a movie," Sophie explained. "You know, *The Princess Bride*, and Wesley and Inigo are having this epic sword fight, and in the middle they stop and it goes like this." She played both parts with the accents, just like Allie remembered it.

INIGO: Who are you?

WESLEY: No one of consequence.

INIGO: I must know...

WESLEY: Get used to disappointment.

"And Inigo shrugs and they start fighting again—great stuff, so funny." Her laugh made Allie ache with yearning to feel like that, to be so satiated with joy that it spilled over and drenched everyone within range.

"So you won't tell me who you are."

"Hmmm..." Sophie sighed. "Instead, I want you to think about this: Who has disappointed you? Is it really me? Don't shoot the messenger, Allie!" She laughed and held her finger like a gun to her own head. Then she became serious. "I want you to think long and hard about my question—don't attempt an answer now—and when you figure it out, you will know who I am." Allie nodded, pondering, wondering.

"Allie, get used to disappointment. You will experience it all your life, and sometimes it will try to convince you that you're unfortunate, unworthy, uncared for, unloved. It's not true. Good has been withheld from you, yes, but it's nothing in comparison to the good already given you, and not even a fraction of what's in store for you. Disappointment is saving up for you things beyond your imagination."

She grasped Allie's hands again as if to gather all her attention. "I don't mind disappointing people. I do it all the time. I disappoint them because I love them too much to do what they expect or give them what they desire. Allie, look at your life. How often have you known what was best for you, like really known? All people are like that, and they do their best to make good decisions, but they don't know, they can't know. They're like sheep without a shepherd." She gazed at her intently. "Allie, it's good and right to disappoint you if it means working toward your best interest, toward the good that you couldn't have known was best, except in hindsight."

They looked steadily into one another's eyes, as if looking into one another's souls. It was the most intimate thing Allie had ever experienced. What Sophie said sounded much like what Jim had once told her. But she realized she had complete confidence in Sophie, and none in Jim. "I believe you. I know what you're saying is true. I feel like… like everything I ever did before was the prologue, and now I'm ready for chapter one. I don't understand it, because I remember a few minutes ago being in the depths of despair. Am I losing my mind, Sophie? Please, please, please be real! Please don't be a hallucination, some figment of my wounded imagination. I need you."

Sophie smiled and looked over Allie's left shoulder. She turned her head to see what Sophie was looking at. The café door opened and a man walked in tentatively, and behind him was a woman with long blonde…

XXIII

"MOMMYYYY!!!"

A streak of golden hair and outstretched hands hurled itself into her arms.

Allie's world turned round and round; she and Laney twirled and twined with one another, and at their vortex swirled the word "miracle," and it was like Allie took her daughter back inside herself, into her womb, and bore her again, and they had this new life now to live and always together 'til death do us part, and Allie cried and Laney cried with her, and they laughed and giggled and sat back panting, holding hands, looking at one another with crazy grins on their faces as if each were saying, wait until you hear what happened to me, but they said nothing; it was all too much for words and that might have gone on a long time, this glad study of one another, but it was only a few moments, and they were gradually aware of other people in the room, watching and laughing and some crying with them.

Jack and Lizzy were still by the door. Jack began to steal back outside, but Lizzy took his hand and led him in. They slipped into the booth across from Allie and Laney, who were still glued to one another. Lizzy set a forgotten teddy bear on the table. At the same time, the men came in—Ted and John and Gerry—and the whole thing started over, shouts and hugs and tears and laughter. And the whole while, Jack sat awkwardly at the booth and Lizzy watched with joy and weeping, then stood and hugged Allie—embraced would be a better word, because they held one another like two empathetic sufferers of the same burden—and they wept and laughed and Allie kissed her on the forehead and forgave them without speaking a word.

Exhausted, they all sat down, crowding chairs around the one booth, everyone talking and no one listening, until Laney sat up on the table and held her fingers to her lips, a small action that brought a happy and amused quiet to the crowd around the booth, and the growing crowd of townsfolk standing around them.

Laney made introductions like a proper lady. "These are my friends, Jack and Lizzy, who looked after me for a long, long time. And this is my mommmmm. And Ted—hi Ted! And I don't know anybody else." Everyone cheered, though the better part of the people from the town didn't know what the heck was going on, and a considerable buzz among them tried to find out.

After a while, Allie turned from the buzz and faced Jack and Lizzy, face glowing. "So much about this, I don't understand. But looking at you, I can't help knowing you're good people, your intentions were good, and we were all caught up in something much bigger than ourselves." Jack's tension noticeably subsided; Lizzy smiled warmly. Allie continued, "I'm so grateful for your care of my daughter, and somehow, you were part of saving us both, I think, though it didn't go the way any of us imagined it would. And I can see hurt in your faces like my hurt, only mine is resolved and yours is not, and my heart goes out to you." She grabbed their hands. "I have no angry, resentful feelings toward you, only empathy... and compassion. And gratitude. Thank you." She hugged Lizzy again and gave an awkward, across-the-table hug to Jack. When he sat down, tears ran down his cheeks.

It took a long, long time to scratch even the surface of their stories, and the stories turned into dinner in the little café, though the waitresses and the cooks stood and listened more than they cooked or waited. "Ted, Ted!" exclaimed Laney. "I've got favorite Bible stories now! Lizzy told me them! Noah, and he builds a big boat and puts all these animals in, and feeds them, and scoops their poop, and they sail right around the world and back again!" Ted laughed, with tears running down his face, and held Laney close. Allie looked at Jack and Lizzy with question marks.

"Sorry," Jack shrugged. "We're Christians. We can't help it!" Everyone laughed, and Allie smirked and ruffled Laney's hair and wondered at this precious little life returned to her, so unexpected and so nearly beyond hope. Allie noticed that Sophie was gone again, as usual. And the good—that she couldn't have known was best—was hers. Like Sophie had said. She wondered if and when she would ever see her again. She wondered, determined to wonder more.

It grew late. One of the townspeople offered their bed-and-breakfast for the night, if they would have it. Everyone tossed around and debated plans. Ted motioned for attention and the room became quiet. "Listen, everyone, this has been quite a day, and we know none of us is going anywhere tonight, and we're all concerned about this earthquake on top of everything else. I say, let's all go to our homes with grateful hearts, and… sure, prayers on our lips for the people suffering on the island and lower mainland, and wait on tomorrow. And we're thankful to our friend—is it Frank?—Frank, who has offered us a place to stay, and we gladly accept. Have a good night, everyone, and thank you all!"

The bed-and-breakfast was quaint but a little tight for them all. They gave Jack and Lizzy the one room, John took a sofa in the lounge, and there was an awkward moment about the other bedroom, where Laney was already asleep crossways on the king-size bed. Allie pulled Ted outside onto the balcony, where the wind was bitter, and kissed him. "Go stay with John, Ted. Don't be an idiot. We have lots of time." He held her head against his chest. "Besides, I'm done with shacking up—didn't go so well for me the last time. I want Laney to know you'll be around for the long haul, as long a time as we have. You told me your life is mine, and that's good enough for me." She looked up at him. "But I want a wedding, Ted! I want the world to come to it, and I want them to know we belong to one another—you and me and Laney, and who knows, maybe ten more!"

"Ten?"

"Okay, twelve then, but that's it." They held one another a long time, and after a while Allie began to sag, and Ted opened the balcony door, picked her up and laid her on the bed, arranged

Laney beside her and tucked them in. As he looked at the two of them, he wondered—wondered a long time—and came to the conclusion that luck had nothing to do with it. He kissed them both, turned and joined John in the living room, sank deep into a reclining chair and knew nothing until morning.

Allie awoke to big blue eyes peeking over the comforter, soaking her in. She had this dream so often—Laney waiting for her to get up, only to dissolve into nothingness—but these eyes seemed so real. Because they were real. Laney pounced, and Allie was ready for her, and they rolled over and nearly off the bed but not quite; wrestling turned into pillow-fighting, then pillow-throwing, and when the pillows were all on the floor, mother and daughter collapsed in a happy pile in the middle of the bed.

"I missed you, Mommy. I watched and watched and watched for you."

"I know, honey. I missed you terribly too. Even when things got hard, I thought about you all the time. I'm so glad you had Jack and Lizzy to take such good care of you, and I can hardly believe we're back together again. Let's stick together now, at least until you're thirty-five years old and want to date someone, okay?"

"Mom, don't be gross. And I'm not leaving home until I'm thirty-eleven."

Ted knocked and came in. "Whoa, what's been happening here? Shoulda told me; I would have brought my pillow!" Laney jumped off the bed, grabbed the nearest one, and hit Ted with it until he was flat on the floor. "Oooh, you got me. I'm done for!" He rolled over and grabbed both Laney and her pillow in a big hug. Laney squealed and squirmed and planted a big slobbery kiss on Ted's forehead, and escaped when he tried to rub it off. She heard the TV in the lounge and ran out to see if someone could find her an animal show.

Allie and Ted gazed at one another. "I've been watching the news—it's non-stop coverage of the quake." Ted shook his head. "Things are pretty bad, and aftershocks are causing havoc with the rescue work in Victoria. Big news this morning is the continued silence from the Directorate on the island. It seems the labyrinth of offices underneath the parliament buildings is completely flooded—something about cracks in the bedrock."

Allie put her hands to her face. She saw in her mind an elaborately decorated room with a raised dais. Long beautiful gowns. An exquisite garden and a man at a desk, powerless to stop the rise of water in his cell. She shuddered. Ted continued, "Speculation is that the entire Directorate fell victim to the quake, making the island without any government. As far as anyone can tell, the flood destroyed most official records, so the remaining government bureaucracy has lost not only its direction but its infrastructure as well. Leaving us like sheep without a shepherd." Allie remembered Sophie's words.

"Both Canada and the US offered to step in with provisional government; then the Brits got upset, saying Vancouver Island is still a crown colony and so it's their responsibility. And now the Victoria Times Colonist pulled together a front page calling for the election of a new government. It will be messy for a while."

He finished his report, got up off the floor, sat on the bed with Allie and held her hands. "I've decided I need to go back to the island."

She looked at him squarely. "We're coming with you."

He nodded. "But you need to know it will be rough; the island's a war zone. It will take years to get all the services going again. One of the things they said this morning is that the entire island has tilted by 1.7 degrees, so every house and building is no longer level. Nobody has any experience with stuff like that. With a new government, no one knows what will happen. It's not a great place to raise a child right now."

Allie squeezed his hands. "Three-quarters of a million people are raising their families on the island right now. We should join them. We can find some way to help."

Ted sighed, "I know. And I have a great network of people who look to me for leadership, and I'm not there. We'll find ourselves incredibly busy before we can even process what's happened to us. It's not the life I imagined with you, those long hours I held you in my arms on the boat. It scares the hell outta me."

"Well, I think what happened to us was meant to be preparation for what we're now called to do." He looked at her uncomfortably. "Hey, I know we don't understand the strange help we received, but it was real! Look at us—alive, together, and Laney is with us! It's like you said—things happened that were absolutely impossible for us. It's the kind of help that won't leave us now."

John walked in without knocking. "Hey, lovebirds. Breakfast is on the table!" He walked out, chewing on a cinnamon bun.

"You're right, Allie. I don't understand any of this, and what I don't understand freaks me out. But I have to admit I like what I see in you since all of this happened. I admire your hope, your... faith."

They joined the others in the dining room and told them what they had decided. After a few moments of uneasiness, everyone agreed they were right, that returning to the island was the right thing to do. As the meal was wrapping up, Jack and Lizzy drew Allie aside. "We want to thank you, Allie, for your understanding and your forgiveness. And for your example." They had told her about their child, lost years ago, and the many young moms and children they had rescued. Allie held Lizzy with tears running down her face. Lizzy took her by the shoulders and smiled. "But you, you never gave up hope, did you?" Allie murmured something about "almost," which Lizzy waved aside. "We were talking together this morning, and we're returning to the island too. We want to rebuild our lives and help out wherever we can. And we want to find Raylene, even if it's too late to take her back again from the life she has now. Thank you for encouraging us to not give up."

Gerry was waiting for them at the Zodiac. "Everyone is already taking advantage of this little quake," he laughed. "The pump charged me twice the normal price on fuel for the boat! Get in everybody—got a long way to go and the morning's passing."

The Zodiac didn't have room for Jack and Lizzy. "It's okay,' said Jack, "The guy who sold me the car is willing to take it back in exchange for a quick trip to Port Hardy. That's where we'll begin our search and inquiries, as far north as we can go and well away from the quake zone. I'm more and more sure we'll find our daughter." Jack hugged Allie, not awkwardly. "Forgiveness feels good. I'm so glad we found you, though we weren't the ones doing the looking. God bless you. We will pray for you."

Lizzy held Allie for a long time. "Ironic, isn't it? Your story and ours, merging this way." She laughed and tears came down her face at the same time. "Don't be sad for me—I'm happy and hopeful. We're not entering this search alone. Please, we must see one another soon! I love you, Allie. God loves you."

Allie fixed a look of sisterly warmth on her. "Maybe you're right. And we'll find you—we're getting good at it."

Laney hugged Jack and Lizzy at the same time with such exuberance that they all fell over on the dock. "Come see me soon, okay? Bring stories! Especially Noah ones!" She gave them her teddy bear. "I don't need him anymore. I want you to have him." They had nothing to give her, this little girl who had so nearly become their daughter. Only hugs and tears. Sometimes doors close unexpectedly, and sometimes it's no use banging your head on them. Especially when others are opening nearby. They would seek the open door that no one can close.

It seemed a quick trip to Han's trawler, waiting at the entrance to the channel. Hans crushed each of them with his hugs, so bubbling with excitement that he couldn't start his engine for five minutes, talking non-stop the whole time, never completing a sentence. "This is so... how on earth could we have... I couldn't believe my ears when I heard that...!" He insisted on taking them all the way to Port Hardy since he still had John's Zodiac on board. John perched on a tall stool, swinging his legs and looking forward, quiet as a zephyr for once. Hans stood at the wheel with a giant of a smile on his face, watching the alpenglow on the mountains, finally with no words left in him. The excitement proved all too much for Laney; she was curled up asleep in a nest of blankets in a corner of the cabin.

The sun was setting as the island mountains drew near. "Well, Fletch? Or do I call you Ted?" Allie snuggled in close and kissed him on the end of the nose.

Ted rubbed the kiss in with the back of his hand. "Sorry, that tickled!" This woman felt so right in his arms, as if she belonged there. "You can call me anything you like. But I'm cooking dinners, okay? I don't like anyone's cooking better than mine. Better get used to it!"

"Sounds like a hardship. Anything else?"

"I kinda like foot massages."

She sat up. "Well, I don't like giving foot massages! Better get used to it!" She snuggled back in and watched the approaching mountains in silence. They had their first argument, and now anything could happen.

ABOUT THE AUTHOR

As a young man, James Badke spent a summer on Vancouver Island providing helpful information to the hundreds of backpackers who wanted to hike the fabulous forty miles of the West Coast Trail. That summer was the beginning of his fascination with the island. Since then, he and his wife and two sons have lived there on several occasions, most recently for the past 28 years. He thought it would be interesting to take a setting with which he was familiar and alter a bit of its history, creating a new setting for what he wanted to say. His inspiration was Joan Aiken's *The Wolves of Willoughby Chase*, in which nineteenth-century Britain under King James III is overwhelmed with the wolves that swarm through the Channel Tunnel from Europe, which of course was not built until the late twentieth century. Nor was there ever a King James III.

Also by James (Jim) Badke:

The Island and i
How do you love your neighbor when you live alone on an island off the wild coast of British Columbia?

As The Eagle Walks
If the Apostle John was still living on the island of Patmos, would you want to visit him?

The Mummy of Fisher Creek
A young couple has found a pair of boots in a cave—and someone is still inside them.

Camp Liverwurst Series
A series of three novels for middle-school kids, set at a camp that is out of this world and a whole lot of fun.

---All available on Amazon---

www.ingramcontent.com/pod-product-compliance
Lightning Source LLC
Chambersburg PA
CBHW031312170626
46807CB00001B/392